LOVE ON SIGHT

A MESSAGE FROM CHICKEN HOUSE

Asli won our Lime Pictures New Storyteller Award with an outstanding novel that is not only gripping, emotional and down-to-earth, but also has something tough yet warm to say about love and London! With great characters, tense action and an authentic voice, this is something truly special. Enjoy.

BARRY CUNNINGHAM
Publisher
Chicken House

LOVE ON SIGHT

ASLI JENSEN

2 PALMER STREET, FROME,
SOMERSET BA11 1DS

First published in the UK in 2025
Chicken House
2 Palmer Street
Frome, Somerset BA11 1DS
United Kingdom
www.chickenhousebooks.com

Text © Asli Jensen 2025
Illustrations © Ali Al Amine 2025

The moral rights of the author and illustrator have been asserted.

All rights reserved.

No part of this publication may be reproduced, transmitted, downloaded, decompiled, reverse engineered, used to train any artificial intelligence technologies, or stored in or introduced into any information storage and retrieval system, in any form or by any means, whether electronic or mechanical, now known or hereafter invented, without the express written permission of the publisher. Subject to EU law the publisher expressly reserves this work from the text and data mining exception.

All emojis designed by OpenMoji, the open-source emoji and icon project.
License: CC BY-SA 4.0

For safety or quality concerns:
UK: www.chickenhousebooks.com/productinformation
EU: www.scholastic.ie/productinformation

Cover design by Ali Al Amine
Typeset by Dorchester Typesetting Group Ltd
Printed in the UK by Clays, Elcograf S.p.A

1 3 5 7 9 10 8 6 4 2

A CIP catalogue record for this book is available from the British Library.

PB ISBN 978-1-915947-86-4
eISBN 978-1-915947-87-1

To teenage dreams

CHAPTER 1

JALAAL

I cycle through the ends and down on to the high street at a fast speed. No helmet. No lights. Just me. And the will of Allah. Not gonna lie though, I don't think about God very much, only when I'm alone with my thoughts. And I don't do that often, cos I don't like thinking about the person that I am right now. I focus on what's important. The pharmacy is closing soon and Habo Hani needs her medication. The pain in her knee has made it impossible for her to leave the yard today.

A strong cockney accent wakes me from my thoughts, 'Oi mate, get off your bike!'

I quickly turn my head back to the two feds pacing up behind me. I don't think I have anything on me, so I press my brakes and stop. Bun going back to them, I'll wait here for them to come to me.

'Right.' The fatter one breathes in my face, his chest rising and falling quickly. 'You know it's an offence to cycle on the pavement?'

I stare at him and say nothing. He ain't serious.

'Please get your hands out of your pockets,' the skinnier, red-faced fed says.

I have one hand placed on my bicycle seat and the other one in my pocket, gripping my aunt's prescription.

'Why? Are you detaining me?' I bite my tongue.

They both stare at me in silence as if I'm stupid.

'I said, are you detaining me?' I lower my voice despite the heat rising within me.

'Right, mate. Calm down, you're being searched under Section Twenty-three of the Misuse of Drugs Act . . .' His voice fades as the fat one grabs my left hand and pulls the right one out of my pocket, securely locking handcuffs on my wrists behind my back. They're tight.

My body tenses as they start digging into my pocket. Everything is happening in slow motion and when I finally process what's going on, my nostrils flare and my muscles contract.

'Wait. What the fuck is going on? I haven't got anything on me.'

Silence.

I try to move, my body slightly twitching. The fat one firms his grip on me, and my body begins to jolt. I hate this feeling.

'Fam, why are you searching me? What have I done?'

They ignore me, speaking among themselves and listing the items in my pocket. Prescription, Oyster card, twenty-pound notes, iPhone. Thank Allah I left the burner phone at home.

'Officer, speak to me!' I shout at them.

Before I know it, I'm on the floor, my back rubbing against the coarse gravel, and palms pinched against the sharp floor. The red-faced officer is up in my face shouting at me, 'JUST CALM THE FUCK DOWN MATE.'

Subhanallah.

There's not many people on the high street but I clock the barbers peering through their windows, old people at the bus stop watching us closely and a few people recording us from across the road. I better not end up on some meme page on Instagram, it's so fucking embarrassing.

'He's clean. Nothing on him,' the fat one finally says. The red one loosens his grip on me and I'm able to fully breathe again, the hard gravel slowly detaching itself from my body.

I exhale as they uncuff me.

'It's your lucky day mate.' The fat one squares up to me. 'Don't worry Jalaal Abdi, we know exactly what you and your mates are up to. Don't get too comfortable, you'll see us real soon,' he mutters quickly before jumping back into his whip, leaving me there bruised and battered like some dickhead.

When I get to the pharmacy, Uncle looks at me sideways. He's known me since I was a young kid and my mum used to bring me here to collect my banana-flavoured amoxicillin. That was a lifetime ago. I wonder if he remembers what Hooyo looked like. I'm slowly starting to forget.

As soon as I enter the doorway and the bell chimes, Uncle runs up to me.

'Jalaal, what happened to you?' He holds my head firmly in his hands, inspecting.

'What do you mean? Nothing has happened to me.' I avoid eye contact and back away from him.

'Come here son, you've got a cut on your eyebrow, let me quickly clean it up for you and give you a plaster.'

A cut. Fucking pigs.

I mumble in agreement. It's not right for me to be rude to Uncle, but I'm angry fam.

He comes back out with his personalized *King's Pharmacy First Aid Kit*. It's bare cringe, but I rate him still. He tells me to sit on the stool and presses the antiseptic wipe against my cut. I wince even though I try hard to suppress any pain.

'There, there, there.' He finishes it off with a plaster. 'All done.'

'Thank you, Uncle.' I force a smile.

'No worries, Jalaal. Let me go get the prescription for your aunt. How is she feeling today?'

'I can't lie, she wasn't doing too good, but I think the meds will help her knee ease up.'

'*Inshallah*, I will make *dua* for her too.' This guy is so blessed.

'Thank you, man, it means a lot.' I take the paper prescription bag from him and walk out the pharmacy.

'And Jalaal . . .' he shouts from the back of the shop. I pause at the doorway and turn back to him.

'Yeah?'

'Whatever happened for you to get that cut, I know you're better than that. It's not my business but I know your mum would have wanted the best for you,' he responds. Hooyo? I can't take this. It's too much for one day.

'You're right, it's not your business!' I slam the door, leaving the bell to chime before he can reply.

I need to get back to yard.

When I reach yard, I go to give Habo Hani her prescription. She's on the phone but immediately hangs up when she clocks the plaster on my face.

'What happened?' She speaks quickly in Somali.

'Habo, it's fine.'

She struggles to get up.

'Sit down, your knee.' I switch to our mother tongue.

'Did somebody do this to you?'

'No, no. Relax, I fell off my bike.' If I tell her that it was the feds, she'll know that I'm back on road. And I'm not tryna stress her.

'I should really get a helmet like you keep saying,' I add.

'You need to be careful, *waryaa*.' She melts back into the sofa.

'I know, I'm bare tired so Ima go sleep for a bit. Do you need anything else?' I hope she says no.

'No, no, it's OK.' She ushers me off. 'You better get that helmet soon.'

I nod before leaving her.

The heat wakes me up.

We're all being cooked alive in our own homes. Twenty-nine degrees is too much for the ends. The sweat patches on my basic white T-shirt have turned yellow. It's the one time in my life when I'm fully annoyed at the council for installing some shit windows in our block that don't even open properly. I swear that's how the Grenfell fire started, the council using cheap material. I bet all those new-build flats for the rich dons who live down the road don't have that problem.

My phone buzzes. A text from Shaah.

Yo Jalaal, party nearby, I need to do a drop off, u on it?

Yh bro, come thru. I notice how big my fingers look against the Nokia keypad.

Kl.

'Habo Hani,' I shout down the stairs at my aunt. 'Shaah is coming over.'

She hates it when people come to our yard unannounced.

'I can't hear you Jalaal-o.' She elongates my name. 'If you want to tell me something, you need to come downstairs,' she shouts back in Somali.

I groan and go downstairs. She's calmly sitting on the sofa, tapping her phone screen with her eyes squinted.

'Habo Hani,' I sigh. 'Shaah is coming over in a bit and we gonna go out.'

Her neck snaps in my direction. 'Going where?' Her eyes don't even blink.

'Just chill innit, probably get munch too,' I try to convince her.

'Don't you have exams to be revising for?' She raises her eyebrows. 'Just because Shaah isn't in school doesn't mean you can be a *dib jir* too.'

She knows I hate it when she cusses me out in Somali and, according to her, I'm a lowlife today.

'Yeah, but I did most of it already and I just need to relax for a bit.' I lie through my teeth.

'I don't ever see you studying.'

'Why are you on my case though?' I snap.

'Don't you dare raise your voice at me!'

'Just let me live my life then.' I suck my teeth together.

'Have you forgotten that you come from a good Muslim family?' She shakes her head. 'Do as you please then . . . as long as you don't end up dead or in prison.'

I hate to think that she's starting to give up on me. I stare at her blankly for a few seconds before returning upstairs.

I don't want to be seen shotting weed at some dead party, but ever since I got kicked out of college last year, I feel like this is all I do. Back when I was at W&A college, things were kind of easier and I wasn't this pressed. Even though some of my teachers were dickheads and used to violate me all the time by removing me from the classroom and picking on me for no reason, I did enjoy a bit of school, like graphic design and media. I even started to design my own T-shirts and hoodies. I bet if I carried on then I'd have my own clothing brand by now. Probably would have had good-quality T-shirts that don't stain yellow with sweat either.

I'm gassed Shaah has come through with a motive at least. He's been my boy for God knows how long. We met at the park on our estate when we were five years old. I remember the day so well. I was sitting on the swing, trying to go as high as I could to get that adrenaline rush. Shaah was playing football with the other kids, and he saw me. His ashy knees came running over and he showed me how standing on the swing would help me go higher. Ever since then, we've been boys.

I quickly get up to close my bedroom door. I don't want my little brother Ibrahim knowing where I hide my drugs. He's only eight years old, he shouldn't even know what drugs are. I dismantle the hairbrush that I hide my weed in. You'll never believe the shit you can find on Amazon. I've sealed it in multiple bags and some cling film, so the yard doesn't smell. Ever since I got bagged last year and the feds raided my room, I've been bare paranoid. When the police did buss down my door, they only found the weed in my shoebox, which they said was *just* enough for personal usage. Then the dickheads made me go YOT, the youth offending team, and it meant I had to do some cannabis awareness classes. Shaah also got the same visit from the feds and had to go YOT, too.

Alhamdulillah, God has my back and I just got a Youth Caution. I never deeped the fact that I could go prison for what I do until that day. And not gonna lie, it shook me. My aunt was mad about the whole thing, *wallahi* she did not speak to me for nearly a whole month. It was peak. I promised her that I would pattern up and I tried for a bit. After college kicked me out, I was going to PRU for a while, trying to do some courses and not staying out late. After a while, I don't know what happened, but I fell off. Habo still thinks I'm at college, but most time, I'm on road or wasting time.

Twenty minutes later, the doorbell rings.

'I'll get it,' Ibrahim shouts as his feet race down the stairs.

'Hello big man, what you sayin'?' Shaah's deep voice booms up the stairs.

'Shaah,' Ibrahim chuckles. 'Isn't it too hot to be wearing a coat?'

I burst out laughing from upstairs. I bet that's what every sane person thinks when they see us lots wearing puffer jackets in the summer.

'Come upstairs, fam. And Ibrahim, you pagan, go do your homework.'

Ibrahim's feet run up the stairs again and he smacks open my door. He stares at me with his eyes wide open. 'Why'd you call me a pagan?'

Shaah comes up behind him and enters my room.

'Shut up Ibrahim, go do your homework,' I say. He pulls a face and turns to leave. 'And close my door.'

He slams my door shut.

'You've made big man vex,' Shaah says, his silver incisor glinting at me.

I shoot Shaah an unbothered look. He doesn't have any younger siblings as he's the youngest in his family. He has no one to protect. I don't want Ibrahim knowing anything about me being on road.

Ibrahim is innocent, enjoys school and plays football. He's an academic little yute so he's going to have to do the whole university thing.

He clocks the cut on my face and raises his eyebrows.

'Feds,' I sigh.

'Did they find anything?' His eyes widen.

'Nah, don't stress man.' I don't want to think about it, and I don't want to tell him about their little threat. 'So where is this party happening again?'

'It's at St Mary's.'

We leave the house and ride our pedal bikes to St Mary's Estate. It's the sister estate to mine, St George's. Two identical estates facing one another – so basically, it's two shitholes opposite each other.

As we arrive, I ask Shaah, 'Yo, this is Shanice's yard, ain't it?'

He smiles knowingly; no wonder he didn't tell me the specifics. He knows how I feel about trying to maintain a good image in the Somali community so that my aunt doesn't get suspicious. Even though Shanice is a true yardie girl, there better not be any Somalis at this party.

Shanice was in my English class in secondary school, and we used to bun weed together sometimes. As far as I know, she still chills with the same circles which means bare exposure for me. For fuck's sake. I need to be in and out as soon as possible.

The blocks here are grey, ugly and chunky. Too much concrete and not enough windows. The whole of Shanice's building is stained with green-turning-black sewage, and you can smell the rotting food from the communal bins. The heat isn't helping either. This is the hood, and the feds are always circling around her ends. The metal entrance door to her block is secured with actual bars. No wonder everyone feels trapped. I notice the 'NO BALL GAMES' sign hanging at an angle off the wall. It's jokes because I'm the one who kicked a football at the sign when I was thirteen years old and angry at the world.

We walk up the alleyway adjacent to the block of flats and towards the communal back garden. We follow the blaring lyrics of Vybz Kartel's 'Summertime'. The scent of succulent jerk chicken drifts up my nose and my stomach rumbles. Obviously Somali food bangs and that's my favourite munch, but I swear, Caribbean food is also top tier. The beef-and-cheese patties are unmatched. These lot are always bare generous with their portions, they're blessed people *wallahi*.

A girl's voice shouts, 'Ayy, party's about to get live,' and faces turn our way.

I swallow my panic. Now it's bait that I'm some established drug dealer.

Shaah and I wait around awkwardly for whoever this drop-off is for. There are bare people at this party. The music is a vibe and everyone is having a good time. I'm not tryna be involved but it's low-key nice to watch people. I'm not the best dancer, though I've got rhythm. But I'm here for Shaah and here to make money. He's stood next to me, chest puffed out and eyes darting everywhere. I don't know why he's on edge, this is a calm barbecue. Like I said, I don't want to be caught slipping here but at the same time, I'm not ready to leave just yet.

I smile and wait.

Just as we are about to leave, I notice Shanice entering the garden with a sweet one. Fuck though, she's the lengest girl I've seen in a long time. Her skin is glowing a beautiful brown. She's wearing a black bodycon dress that hugs her figure perfectly, accentuating her slim waist and curved bunda. I must look like a wasteman just staring at her, but I can't help myself. Even though she's at a distance, I notice the small freckles around her cheeks as she observes everyone in the garden with her wandering, wide brown eyes.

She paces slowly behind Shanice. She's shy. There's something bare alluring about her. It's like she's cautious and thoughtful at the same time. I can't help but feel drawn to her, Ima have to chat to her.

Out of nowhere, her eyes lock on to mine. She holds my gaze for a second before looking in the opposite direction. For that brief moment, something inside me shifts. As if there are suddenly bare possibilities. I don't know, maybe I'm bugging out.

I pat Shaah on the chest while staring at this beautiful girl. 'Who's the lengers next to Shanice?'

Shaah smirks. 'That's Sabrina fam, we all used to go college together . . . you probably don't 'memba her cos she's in the year above and she's a good girl. Just keeps to herself if you get what I mean.'

I zone out as I continue watching her. Sabrina.

CHAPTER 2

SABRINA

I'm seriously contemplating going to this party. It's Shanice's eighteenth birthday and even though we chill together sometimes, we're not close friends. I only know her from the youth club we went to as kids. But then again, it's always a vibe when I'm with her. I'm sat in her room with two of her hood friends who are beating their faces with foundation. They're both wearing matching bralettes with denim shorts. They practically look the same except that one of them has a bulging mole on her eyelid. I watch them intently.

I made a pledge to myself that I'd unwind and get out there more. My sole personality trait can't be studying to ace my A Levels and leave the ends. Ever since the whole thing with Mum happened, I haven't gone to all these parties. I just never felt like socializing and being outside. I've been hyper-fixated on getting the best grades to get into a university that's far away from London. And far away from the turbulence of the past two years. So, when Shanice invited me to her birthday, I decided to get out of my comfort zone. To feel more like myself again.

I turn my head to the window and observe what's going on outside. I watch all the people at the party drinking out of their plastic cups, while eating their jerk chicken and curry goat. My mouth salivates. Now that I'm thinking about it, it's strange that nobody has seen me glaring down at them from the top window. I'm such a creep. I focus on the mirror placed on the windowsill and use my stippling brush to *lightly* apply my foundation. My skin is oily and I'm praying the foundation stays on in this heat.

'Are you all right Sabs?' Shanice asks me.

Her two friends, whose names I genuinely don't remember, cock their heads towards me, both raising their eyebrows. I swallow my anxiety.

'Yeah, I'm good boo. Just really need a joint!' I smile back at her. I have no idea why I addressed her as boo, that is definitely not like me.

'Yes, turn up!' the one with the mole on her face squeals at me.

I internally roll my eyes.

'Are you not drinking, Sabs?' someone asks me.

I know better than to mix weed and alcohol together, nothing good ever happens. My A Level exams start in a few weeks and the last thing I need is a messy night to fuck up my head.

'Nah . . . I love my ganja, but I can't be getting yakked too.'

'You're too much of a good girl,' Shanice says.

'Aha, trust me. I can't be as wild as you.' I try to deflect.

'Fam, you're getting lit and you're definitely bussin' a wine or two!'

You shouldn't be here, Sabs. I laugh it off. To be honest, I'd rather be at home with my best friend Liyah, watching *EastEnders* and babysitting my younger sisters.

I tap the home button on my cracked iPhone screen to unlock my phone; I'm hoping that Liyah has sent me a funny TikTok. No notifications. I sigh. My wallpaper stares back at me and I smile. It's a photo of my grandad in the late 1970s when he first immigrated to

London. My dad, who doesn't look older than five in this pic, is stood smiling with his missing tooth and oversized farmer's hat, right next to Grandad and his older sister Maureen. I send him a text: Hey Dad, I hope you have a great shift at work. Thanks for everything you do for us. Love ya loads. ♥

Shanice's two friends finish their make-up looks and go downstairs to join the party. I'm sure that they'll get all the attention they deserve. *You're being so judgy, Sabs.*

I stay with Shanice as she finishes her look by applying fake lashes.

'Soooo . . .' She twirls and flashes a smile at me. 'How do I look?'

'Girl, you look fire.' It's the truth. Her make-up looks flawless and her white co-ord complements her dark complexion. She looks like she could be an Instagram influencer – all she needs is for House of CB or PrettyLittleThing to sponsor her.

'Thanks Sabs, gotta look on point sometimes,' Shanice says. 'You look peng too! Can you take some pics of me for Snap?'

She hands me her phone with Snapchat already open. She stands in front of me with the window directly behind her. The lighting is terrible.

'Shanice, I think we should swap places, so you get better lighting.'

'This is why I invited you babes.' She runs over to the other side of the room.

She places one foot in front of the other, arching her back so her bunda appears bigger and her waistline looks snatched. She knows her angles. I crouch on the floor and snap photos as she changes her poses, capturing all of her beauty.

'That's enough now, let's go downstairs.' She grabs her phone and walks towards the door, ushering me to follow her.

I glance in the mirror and give myself a final look over. It's been a while since I've dressed up, but I know how to look good. My hair looks smooth in a curly bun and not gonna lie, my edges are slayed. I assess my red open-toe heels from New Look, mentally preparing for blisters.

'Stop watching yourself, let's go!' Shanice tugs on my arm before letting go.

My heart drops for a split second before pouncing back to normal. I swallow my anxiety and head downstairs. *Good vibes only, Sabs.*

As we head out into the communal garden where everyone is, I quickly steal a look at myself through the reflection in the window. *I can do this.*

'Ayy, turn up, turn up,' I hear Shanice shout before I follow her into the garden.

The area is filled with people. It's a concoction of the world. That's one of the few things that I love about our ends. You live in a block of flats, but each household represents a different part in the world. You wake up in the morning to go to school not knowing if you're going to smell empanadas, plantain, roti or even a fry-up. Sometimes it's a combination of all.

Even though my body tenses up in response to the large crowd of people, I'm at ease when I notice recognizable faces and happy expressions. There are two faces among the crowd who seem to stand out. It's not so much what they're wearing, it's more their body language. It's how their eyes are attentive to their surroundings, their hands fidgeting in their Armani messenger bags and how they are watching people suspiciously. You can feel the apprehension. It could not be more obvious that they're dealers.

They both catch me staring at them at the same time. I quickly glance in the opposite direction. Shanice has started dancing before she's even had a proper drink. If this is how the night is going to go, maybe I should reconsider my sobriety.

After making small talk with a few people from secondary school and loading my plastic plate with more food than I can eat, I stroll to a quiet space to enjoy my feast.

'Hey,' says a voice.

I put down the jerk chicken I was about to devour and slowly turn around, convincing myself it's not the roadmen.

But it *is* one of the dealers. 'Hey,' I reply awkwardly.

I look at him closely. He's surprisingly cute. And dressed really fresh. I appreciate how he's paired his grey Nike jersey shorts with a white T-shirt and clean white trainers.

'It's Sabrina, isn't it?' He smiles with dimples.

'How do you know?' I raise my eyebrows while noticing the cut above his eye. I wonder what happened there.

I'm genuinely baffled as to how he knows me; I mean, he's not somebody whose path I would intentionally cross. It's embarrassing to be outwardly associated with drugs.

'You don't recognize me?' Something between shock and disappointment plasters his face.

His skin is to die for, smooth and clear. My eyes focus on his big, wholesome lips. I can't help but imagine what they would feel like against mine. *Sabs, relax gurl!* His ears are hidden under his swooping 3C curls, but I notice the glimmer of his diamond stud on his left ear. The only thing missing is a gold chain. *Stop being so shallow, Sabs.*

He is cute, though. And he looks oddly familiar.

'Nah . . . I know your face and your voice . . . but I'm just unsure where from,' I answer honestly.

'Oh . . . is it like that?' He towers over me, a hint of a smirk pulling at his lips.

I don't know why he's taking it so personally. Or is he pulling my leg?

'We went to the same college, but I stopped going late last year,' he says.

So that's where I recognize him from. I guess he picked the road life.

My face slightly drops but I give him a half-smile and ask, 'How comes?'

'Long story.' He avoids eye contact momentarily. 'It wasn't for me, so I left.'

'Oh, cool.' I don't want to pry.

'Uh anyways, you want some loud?' he smirks.

The way his dimple deepens is distracting me from the conversation. There's a flutter in my belly and just like that, I remember him. The cute Somali boy who I saw in the corridor a handful of times at college – Jalaal. He disappeared after a while, and I almost felt like I had imagined his existence. *Sabs, this guy is bad news, but boy is he fine!*

'Yeah sure, how much do you have?' I manage to string together.

'There was me thinking you were a good girl,' he tuts.

I roll my eyes. 'Who doesn't like the occasional smoke?'

'True that B, yeah so, it's going to—'

'Stop.' I halt him. 'Don't call me B, I'm not your bitch, you don't know me like that, Jalaal.'

He chuckles.

'What's so funny?'

'Looks like you remember my name.' He laughs louder.

I didn't even realize that I had said his name. My cheeks heat up. He hands me a small baggie.

'It's for free – you're too funny, Sabrina.' He smiles and walks off.

'Wait . . .'

I hear his friend say something along the lines of: 'Bruv, she's bare . . .' and the rest drowns out because Shanice grabs my arm and pulls me towards a group of people doing the drift dance. My eyes go fishing for Jalaal through the crowd. He's left already. Once I finish dancing in the heat, I tend to my food and my joint.

I wake up the next morning to the booming sound of my dad's voice. His subtle Bristolian accent penetrates our small hallway and my heart thumps in retaliation.

'Get up now, you lazy gyal!' he demands.

As I open my eyes, my two sisters come into my room and hover over me.

'Sabs, I'm not tryna be rude or anything but SIS . . . you look a mess,' Natasha says as she sits on the corner of my bed. Natasha is always so bloody honest. I adjust my back against the bed frame to make space for her, and that's when I notice I'm still in my black dress. *The fuck?*

'Sabreeeena,' Isabel whines. 'Your hair looks so funny,' she giggles as she clenches her fists in front of her face, trying to conceal her wide grin.

'Guuurl, you better clean yourself up before Dad sees you cos he won't be happy.' Natasha acting like this makes me wonder if I'm really the eldest sibling. She's only fourteen years old.

'Shit man, what time did I come home?' I scratch my head and

I'm disgusted by how static my hair feels.

'You came home at 4 a.m., right before Dad came back from his night shift.' Just as I open my mouth, she adds, 'Shanice's brother dropped you off.'

I bet she was up on TikTok at that time. I was in such a haze, but I do remember Shanice's older brother dropping me off home. It amazes me how responsible Natasha can be at certain times. Then again, she's probably learnt it all from me. I'm the strict big sister keeping the house going, seeing as Mum's not around to do it. I wonder where Mum's at now. *You've got other things to worry about.* I bury her inside.

Natasha has a smug look on her face and silently crosses her arms. She wants her payment. *Shit.* I fumble into my purse and hand her a ten-pound note. Isabel watches the exchange and raises her eyebrows at me. These two are really trying to finesse me. I hand Isabel a five-pound note. What's a seven-year-old going to do with five pounds anyways? They both high-five each other.

'Sabrina, don't make me ask you again.' Dad's voice echoes into my room. He's not playing around today.

'OK, Dad.' My voice is hoarse, and my head is foggy.

Natasha and Isabel leave, financially satisfied. Last night really was a myth. Good news, Dad doesn't know I was doing a madness last night. Bad news, I smoked and ended up being driven home by an older. You can tell I haven't done this in ages. On my small desk, a whole bar of Galaxy Cookie Crumble is empty, and I'm talking about the large-sized one. *You really indulged last night, Sabs.*

I unlock my phone. It's 1 p.m. and I see a notification.

Jalaal has added you as a friend on Snapchat!

CHAPTER 3

JALAAL

My eyes widen to the pounding sounds of Habo Hani slamming her crutches on my door.

'*Waryaa*, wake up, it's almost 5 p.m., you think it's OK to sleep at these stupid hours?' She whacks harder and I groan into my pillow.

'OK, OK, Habo!' I shout. 'I'm up!'

I'm not bothered for another lecture about disobedience or how I'm losing *ajr* by not waking up early, because apparently, being up early means I'll get more rewards to go to heaven.

My head is fucked. I don't believe it's 5 p.m. I stare up at the ceiling, giving my eyes time to adjust to the blazing sun, but they're still stinging. I focus on the bumpy pattern on the ceiling. It looks like someone got bored painting and left the droplets to dry. I swear I saw my ceiling on an Instagram meme of different 'hood ceilings'.

Sabrina slides into my mind. I never deeped how beautiful she is. It was such a mad experience seeing her yesterday, I don't even know what came over me because I *never* move to gyal like that. When I clocked who she is, it reminded me of college days when everything was just calm. All I had to worry about was arriving at college on time. I want to feel like that again. I wonder what she's up to in college. I bet she's smart and going to Oxford or Cambridge or some shit. Those are the people that really make it in life, when you elevate. Not gonna lie, I'm kinda curious about her. She's drawing me in.

'Jalaal!' Habo Hani shouts.

I smell my aunt's *baasto iyo suugo* and my stomach begins to growl. Nothing I love more than lamb stew and spaghetti.

I drag myself downstairs to the dining table in our living room. It's meant for two but we all squeeze in. Me, Habo and Ibrahim. Our living area is a typical Somali set-up, decorated with dark brown curtains that force us into unnecessary darkness. Habo says that they mesh well with the golden Turkish-style sofas. But if I try sit on them, her slipper is coming off.

Ibrahim is already sitting down waiting to eat, clenching a fork in his fist. He's giving me cuts like I've done something wrong. I smirk at him.

'Why you laughing for?' he questions me.

'Did you hear me laugh?'

'No, but your lips were smiling.'

'So smiling is laughing now? Is that what they're teaching you at school?'

He scrunches his eyebrows. 'Shut up.'

Habo walks to the table with two piping-hot saucepans in her hands, one filled with *baasto* and the other with her *suugo*. She isn't bothered to place it in different fancy bowls; it's unnecessary dishes for her to wash and too much fairy liquid being wasted. Every time I try help in the kitchen with cleaning, she always cleans after me. I don't know if it's OCD or if I'm genuinely shit at cleaning.

'*Waryaa*, why did you come back very late this morning, you think I didn't hear you?' She refuses to open the saucepans until I answer her.

I can see the hunger in Ibrahim's eyes.

'I was revising with my friends, Habo, you already know this.' I lie through my teeth and pray she believes me.

'But you were with Shaah, and he doesn't go to college . . .'

Neither do I.

'Yeah, I left him and went with my other friends.' I avoid eye contact.

'OK Jalaal-o, I'm glad you were studying,' her eyes soften.

Guilt washes over me as she opens the saucepans; she really believes the lie. As the steam fires upwards, the lamb emerges from the thick burgundy sauce. My eyes widen in anticipation as Habo mixes the pockets of oil sitting on the surface. She quickly runs to the kitchen and back, placing the jar of *shidni* on the table. A meal is never complete without chilli sauce.

'Liar liar,' Ibrahim grins.

'Shut up, I'm not lying.'

'Why did you come home late then?'

'I told you. Revising.' I dip my head.

Truthfully, after the party, Shaah begged me to go to the traphouse with him. I felt bad when he mentioned going alone, so I ended up tagging along with him, as usual. I regret it cos this crackhead rattled me when she started having a seizure. *Wallahi*, I thought she was going to die, and I didn't touch her because I'm not catching whatever diseases she had. Those needles scare me. Even Shaah was bugging out, pacing up and down, sidestepping over her spasming body. *Alhamdulillah* she came back to her senses, but only after she was spitting white stuff from her mouth for about ten minutes. Imagine she had died though. That would've been an M charge for me. I know someone from the estate who got sent to pen for something called joint enterprise, because he watched his friend stab someone up.

This is why I told Shaah I'm only shotting weed, nothing else.

Fuck. I hate that shit. I bet Sabrina doesn't go to traphouses.

I glance up at Ibby. 'Eat your food, bro.'

'Stop arguing, I didn't raise you boys like this!'

'Sorry Habo,' we both say.

I dig into my food as my phone pings. A Snapchat notification.

Sabrina has added you back.

I'd be lying if I said I wasn't gassed. I put my fork to the side, momentarily forgetting my hunger, and unlock my phone. I open her Snap story and see a few videos from the party last night and a picture posted three hours ago of an empty Galaxy chocolate wrapper with the caption, 'No more 🍫 for me'.

I reply to the picture in the chat. Where's my thank you?

I feel Habo's stare.

'*Waryaa*, who has you smiling at your phone?'

'I'm not smiling, why are you making me sound moist?' I fake a poker face.

'Ohhhhh, so it's a girl.'

'No.'

'We're eating. Get off the phone now.'

I put my phone on silent and slip it into the pocket of my grey joggers. I know I've sent a risky reply, and I'm already tempted to take my phone back out. But I'm already in deep shit with Habo; I won't piss her off more than I need to. We eat as Ibrahim relentlessly talks about how his school football team voted him to be the captain.

'Habo, how come the kids in my class have their hooyo and abo pick them up? Can I have Hoo— I mean Abo pick me up?'

Anger pulsates through my veins. I know my habo always finds a delicate way to answer Ibrahim but sometimes, I wish she would just be straight with him so he would stop thinking our dad is innocent. Because he ain't.

My mum passed away eight years ago because of complications during Ibrahim's birth. He never met her. The worst thing about him knowing she's not alive is that he keeps asking about Abo, our dad who might as well be dead (to me). He chose to live in Somaliland after Ibby was born, to start his 'business', and said it was better to send money to us from afar. Habo Hani says he sent money for the first few years but I haven't ever seen a pound. He came back once or twice after he left, and took me and Ibby out. Ibby doesn't remember though, he was like a toddler or something. I don't really chat to my dad like that but I think Ibby and him FaceTime. They do it when I'm not at home. He called me last year to wish me happy birthday. I didn't say too much on the phone. I know deep down he's just one of those deadbeat dads who go back 'home' to their other wives and families. I know a couple other Somali bredrins from the estate whose dads are back home with their young wives. It makes me sick to think that me and Ibby are the same.

My aunt sighs. 'Ibrahim, your abo is working really hard, he will come see you soon.'

I don't know why she even bothers to defend him. He is her brother-in-law. Not even blood siblings.

'I'm going upstairs,' I announce to them as I take my phone out.

They both turn quiet, and their eyes pierce my back. I shrug it off.

I open my chat with Sabrina on Snapchat. She still hasn't responded but I don't care.

Wuu2? Besides eating chocolate . . .

Sabs
Are you trying to be funny?

Is it working?

Sabs
Answering a question with a question . . .

Are we gonna fight?

Sabs
Try be more original, we all know what fighting means.

Lol is that you Sabs?

Sabs
Who gave you permission to call me Sabs?

Sorry . . . Sabrina*

Sabs
Thx!

Wuu2 then?

Sabs
Nothing substantial.

OK miss, gonna bell you in 5.

Sabs
Good luck 😂

Before I call her, I cover my curls cos they're starting to look a bit dry. I pull out my purple durag from under my pillow and tie it around my head. I look at the reflection on my phone screen, satisfied with this improvement. The normal me would never be doing this.

I call Sabrina and she doesn't answer. Prestige mixed-race-girl behaviour. I have absolutely no shame and ring her again. She answers but the screen is black. Am I a dickhead for being on here with my purple durag?

'Am I gonna see you or are we doing black screens?' I ask her.

'Hold on, one sec, my room is a mess.'

'Am I on video chat with you or your room?'

She snorts. 'You're low-key funny, you know that?'

'It's not low-key if you're laughing though, is it?'

'Oh, shut up,' she sighs, 'nice durag by the way.'

'Thanks.'

'Hiding the dead trim, right?'

'You're not funny.' I roll my eyes.

Without warning, she appears on my screen in an oversized black Trapstar hoody with the slogan in a gradient blue colour. She must've just woken up because her hair is tied in a messy bun and there are wisps coming out in different directions. Her Wi-Fi connection must be elite because her face is so clear that I can see the smudged mascara around the corners of her eyelids, and a delicate gold chain around her neck. She squints at me and the freckles on her nose and cheeks rise. The freckles look prettier than they did last night. She's beautiful.

'Are you frozen?' Her voice wakes me up from my trance.

'Nah, just deeping how peng you are.'

I wasn't expecting her to be make-up free. I can't lie, I'm so used to the long nails and eyelash extension look – which I do love and appreciate – but this is different.

'Ugh, you make me cringe.' Her shoulders drop and she starts playing with her necklace.

'If I'm cringey, then why did you accept my request?'

Her eyes dart around her room and I use the pause to spy what's behind her. She has a chest of drawers with a line of hair products. I can't really tell what they are because of the distance, but I recognize the Sunny Isle Jamaican Castor Oil and line of Shea Moisture products. There's also the Galaxy wrapper from her Snapchat story. I wish I could see her ceiling. It would be jokes to know which hood ceiling she has.

'That's a good question you know. I don't know why I accepted.' Her sweet voice turns my focus back to her face.

'So, you're saying that you don't let man move to you?' I raise my eyebrows at her.

'Nah, it's not that. It's just that when I saw you at the party and umm,' she stumbles on her words, 'I don't know, something just compelled me to accept you.'

'Compelled? Are you Shakespeare now?'

She sighs. 'Sorry, I didn't realize speaking English was a crime.'

I chuckle. Like a little boy.

We get off the phone at midnight because Sabs has college. I clocked we'd been chatting for a while when I had to lie down at an awkward position to make sure my phone charger reached the socket. I don't know what I was expecting from our conversation, but now she's gone, I want to talk to her again. She's so calm. I wish I made the effort with her in college – maybe things would've been different for me.

The convo did get a bit sticky when she asked me what I do now. Obviously, she knows about the shotting, but I told her I also work part-time at Sainsbury's, which is the truth. Mainly to avoid suspicion from Habo about where the money I give her comes from. It was weird though; Sabrina didn't say anything that showed judgement, but she did give off a vibe of disappointment. It's not that deep though. If it *really* bothered her then she wouldn't have accepted me.

Shaah left me a missed call. I bell him back.

'Yo wagwarn.'

'What you saying my brudda, you're not answering my calls.'

'I was just helping my aunt,' I lie. 'What you saying tho?'

'Do you wanna come smoke a zoot in St Mary's Park?'

'I don't know if I'll smoke, but I'll come chill with you. I got things to tell you about that gyal from the motive yesterday.'

'You making movements bro?'

'Fam, just wait till I see you.' I hang up the phone.

It's 12.30 a.m. Ibrahim and Habo are fast asleep. I put on my Nike Tech hoody and go downstairs. I take my Emporio Armani aftershave and place it in my back pocket as I slowly creep out the yard, leaving the door behind me on latch.

CHAPTER 4

SABRINA

I can't believe that I video-chatted with Jalaal on Snapchat last night. Me? Entertaining a guy like him. A roadman. *Or any guy really, if you wanna be honest, Sabs.*

It definitely was a 'why not, fuck it' type of moment. But the truth is, I enjoyed myself and I don't know, his persistence was endearing, like he genuinely wanted to get to know me. Still, I was reeling from the side effects of smoking so I may or may not have had my common sense inhibited.

I know how these roadmen are, I've seen what they do with the girls they lust over on Instagram. Stunt on them with the cash and cars (which they can't drive legally), take them to overrated steakhouses, buy them all the same Gucci bag, maybe engage in sexual activity (if they're lucky) and then ask them to hold stuff for them in return. *You're being judgy, Sabs.* They're unserious candidates. But Jalaal was able to hold a conversation that didn't involve him talking about what designer items he owns or anything remotely materialistic and shallow.

Low-key, I was surprised by how family-orientated he was when we spoke. He even had to pause our video call at one point to go help his aunt with something, and then his brother came into his room asking for help with his homework.

I didn't go bed until like 12 a.m. I'm pissed now because it's 7 a.m. and I'm absolutely knackered. The sun blaring through my window is only making me more agitated. I have to sort Isabel out for school before I head off to college.

I crawl out of my bed, giving myself a moment to breathe so my brain and body have time to wake up properly. I stretch my arms downwards, yawning as I rub my hands against my bare prickly legs. I literally just shaved two days ago, and I'm covered in hair again. So annoying. I get up and slowly open the door to Isabel and Natasha's room, tiptoeing to make sure I don't wake Dad up. He needs his rest after his night shift; the 18 bus route is his worst.

'Isabel,' I softly say, 'I'm gonna get your stuff ready – go brush your teeth and pack your school bag.'

'Isn't it Sunday?' she mumbles, clenching her fists like a baby.

'No sis, get ready quickly and don't wake Natasha.' She's fast asleep on the top bunk and doesn't start school till later. Waking her up would cause unnecessary beef.

Once downstairs, I grab Isabel's uniform from the washing line outside. The air is muggy and the neighbours are shouting in Arabic like always. I take a moment to evaluate myself. *Was late-night pillow talk with Jalaal worth this tiredness, Sabs?* I am responsible for my own suffering. I swore to myself that I'd never be that girl who put boys before sleep and yet here I am, failing at the first hurdle. *Do better, sis.*

I turn the kettle on and dash some instant coffee into a mug. I pour Coco Pops and semi-skimmed milk into a bowl for Isabel. She won't eat the food at breakfast club. She doesn't like her cereal cold, so even though it's boiling hot outside already, I pop the bowl into the microwave for a minute and thirty seconds. It'll be hot when it comes out, but warm by the time she makes it down. The creaks from the floorboards above reassure me. I wait for her at the long dining table until she comes downstairs.

While Isabel devours her breakfast and gets changed, I go back upstairs to brush my teeth and get ready. I tie my hair up in a neat bun using my slick brush. My baby hairs won't be making an appearance today, and that's the suffering they will endure because of the selfish decisions I made last night. I put on my high-waisted jeans with rips on the knees and my white crop top. I creep back into my sisters' room to leave Natasha her lunch money on her desk like I usually do.

After I drop Isabel off at her school, I WhatsApp Natasha to remind her that I've left her lunch money on her desk. The last time I forgot to do so, she made a big fuss and Dad wouldn't let me hear the end of it. Apparently, it's my responsibility to remind her to feed herself. It's moments like this that I wonder how things will be if I get into Warwick University. I'm the glue holding our family together. How will they cope without me? *Focus on yourself, Sabs.*

I bury my doubts, plug in my wired headphones and walk towards the bus stop. It's packed with mothers and pushchairs. I let them on first and get on last, allowing myself to be squished against the driver's flimsy plastic door with RAY BLK's 'My Hood' blaring into my eardrums.

I wait for Liyah by the Paddington Station exit near Sheldon Square. She arrives quickly. I thank God because the boys from St Augustine's were hovering way too close to me. There's something about a girl wearing headphones that screams 'come harass me' to horny sixth-form boys. Liyah wraps me in a big hug. She's also wearing her white Air Forces but they're definitely in a better state than mine. The creases in my trainers are so deep, you'd think someone drew a line across them in black ink. Liyah is dressed in a burgundy blouse and black denim skirt. She has her pale legs on show, but I'm sure the sun will colour her North African skin by the end of the day.

'Hey sis!' Her tired eyes smile.

'Guuuurl, I am knackered,' I reply.

'I can tell. What happened to your baby hairs?'

'Let's not even go there.'

Making our way to college, I fill Liyah in on Shanice's party and everything else that went along with it. Unsurprisingly, Liyah is shocked about Jalaal.

'Roadman? Your type?' Her mouth is wide open. 'Video chats as well?'

'Close your mouth, you'll catch flies!'

She covers her mouth. 'Rewind, really, a shotter?'

'I know, Liyah! We just sort of started speaking and he's all right ya know.'

'But he's on road. Your dad won't allow it.'

'To be honest, who isn't on road these days?' I surprise myself in defending him.

'OK but isn't he like Somali?' She raises her eyebrows.

'And . . . ?'

'You're Jamaican?'

'And half English!' I correct her.

'He's also Muslim . . .'

'And I'm Christian,' I state matter-of-factly.

'How's that gonna work? You'll convert? Your dad'll love that. So will your Auntie Maureen. Let's not even start on his family. You think you lots are Romeo and Juliet. Wake up, sis.'

I hate that she's right.

'I'm not thinking that far ahead. And it doesn't matter anyway, I haven't heard from him today.'

'Fuckboy!' she sings.

Our college is a reflective glass building with different-coloured window panels. In all honesty, it looks like an upside-down spaceship. The entrance is a revolving glass door, protected by standoffish security guards and a metal detector. Sometimes I question whether I'm at school or in prison. I know my motivation though. It's the only way to leave the ends and start this new chapter of my life at university. I'm gonna do it, and no one's going to stop me. *Nobody can stop you.*

Outside the entrance of the reception, large concrete steps lead down to a small courtyard. The teachers usually smoke on the bottom steps before and after school, always the English teachers with their coffee-stained teeth. Weirdly, some of the boys smoke weed outside at the same time as the teachers. It's awkward because the teachers never say anything to them, even though they come to class high. *Sabs, you cannot be making judgement after your antics.* But then again, when the police do their 'random searches', the smoking teachers are coincidentally nowhere to be seen.

As Liyah and I stroll into college, some of the Business BTEC boys in our form class are smoking outside. Cigarettes make me feel sick.

'Ugh, they're so jarring,' Liyah whispers to me.

'Trust me.'

They're all dressed in black jeans and wearing variations of branded jumpers, Hoodrich, Trapstar, Adidas and Nike. Their eyes peer our way and I feel the discomfort in the pit of my stomach.

'Ay, bunda looking sweet,' Ahmed comments.

'Shut the fuck up, you fucking perv,' Liyah spits back at him.

'You're a fucking slut anyway Liyah, I was chatting to your lightie friend.'

He's talking about me. *Shit*. I fiddle with my gold cross necklace. The gift passed on from Grandma to me, the only thing that calms me down.

'You think she'd look twice at you? You fucking tramp.' She has the venom of a snake.

'Shut up, you Moroccan whore.'

I can feel Liyah beginning to shake with anger; I have to interject. 'Thanks for the compliment but unfortunately, my ass isn't as big as yours.' My voice is calm and collected.

His friends immediately 'OOOOH' him. I pull Liyah by the arm and rush her into the building. I can hear them in the background: 'Are you gonna take that?' and 'Did you just let a girl violate you?'.

Boys make me sick.

I take Liyah to the disabled bathroom to give her the space to cry, rant, scream or do whatever she needs to do to let it all out.

'I'm sorry but who the fuck are they calling a Moroccan whore, watch when I get my cousins to sort them out, fucking pricks.' She inhales. 'Fucking uneducated idiots.'

She starts mocking their voices and I can't help but chuckle. She stops to look me dead in the eye.

We both burst out laughing.

The bell rings and reminds me that it's only 9 a.m. We've got our first lesson of the day. Sociology. Liyah and I do the same subjects:

Sociology, English and Politics. We developed an interest in activism, or, as Liyah would like to say, 'became woke', after the Grenfell tragedy. Liyah's aunt lived in one of the flats and managed to escape when it happened. The council didn't move her to permanent accommodation, and she couldn't live in the hotels they provided because they were so far from the school she taught at. So, her aunt came to live with Liyah for six months. After speaking with her and seeing how it impacted her, it changed us.

Liyah wants to protect people like her aunt and get into policy-making. I'm not sure where I want to go exactly but I want to protect people too – I can't imagine what we would have done if that happened to me. Having our mother abandon us is one thing, but losing our home too? I'm glad I have my sisters. They are my everything and I'm low-key doing this for them too. I want to be their role model and show them that they can do anything they want in this world. They can go anywhere they want. It's not confined to our postcode.

Anyways, we are doing the same subjects but we plan to go to different universities. I want to get out of London and go to Warwick to study Philosophy, Politics and Economics, and Liyah wants to stay in London studying the same degree. Her parents don't feel fully comfortable with her moving out and she explains 'it's a Moroccan thing' so she must stay here. My dad is a bit more chilled and says as long as I'm following my dreams and not getting into trouble, he's got my back. Mum was also on the same vibe as Dad until she changed and decided to go away. *You can't think about her right now.*

'Hello, ladies.' Ms Ross welcomes us in.

'Hey, Miss,' we both reply in unison.

'How was the weekend?'

'You should ask Sabs, she's the one who's been partying all weekend.'

I give Liyah a death glare.

'Partying, eh?'

'Barely Miss, I was just hanging out with some friends.'

'Friends or frieeends?' She raises her eyebrows. My teacher can be so jarring sometimes.

'MISS, no!'

She laughs. 'No distractions, Sabs. You're at the last hurdle and only have three weeks until your exams. Keep up the good work ethic.'

'Will do, Miss.'

'You too, Liyah. I'm expecting the best from both of you.'

We take our seats at the back of the classroom and Ms Ross starts the lesson by going through one of the past papers on socialization. Three weeks until exams. I can do it.

CHAPTER 5

JALAAL

My body needs munch before I go to work. My manager at Sainsbury's is seriously trying to run man down; I don't know why they gave me a 6 p.m.–12 a.m. shift. Making my life long for no reason.

I'm feeling to eat some crisps and chocolate. If Habo knew that's what I was eating outside of the yard, she'd flip her shit. I don't care though; I need the energy to get through this long shift.

My feet carry me to my busted wardrobe and I throw on a pair of black jeans, my maroon-coloured work shirt and a Nike hoody. There is absolutely no chance you will catch me slipping in the Sainsbury's fleece. My manager Steve is always on my case, but I'd rather freeze in the shop than wear that ugly fleece. I'm not some wasteman. One thing about me: my drip has to be on point.

I walk into Ibby's room. He's reading one of his books from *A Series of Unfortunate Events*. I don't remember the last time I touched a book. Every time I look at my brother, I know that he will not end up like me. He is better than me. He never gets into trouble at school and is always caring towards other people. Ibrahim has no bad bone in his body. Even though it does sometimes baffle me how different we are, I am proud that he's my little brother.

'Ibby.' He looks at me, curious. 'I'm going to the shops; do you want anything?' I ask.

'Salt and vinegar crisps please.' He shifts his attention back to his book.

Rah. It's like that? Say no more.

I close the door silently and make my way towards the living room. I hear Habo's favourite Turkish TV show blaring. I don't get what it is with her and watching TV shows that are in languages she does not understand.

'Habo.' She doesn't hear me over the loud volume. 'Habo!' I shout.

Her neck swings in my direction and she gives me cuts. She hates it when people shout in the house, even though she legit screams on the phone every day. Make it make sense.

'Going shops, you want anything?'

'Yes.' She straightens her back. 'Get some teabags. You know the ones?'

Of course, I know it's PG Tips. It's the same tea that we've been using for the past eight years. Even Ibby drinks it with his toast in the morning.

'OK, safe. See you in a bit.'

She presses play on the remote and continues watching her incomprehensible show.

I consider taking my bike to the shop but talk myself out of it, because I've got time to kill before I'm expected at work. Let me even go to the shops further away.

I put my hands in my pockets, start walking, and allow my mind to drift away. Not too much though. I always need to be alert.

CHAPTER 6

SABRINA

I split ways with Liyah at the roundabout; the same spot for the past ten years.

School was proper hectic today. Not that long until I start my exams. Going over the syllabus with Ms Ross made me realize how much I've got left to do. I'm gonna have to be knee-deep in these revision notes for the next month.

My stomach rumbles. I ignore the slight guilt for not asking Liyah to join me, but I prefer eating alone when I'm this anxious. It's nearly 5 p.m. and the flashing lights of Chicken Cottage are calling me. Who knew greasy wings and chips could make one so happy?

I glance at myself in the glass reflection of the shopfront – God, I look a mess. My mum always made sure that I didn't 'look rough'. It's a shame that she isn't around to police what I wear. Her other *priorities* are responsible for her absence. *Sabs, you can't think about her when you're in the middle of exams. It's not your fault. She made those decisions.* I push her out of mind; I'll deal with that later. To give myself credit, I have been up since 7 a.m., so I'm allowed to look dishevelled. Partly due to Jalaal and our yapping all night.

Inside the chicken shop, I'm hit by the aroma of hot oil and crispy batter. The smell is nostalgic. I scan the menu above bossman. I know for a fact that these photos are not what I'm going to be served. I don't know why I'm even looking at the menu when I already know exactly what I'm going to be ordering.

'Hi, can I have six wings and chips please?' I would never call him bossman to his face. It's what the mandem do. Not me.

'You want a drink too? Only add 50p?'

I'm quite anti-fizzy drinks due to my current skincare routine but I think I might need one today. *Fuck it Sabs.*

'Yes, sure – can I get a Coke please?' I smile.

'OK, wait two minute.'

I go and sit on the ledge outside while he prepares my order. I swipe open my phone and see a notification. Jalaal.

What happened to 'I don't like junk food'?

Huh?

Oh shit! My stomach flops.

I slowly look up from my phone. Jalaal is lingering outside the corner shop next to me. *Girl, he better not be stalking you.* He's holding a black plastic bag in his hand and is dressed in dark trousers and a hoody. His creps catch my eyes. He's flexing these cool custom Air Force 1's with an interesting combination of colours and Arabic inscription.

Before we can even exchange words, bossman yells, 'Wings meal ready.'

I run into the chicken shop, throw three pounds at bossman and grab my food. I straight away remove the Coke can from the bag. I hate it when they do that – like don't you know a cold drink will make the chips go soggy and stale. Proper annoying.

Outside, I'm relieved to see Jalaal waiting for me. The universe is crazy. It's only been two days since the party. He's a handsome guy, like he could be a model. I look him up and down intently as I approach him. His brown skin is glistening. He really is so cute.

'Are you stalking me?' I joke.

I'm not sure whether we are meant to hug, so I smooth my fingers against my cross necklace instead. *Stay cool, Sabs.*

'You wish.'

I guess there's no hug then.

'Coincidence that you're here though.' I raise an eyebrow at him.

He ignores me and gestures towards my food. 'What you eating?'

'Wings meal duh. What have you got?'

This small talk feels awkward.

'Unhealthy shit, just like you. Do you wanna sit down and eat?' he asks, his eyes earnest.

Butterflies. *Ignore them – poker face, Sabs.* 'Sure. Shall we go sit on the wall?'

'Lead the way.'

'So you can pree me from the back? I think not.'

He laughs and plants himself on the wall.

I sit down beside him but keep some distance between us. He uses the space to place his munch down. He takes out a can of KA Pineapple, McCoy's Thai Sweet Chilli crisps and a Kinder Bueno. You know what, his taste ain't that bad. I give him ratings for it. I open my box and start with the chips.

'So, what brings you here?' I ask.

'I have work in a bit so thought I'd get some food before my shift.'

Why is he talking about drug dealing as if it's a proper job? A bit weird.

'Work?'

'Yeah, Sainsbury's.'

I completely forgot he worked there. It was like his redeeming quality. *Don't be so judgy Sabs.*

'Oh yeah, sorry, I forgot. Well, I had some revision thing after school, kinda long. Thought I'd treat myself to this shit.' I can't believe I'm calling this food shit when I'm clearly enjoying it. *Why you acting up, Sabs?*

'Shouldn't really call food shit. What were you revising for?' His eyes are curious.

'Sociology.'

'Ms Ross?'

'How did you know?'

'You do know that I went to your college for a bit right . . .' He tilts his head.

'Yeah, but how do you know her? Did you take her class?'

'She was my form tutor,' he explains.

'Oh. Makes sense,' I nod. 'Yeah, was doing some revision and stuff.'

'So, sociology. Is that what you wanna do in the long term?'

'Yeah, I guess so. I'm more interested in disproportionality of wealth in ethnic communities. And how household structures affect that. But yeah, that kinda stuff.' I hope he catches on. I don't know why I'm presuming he's dumb. But he is a roadman after all.

'Ethnic communities in general or specifically black?' he narrows his eyes.

'Specifically black.' I stop my jaw from dropping. So, he does get it. *Sabs, maybe you should give Jalaal more credit.*

He still catches my surprise as he says, 'I'm not dumb you know.'

'Is that why you're not in college then?' Shit. *How can you let that slip out, Sabs?*

'Got bagged for having hella weed. They told me to leave, or they'd kick me out.' He shrugs his shoulders.

'Oh, wow.' I guess it's more weed than the spliff Ahmed and his broke mates share outside colly.

I didn't expect him to be so honest. I thought that he would make up some shit.

'What?' Jalaal says in a half-polite, half-annoyed way.

I realize I've just been staring at him, mouth wide open.

'Sorry. Do you think you'll go back?' *You can salvage this, Sabs.*

'Maybe, we'll see what happens.' He looks away awkwardly.

I don't know what to say so I take a big bite of my chicken wing and hope that my chewing is enough to fill the silence.

Jalaal starts laughing midway.

'What?'

'You're bare dramatic you know.' He continues to chuckle.

'I'm not good with awkward silences,' I confess.

'I can tell,' he smiles. 'Don't worry, you'll be good with them soon enough.'

'What's that supposed to mean?' The tips of my lips curve up.

'Don't worry,' he repeats and winks at me.

I shift my eyes down and analyse his Air Force 1's properly. The white Nike swoosh has a black star in the middle, the heel counter is filled in red and the collar is green with Arabic inscription. The shoes are proper wavy.

'Your shoes are banging, where did you get them customized?'

His face lights up in a way I haven't seen yet, like he's not used to being complimented. 'Swear down? Thanks. I customized them myself to look like the Somaliland flag.' His dimple deepens.

'That's amazing. You're sick, Jalaal.' *So he's an artist!*

We continue talking until I finish my food. Jalaal needs to run back home to drop off stuff to his family before he goes to work. He doesn't want to be late and seems kinda pressed. We walk together to the bins to throw our rubbish away and I literally have a meltdown when I see him put his canned drink into the normal bin instead of the recycling bin.

'Do you not know how to recycle?'

'You're a control freak.' He shakes his head, chuckling.

I stop dead in my tracks.

'OK, OK, I'm sorry.' He holds his hands up in surrender before taking the canned drink out of the bin and putting it in the recycling one. Admirable, seeing as the bin smells rank.

'Anyways, I'll catch you soon?' He holds out his arm for a hug.

I quickly push myself in and out of his embrace.

'We'll see.' I play it cool.

Even though I probably shouldn't see him again, I know that I will.

'All right then, bye Sabs.'

We walk away in different directions.

Don't look back.

After eight seconds, my resilience fails. *Fuck*. He's turned around at the same time. We smile at each other and quickly face back to the direction we are heading. I can't deny it. The butterflies in my stomach are real.

I quickly pull out my phone and text Liyah.

Guess what?

CHAPTER 7

JALAAL

It's been three weeks since I bumped into Sabs at the shops. We've been messaging and FaceTiming at least every other day. I'm deep in the talking stage. I'm rattled by this version of me; I've never been the guy to consistently maintain a conversation with a girl, especially when she's not Somali. At first, I thought she was just so leng. Now here I am, three weeks deep, invested. It sounds bare cringe but *wallahi*, things are a bit different with Sabs because I've *never* acted like this before. She's not judging me, she's taking me as I am. There's no need to pretend, I'm just me. It's new.

Even though Sabs is starting her exams now, I seriously appreciate the time she's given me. She wants to do well, and I respect that. She'll go on to do big things. If only Habo Hani knew that I was speaking to a mixed-race girl. Forget having to be from Somaliland, she's not even from the same continent. Habo would never accept it. I know how traditional Somali people are – they stick together like glue. That's why I can never tell her. It's not that deep though. It's calm. We're just talking. For now.

Time drags on. I'm either working odd shifts at Sainsbury's or posted up somewhere with Shaah, selling to a friend or a friend of a friend. But recently, he's been carrying white and brown. I'd be lying if I said it wasn't mad weird. We always do things together but now he's beyond me. Them man are always asking me to level up but I'm not banking packs. That's where I draw the line. I'd rather eat pork than shove those wraps up myself. Plus, a charge for Class A is worse than Class B, I ain't tryna go pen. I'm not leaving Ibrahim. There's more to this life than just me.

The truth is, the olders almost made me go to Norwich when the police seized my weed. It was worth about £860 but I managed to pay that off with some of the money from work. I can feel it though, they're gonna find a way to make me go soon. They're waiting for me to slip up, to catch me out. The olders are on to me. The man inside me makes me want to step up and just firm it. But after chatting with Sabrina and listening to all her dreams, I'm a bit like rah, I kinda want that too. I don't know man, it's bare difficult.

I've been tryna link Sabs but she's always revising. I even offered to pick her up or study with her, but she's not on it. She said after her exams . . . 'maybe'. I guess I'll have to be patient then. Nothing else to do. She has to succeed.

'*Waryaa*, Jalaal.' my aunt's shouting disrupts me.

'Yes, Habo Hani.'

'Can you pick up Ibrahim please?' Her voice shakes. 'My knee is in pain.'

I haven't picked up Ibby from school for a hot sec.

'Don't worry Habo, I'm going now.'

Ibrahim's school ain't that far away, but the area is a bit bait, so I pull my hoody over my head while I wait outside his school gates.

The parents standing outside have their arms crossed and are waiting patiently for their kids. Some of them give me awkward looks. One lady even nudges her elbow on her man. He looks at me apologetically. I swear down these lot just see a black boy in a hoody and think I'm some hoodrat. I consider taking off my hoody to make them more comfortable but I deep how tapped that actually sounds.

Finally, an older Indian woman marches out the main reception with a bell in her hand and starts clinking it loudly. My ears are gonna be finished. I don't even know which classroom Ibby is coming out of.

Within seconds, all the kids in their white polo shirts and red cotton jumpers run out the classrooms. They are telling their teachers, 'My mum is there', 'There's my dad', 'Mummy' and 'Daddy'. There are so many kids. I'm bare confused. I recognize a short mixed-race girl who is an exact copy of Sabrina – it must be her little sister Isabel. I had no idea she and Ibby went to the same school. She escapes my vision as quickly as she entered and my eyes scan for a little Somali boy with tight curls like mine.

I can't see him, but I can hear him. 'Miss, miss. There's my brother. He's over there, can you see him?' I finally clock him outside the classroom on the far right, tugging on a white woman's beige cardigan. She's a short woman with thick thighs and cropped brown hair with blonde highlights. She's got huge specs on her face. And the way she's wrapping her cardigan around her chest, there's no mistaking she's a teacher.

'Well, Eee-bra-him,' she butchers his name, 'let's just wait a moment to double-check this is your brother.'

I walk over to them, trying not to swagger too much. 'Yo Ibby, you ready to go?' I ignore her and address my brother.

'Jalaal, Miss said I can't go with you.'

My eyebrows furrow.

She looks me up and down, anxiety filling her eyes. 'Well, I didn't actually say that exactly. You know, we have procedure here and I don't recognize you. I know Eee-bra-him says you're his brother, but we just don't know these things sometimes.' She takes a breath. 'Also, you look quite young so I'm not really sure if we are allowed.'

'Look, do you want me to call my aunt? She can't really come here as she's not feeling too good.' I thrust my hands into my pockets, searching for my mobile phone. I pull it out, purposefully sighing my annoyance. I swipe the screen to call Habo Hani and the background picture of Ibrahim and me lights up. Her expression immediately eases. I slide my phone back in my trousers.

'No no no, no worries, I can tell by how Eee-bra-him is reacting to you that you're his brother.' She crouches down to Ibrahim and tells him to have a good weekend.

I kiss my teeth at her and tell him, 'Come on Ibby.'

My phone buzzes in my back pocket. Must be Habo Hani. I legit just picked up Ibby, I don't understand why she gets so worried sometimes. I ignore the call.

Ibby holds my hand as we exit the gates.

Once we get home, Ibrahim rushes upstairs to get on my PlayStation and I go to Habo Hani in the living room. She has a glass of water placed by her medication on the coffee table.

'How are you doing Habo *macaaney*?' I call her sweet aunt.

'I'm Habo *macaaney* now? You're crazy!' she laughs.

'Seriously Habo, are you feeling better?'

'Don't worry about me. *Inshallah* God will give me good health.' She's so righteous sometimes.

'*Inshallah.*' I sit on the sofa beside her, and she looks at me curiously.

'Thank you for collecting Ibrahim, so much *ajr* you will get from that.' She reminds me of the rewards I will get for my good deeds.

'His teacher is so rude *wallahi* though, what the hell was wrong with her? She's kinda racist still.'

'The white one?'

'Yes, the white lady,' I laugh. 'She didn't let Ibrahim go for ages and she didn't believe that I was his *walaalo*.'

Habo Hani smirks.

'What's so funny?'

'Did you go to the school dressed how you are now?'

'Uh yeah, what's wrong with it?' Is she OK?

'I wouldn't give my student to you if you came saying you were his brother.'

'What's that supposed to mean?'

'You look like a, what do you call it, road man? Jalaal-ay.' Her broken English is jokes.

'What?' I can't believe she's violating me like this.

'You look like a criminal *waryaa*!' She goes on a rant about how my clothes look like I'm about to rob someone and that I look like scum. I wish I never brought it up with her now. She doesn't understand that how I dress is my drip. My expression. It's not my fault that she associates it with real criminals. I think the problem isn't the clothes, it's who is wearing it.

My phone pings. iMessage notification from Sabs. There's also the missed call from earlier from a random WhatsApp number with a +252 code. I guess it wasn't Habo then. Must be some scam.

Sabs

This exam has taken the life out of me. Wanna get munch?

Not gonna lie, excitement jolts in my body.

> Stress. Where u at?

I keep my cool despite my immediate reaction.

Sabs

At college still. Gonna finish up in 30mins. Meet me outside?

I am gassed. I wasn't expecting this, and I ain't gonna miss out on this opportunity to see Sabs. Fuck though. I'm not tryna go around W&A college ends. The last thing I need is for someone to catch me slipping, or even worse, for some of the teachers to see me hanging around like some dickhead. My worst nightmare is being the 'excluded' yute who hangs around his old school.

Snm, see you in a bit sweet 1. She's gonna cringe at that.

She replies.

Cringe.

'*Waryaa*, who has you smiling again?' My aunt raises her eyebrows.

My hushed response is enough to confirm her suspicions.

'What are you talking about?' I fake confusion.

'I'm not stupid.' She shakes her head, leaving the room.

I desperately look for something decent to wear, especially after the attitude towards my outfit today. I put on a pair of black jeans, a Trapstar T-shirt since Sabs loves the brand so much, and my Burberry messenger bag. It's a good fit. I pace downstairs, put on my shoes and tell my aunt I'm leaving the house.

'*Waryaa*, wait,' she shouts at me.

'Yes Habo Hani.'

'What's that smell?'

It's Creed cologne.

I smile at her. She knows.

Before she can continue her interrogation, I bolt out the house, making sure not to slam the door. I order a cab on my phone and make my ways to W&A college.

CHAPTER 8

SABRINA

P*ing.*
Jalaal
I'm here.

I'm surprised he managed to get here in thirty minutes. I'm flattered. *He's got good timekeeping, tick.*

Today has been so exhausting. The English exam on *Hamlet* was actually long and all I can think about is food and rest. Jalaal has been dying to link up but has also been respectful of my exam period. I need to relax a little bit and to be honest, I kinda want to see him again. Three weeks of messaging and FaceTime revision sessions are getting boring. And I'm not going to include the random day we bumped into each other at the shops. That doesn't count. I'm not sure why I'm explaining myself. If I want to see Jalaal, then I will.

OK coming out now.

Jalaal
Come to the blue Prius by the bike storage.

You're driving a Prius?

Jalaal
No, I'm in a cab.

> Yeah, can't lie – I'm not tryna get ina cab wit you.

I type back quickly. There's something really unsettling about being in a cab, especially with someone I don't fully know.

Jalaal
Ffs, but I've paid for it.

> So? I didn't ask you to . . .
>
> I tap the send button with frustration.

Jalaal
Dw sorry, I'm coming out now.

Outside of the college building, Jalaal walks over to me. Even though his body is facing me, his eyes are scanning his surroundings. He's cautious. *Shit*. I completely forgot that this might be an awkward encounter for him. *Sabs, you're too absorbed in your own world sometimes*.

I go to him, my heart beating fast. I don't want him ending up in an altercation right now because of me. I'm steps away from him when he abruptly stops and smiles at me. The same cheeky smile from the night when we first met. I leap forward and wrap my arms around his neck, tiptoeing to reach him. I don't care if anyone at college sees.

'You smell good.' I unhinge myself from him.

'Always.' He winks.

'Don't make me cringe. Sorry about the cab issue. It just feels a bit weird to me.'

'Nah, don't worry 'bout it. I understand. I ain't been on TfL for a while and it's a bit of a sticky one for me.'

'I was being insensitive. How about we just walk to Paddington

Station and decide what to do from there? It's not that bait for us, and plus, it's rush hour time,' I suggest.

'Anything for you, miss.'

Butterflies flutter in my stomach. Jalaal is towering over me, shielding me from the sun. He's still focused elsewhere though, glancing in every direction with his feet spread apart, ready to pivot in any direction.

I cough to get his attention.

He double-takes at my shirt. I hope I haven't got a stain or a hole.

'You support Chelsea?' He raises his eyebrows.

'Of course, West London born and bred. What about you?' I sigh in relief.

'I'm not really into football, unless it's the World Cup or Euros. I prefer watching the NBA. Back to you and Chelsea, though. Tell me more.'

I grin. I tell Jalaal the fact that I'm a big Chelsea fan and the funny story attached to it. When I was younger, my dad, an Arsenal fan, would take me to the park to play football, having decked me out in his Arsenal kit. One day, while watching Arsenal and Chelsea play, it infuriated him that Chelsea had won. I kept teasing him and he got so pissed. What really set him off was when I started commenting that Chelsea had a better kit. It was hilarious. For entertainment purposes, I chose to support Chelsea but eventually I got into the club and committed to being a supporter. Dad took me on a tour of Stamford Bridge for my tenth birthday and that sealed the deal for me. We have an arrangement though: if we ever go to games together, we take alternate turns. So I'll go with him to Arsenal games and vice versa.

'Do you kick ball too?' His eyes widen.

'Yes I do. You don't think a girl can play?' I tease.

'Girls can play . . . just . . . that's so cool, still.' He rubs my shoulder.

'I know, you're gonna be a Chelsea fan soon, trust me.' I rub his shoulder back.

He rolls his eyes. 'Anyways, give me your bag, please.' He reaches for it.

'Why?' I side-eye.

'So I can carry it for you?' His eyes are quizzical.

'Oh no, don't worry. I got it. Ain't it weird carrying a girl's bag, anyway?'

'You think I care?'

His arm remains outreached so I hand over my heavy bag and watch Jalaal easily clasp it in his hands, unbothered, the veins in his forearm slightly protruding. *Sabs, a boy who isn't afraid of being emasculate – you know you love this.*

At Paddington Station, there are so many bloody people. Tourists with backpacks on their fronts, heads tilted back glaring at train times on the board. Plenty of middle-aged men in suits and women clicking their heels in their pencil skirts. Everyone is pacing in different directions. It's crazy. And there's a random Burger King here. I can't believe that place still exists. Even though I regularly meet Liyah outside the station, I only ever go inside to take the train out to Bristol to see my family on my mother's side. My sisters and I always go during Easter or Christmas to spend time with our cousins up there. They love us endlessly. I'll be visiting them again just before I leave for university. Dad has the week off work, so I won't have any babysitting duties. I can't wait.

Jalaal's wariness is obvious.

'Wait, where are we going?' I shuffle.

'Sabs.' He peers around the station in amazement. 'How can we get to Oxford Street? I don't want to ruin the surprise, but we need to get to them ends.'

He's too adorable.

'Let me look at maps to double-check. What's the surprise though?' I smile.

'Don't worry 'bout it sweetheart,' he jokes but his eyes are still examining the station.

I wonder if that's what he must always feel like. He told me that he doesn't have opps and he's not into *that* kind of road life. Maybe he's worried about getting robbed. Now I feel bad for making him take public transport; we should've just got into the cab that he was in. *Damn, Sabs. Why you gotta be so extra?*

After quickly looking at the map on my phone, I figure out that we need to take the Bakerloo line to Oxford Circus. I tug on Jalaal's shirt and tell him, 'Come on, it's this way.'

We wait outside Oxford Circus, the breeze cooling us from just being baked in the Bakerloo Line. Jalaal smiles at me. Despite being crowded in the masses of people, I feel safe in his proximity.

'Where are we going now?' I ask.

'Umm one sec, I need to get my maps out.' He fumbles around his pockets, pulling out his personal belongings, including a Nokia brick phone and then his iPhone 7. He quickly slides his trap phone back into his pocket and I pretend to look away. My gut clenches at the thought of Jalaal selling drugs.

'Umm, Sabs!' He snaps me out of my mental spiral. 'Just follow me yeah, it's like a two min walk.' He pulls out his hand for me to hold.

I look up at him. It's too soon.

'I'm OK, I don't need a guide dog.' I regret the words.

He's quick to make a joke about it, 'Didn't want you getting lost, but say no more.'

He walks ahead and I follow him like a stray dog.

Vapiano.

The famous Vaps.

'You ever been?' Jalaal asks me as we wait in the queue. He knows I haven't been. I scan around the place, trying to mask this feeling of foreignness in my face. The truth is, I haven't been taken to eat out in central by a guy before. Ever. I have been to a few nice restaurants for birthdays but never with a guy, never just the two of us.

'Nah, I don't think so, but I hear everyone rave on about it.'

'I think you'll like it.' He nods to himself.

'You don't even know what kinda food I like.'

'Everyone likes Vapiano.'

'"Everyone likes Vapiano",' I mock him.

'You're jarring, you know that.'

'You love me though,' I say too fast.

He rolls his eyes.

'Not yet,' he says under his breath, thinking I can't hear him.

Vapiano is packed with young people of different ethnicities. Loads of black people here too. I embarrassingly thought that we only go to places like Chicken Cottage and Morley's. And that the only black people who come to dine in central regularly are the sell-out middle-class ones. *Sabs, why are you negatively stereotyping your own people?* Yet here I am, with Jalaal, a roadman of all people.

The employee gives us a card to order our food and explains that payment is taken when we leave. Jalaal and I head towards the food counter. It's airy and spacious and the air conditioning cools some of my nerves. He tries explaining the menu to me but I'm really struggling to understand all the pastas and sauces. Plus, I'm dazzled by how the chef is tossing all sorts of ingredients in his pans. I point at my favourite pasta, tagliatelle.

'I don't know what sauce to get.' I'm absolutely overwhelmed.

'Try the arrabbiata,' Jalaal tells me.

'What's that?'

'It's like a tomato sauce but spicier. Can't go wrong with it.'

'All right, I'll get that then.' I love that he's taking the lead and helping me decide. It's like, I'm always deciding what we eat at home and getting school stuff ready. It feels good that he's doing it for me.

'Do you want cheese on top?'

'Of course.'

We haven't had to go through the pains of paying. Yet. Obviously, I'll pay for my meal and Jalaal will pay for his. This isn't really a date, I asked him to meet up for munch and we just happened to go to this place in central. This is better than the Nando's that I was expecting.

When the man gives us our trays of food, Jalaal is adamant he can hold both. He ushers us upstairs where it's quieter, and he sets our trays on a table. We sit opposite each other, me facing towards the wall, and him facing towards the rest of the restaurant.

'So, why did you suddenly wanna link up in the middle of your exams?'

'Am I not allowed to see you?'

'Nah, it's not that.' His muscles ease from their tense position. 'It was a nice surprise still.'

'Don't ask questions then, let me try this pasta you been raving on about.'

I pick up the fork and stab the pasta that is covered in parmesan cheese, noticing the pressure of Jalaal's gaze. If this pasta isn't good, I'm gonna be fuming.

I place the tagliatelle in my mouth, eyes directly locking with Jalaal's.

'You can't even lie, it tastes good,' he says before I chew.

He's right, but I can't let him know.

'Yeah . . . I mean pasta isn't that much of a difficult dish to cook though.' I try to minimize it.

'You're jarring, can't you just admit when you're wrong. I'm telling you, it's some mixed-race privilege thing.'

I roll my eyes as he begins to dig into his food. I don't know what he ordered but it is penne with some sort of white sauce, chicken Alfredo maybe. I wonder if it's halal but I'm too shy to ask. It looks quite appetizing; I'd love to taste it, but I'm not brave enough to ask.

Jalaal clocks me staring at his food and asks, 'You wanna try it or summin?'

I sheepishly smile at him, and he wraps the pasta string around the fork, pierces a piece of chicken and holds it out for me. I move in closer, opening my mouth as Jalaal holds my chin with one hand and uses the other to put the food in my mouth. I scrape my teeth against the fork, making sure to consume everything.

He sits back and waits knowingly.

'Mine's better,' I tell him after I swallow my bite.

'At least you're admitting you like the food.'

I shake my head with a smile.

*

After taking the last bite of my pasta, I wash it down with water.

'Where exactly do I pay?'

He laughs at me.

'What?'

'You ain't payin'.' He brushes me off. 'And . . . don't even try say anything. Nothing to do with feminism. This is my treat since I picked the place.'

I bite my tongue. Hard. I don't think any guy has ever paid for me. Especially not a part-time dealer. *He's part-time now, eh?*

'Are you sure?'

'Don't worry, B.'

'Ugh.' Ruining the moment. 'I'm not B.'

'O-K, Sabrina,' he mouths slowly.

We leave Vapiano and linger outside.

A silence falls. I don't know if it's about getting home or if there's something else going on.

'Why are you stood so far?' Jalaal quizzes me.

I'm stood by the kerb, hopping up and down from the pavement to the road. *Get it together, Sabs.*

'Am I not allowed to stand afar?' I throw the sass back.

Jalaal shakes his head before setting his gaze on me. His stare feels purposeful. I stare at him back. I'm not afraid to give him the same intensity he gives me. Just because he's paid for my food does not mean he can be all handsome and intense.

'Come closer.' He holds his arms out.

I don't know what possesses me, but I find my legs walking towards Jalaal. He places his hands on my arms and softly pulls me in. His face is inches above mine. I feel seen. Too seen. I wonder if he can see my moustache; I haven't waxed my upper lip in a hot sec. *Sabs, get out of your head.* Before I can convince myself that he's staring at my small hyperpigmentation marks, his lips are on mine.

I haven't kissed a guy in so long, I forget what it feels like. Jalaal's lips are soft and when I press into them, they feel like two cushions swallowing me in. His arms snake around the dip of my back and pull me towards him. I'm enclosed, wrapped up in him.

I wonder if anyone is watching. *Get out of your head Sabs and enjoy the kiss.* I feel something wet at the tip of my top lip. His tongue. I slightly part my lips and let it inside. I'm expecting pasta sauce, but I can taste the fresh mint. He dips his tongue on the roof of my mouth and licks it smoothly over my teeth. I don't know what he's doing but it feels good, and I part my mouth open wider to let out a soft moan.

Unexpectedly, he draws back and chuckles at me.

'What?' I mumble before putting my forehead into his chest, hiding my embarrassment.

He wraps me in a hug. 'Nothing Sabs. You're just bare adorable, you know that?'

This feels good. This feels safe. In his arms. I don't want him to let me go. I don't want to let go.

'So,' he whispers in my ear and a shudder runs down my spine. 'We gonna get a cab home or what?'

I laugh before slapping his chest and moving away.

'You cheeky—' He cuts me off by kissing me on the lips again.

'Guess it's a yes,' he mumbles into my lips.

I groan in agreement.

CHAPTER 9

JALAAL

I arrive at yard after dropping Sabrina off first. The lights are off when I get into the house.

I'm gassed that Sabs holla'd at me to get some munch and I'm glad she was satisfied with Vapiano. Lipsing her was my way of showing that I like her. And it's good to know that she's feeling me too. It helps bare that she's also a good kisser.

Ping. I know it's Shaah messaging. I don't even have to look at my phone. I bet he's gonna call me now.

Ring.

'Yo,' I mutter.

'What you saying bro? You haven't replied to me all day. Were you with that ting?'

'Put some respect on her name please. She's not a ting.'

'Ay sorry fam, I'll keep my mouth shut. You coming out? Some guys want a re-up.' He's always got something lined up.

'Say no more. Ima meet you outside your block, I'm five mins away.'

'Bless.'

Shaah is inseparable from his Moncler jacket even though it's still so warm outside.

'Yo, my brudda,' he calls out to me. His beard is starting to grow out and the swoop of his hair is now covering his forehead.

I walk towards him, fists clenched ready to spud him.

He surprises me with a hug. 'Fam, I haven't seen you in time.'

'Say *wallahi*? It's only been like two days,' I joke.

'True say. Anyway, need to do pick-up now.'

'Who is bringing it?'

'Big H.'

My heart sinks. Big H is the plug. But he's also the guy who was trying to get me to run lines up north. Not ideal. I can't even let Shaah know too much because he idolizes Big H. Shaah's trying to move up and it's not my place to stop a brudda from making P's.

Engines roar. A black BMW 1 Series swerves around the block – it slows down as it approaches us and its black windows wind down. Big H.

'Young bucks.' His teeth are covered in gold grills.

I stride over to him, imitating the confidence I don't have.

'Yo.' I deepen my voice and pull out my fist to bump him.

He looks me up and down before bumping my fist with extra force. OK bro, I feel the animosity.

'I can't always be selling you a Z, Jalaal, you're making small profits from my line,' he tells me straight.

He isn't wrong though. I am buying from him and making profits. Not as much as I could be making though. Just enough to buss myself and sort Habo out.

'I know bro, but you know this is how I wanna roll.'

'I don't know about that still. I'll allow you for now, but I don't think it's going to be like this for long.'

'Say no more.' I shrug. I'm not gonna allow him to intimidate man. I'm not some dickhead. You would never think that when I first started shotting, Big H used to treat me like I was his little brother. Always looking out for me and getting me new creps. Took me under his wing. And the way people on the estate would respect me was mad. It's not like that any more.

'Get in then, what are you man waiting for?' he commands.

We both hop into the car, Shaah at the front and me sat at the back. I zone out as they both immerse in conversation. The AC is on full blast, but my body still feels hot.

I look at Big H. Driving a nice whip, dressed head to toe in fresh garms, has bare girls on to him, hotels, parties. Everything. Here I am. Too much of a pussy to sell the white and brown. Doing nothing with my life. No real ambitions like Sabs. She's got her life put together. I'm not tryna go uni. But what else am I gonna do? Is making small profits from selling weed and working at Sainsbury's the life that I want? Sometimes it's too much effort to even think about that.

I come back to reality when I notice Big H hand over two big wraps to Shaah.

'You need to be careful still, the CTOWN gang have been robbing a few youngers,' he warns Shaah. 'You don't wanna be in debt to me.'

'Don't worry fam, Ima need a re-up soon,' Shaah tries to assure him.

'You're gonna be doing big tings soon. I can feel it,' Big H gasses him. I don't get how he's bigging Shaah up like he's gonna be prime minister or something. 'Big tings' is not running lines. And bare man do that.

I see the gleam in Shaah's eyes, and it annoys me. Can't Shaah see that these man will say anything to you?

I cough to remind them of my presence.

'Nearly forgot 'bout you back there.' Big H fumbles under his car seat, and we exchange weed and money.

I don't know about Shaah but I'm ready to get out of here. The vibe is mad off and I'm starting to feel suffocated.

'Mandem,' I announce, 'I need to get out of here, family ting,' my hand already on the door handle.

'I can drop you off,' Big H offers.

'Nah, I'm good still – it's quicker to walk.'

I'm sure the dickhead already knows where I live.

Before they can respond, I fly out the car, making sure to close the door behind me carefully. I don't want to give Big H any reason to be on my case.

I need something to calm me down.

I roll myself a joint and stroll back home.

The front door struggles to budge and that's when I spot the Dunlop suitcases on the floor inside. *Who the fuck is here?*

'Bro, you actually stink.' A familiar voice.

'Excuse me.' I peer up the stairs.

She emerges from the top of the staircase, dressed in jorts and an oversized Champion T-shirt. Halima.

'When did you get here?' I ask her.

'Drove down earlier today. Where have you been? I've been waiting ages.' Her feet thud down the stairs.

My eyes dart between the suitcase and her. 'Looks like you're gonna be more than a guest.'

She ignores me. 'Come give your fave cuzzy a big hug.' She embraces me in her thin arms.

She unwraps herself but remains in front of me.

'Bro, you actually stink. What the fuck?'

I can see her clearly now. Her once burnt straight hair is tied up in a loose bun of curls. Is that a silver septum piercing? And Habo Hani hasn't said anything? She's got the slightest crease around her eyes, but she still looks as young as when I last saw her. I can tell she's lost weight though; her cheeks are more sunken. Not in a sickly way, but noticeable.

'Allow me.' I shrug her off and kick my shoes away.

'Aren't you happy to see me? You're in a mood.'

'Allah! You've only been here two mins and you're already on to me. I thought you moving out for uni would give me a break.'

Halima is technically my aunt. She's sisters with Habo Hani and Hooyo. Obviously, Halima is bare younger than them so there's no way I'm calling her habo. She used to live with us but moved out to Bristol for university like two years ago. She says it's more 'progressive' and doesn't come back home as often. That's why I'm baffled she's here. I guess it's summer though.

Halima is cool. She isn't like some of the Somali girls from the ends, she's more into this liberal social activism stuff. A bit like Sabrina. I reckon that the both of them would get along.

'*Waryaa*, I'll never not be on your case. Get used to it. But seriously, you stink . . . of weed?'

'Don't call me *waryaa*, you know I don't like it. And since when did you have a septum piercing?' I deflect.

'I don't really get your point.'

'I don't get yours either.'

'Have you been in a bando, shotting?' she asks.

'Firstly, that sounds so weird coming out your mouth. Secondly, what the fuck? No!' I straight out deny. She can't think that I'm that tapped.

'You better not be on no dumb shit, we all ain't breaking our backs for you to be some hoodrat.'

I don't know why she gotta say it like that. As if she's sacrificing her whole life for me. It's bare pressurizing for no reason.

'Nah, nah,' my voice falters, 'you know I'm not on them tings deya.'

'Then why aren't you going college any more?' she whispers, so no one overhears.

'What?' I fake shock.

'Deqa's little sister told me you got kicked out or something, but that's not the shocking part. The surprise is that my sister still thinks you're at college. Now tell me how that's working . . .'

Shit. Fuck.

'Hals, Cuzzy. Can we talk about this tomorrow please, I beg you? Today has actually been long,' I plead.

Hals knows when I'm chatting shit and when I'm being serious. I hope she notices that I'm not capping.

'Fine. Gives you time to come off whatever you've taken. *Dib jir.*' She side-eyes me.

I refrain myself from kissing my teeth at being called a lowlife. I'm not wanting another lecture. I slide past her and walk into my room, slowly closing the door behind me. It's 3.13 a.m. and I'm tired fam.

I'm at peace sitting at the kitchen table alone, eating my Coco Pops and drinking tea. I know it's bare childish to eat cereal at my big age, but it bangs. Nothing beats a cereal in the morning. Ibrahim is upstairs on the PlayStation and Habo Hani is in the living room shouting to somebody in Hargeisa on the phone. I'm enjoying this alone time to relax and play around with sketches on my iPad.

'Well, well, well.' Hals emerges from the corridor, ready to disturb my peace.

She's wearing a thin *shiid* with her collarbones poking out. The septum piercing is so prominent on her face – much more than it was last night.

'You gonna tell me or what?'

'I was with a girl.'

'And that's why you stunk of weed?' She doesn't look impressed.

'Not really, I think it's bummy to only smoke with girls. I linked Shaah after.' I intentionally miss out the part about linking Big H to get a re-up.

'First of all, what's that supposed to mean, "bummy to smoke with girls"? Is that some twisted way of dictating what women can and can't do? And why are you smoking anyway?'

God, this girl and her extreme feminism shit.

'No actually,' I correct her, 'it's cool to smoke with girls but it's bummy if that's *all* you do, because why should we need to get high to enjoy each other's company? And can you keep your voice down, Habo understands what weed is for fuck's sake.'

'Answer me then!'

'I had to do a quick drop-off.' I regret the words as soon as they come out of my mouth.

She doesn't blink. 'Is that what you want to do with your life?'

Of course it isn't. But what else am I meant to do? There ain't much to do that pays good money and I'm not tryna go university. They kicked me out of college so what am I actually supposed to do?

'Umm. Nah.'

'So why the hell are you doing that shit?' She flares her nostrils.

'Need to get my P's up.' I crack a smile that isn't reciprocated.

'Jalaal, that's not even funny. You come from a good family, you're a smart boy and actually had mad prospects. You still do. You got all A's and A*'s in your GCSEs. I don't understand why you are jeopardizing that to make some extra cash. You can do better.' She takes a breath. 'Trust me, I'm not one to lecture, we all have our phases. But you know better than that and you have a lot to lose.'

'Like what? What am I actually gonna lose? Cos I already lost Hooyo, and Abo is never coming back.'

'And I'll never know what that feels like. But you have a supportive network and a little brother who adores you. *Wallahi*, we need to appreciate what we have more.' Her big eyes water.

'You don't need to bring Ibby into this. Let's change the subject,' I cut her off.

She looks at me with pity. Actual pity in her eyes. I'm not some loser and emotional wreck, I don't need her fucking sympathy.

'Fine,' she switches, making my head spin, 'tell me about this girl then.'

'What?'

'The one you met before your lil' Afghan friend.' She's firing shots.

'Ohhhhh, Sabrina. That was calm.' I downplay it.

'She isn't Somali?' She raises her eyebrows and smiles.

'Nah . . .'

'What *cadaan* girl has you smiling? I'm shook, always thought you'd end up with a Somali girl. Spill the tea.'

'All right.' I give in. I've been waiting to share this with someone who will understand.

I tell Hals everything and don't leave anything out. Bare mandem don't understand how I can tell my cousin all about my life. She's probably one of the only people I can really trust, and she gives mad good advice. The best thing about Hals is that she listens to me. Like, properly listens. She doesn't zone out like some of my boys.

I start from the block party up until now. I emphasize the good parts about Sabrina, which is basically everything, like how she's tryna get into Warwick University, she's doing her A Levels, she takes care of her two younger sisters, helps around the house, how her mum's family live in Bristol. I mention that Sabrina hasn't seen her mum for a couple years, which she briefly mentioned on FaceTime. It made me think, is it better to have no mum, or a mum who isn't really herself and you never see? Imagine having to live with that disappointment? Is it worse than me, having to live with emptiness? Anyways, Sabs is not neglecting her mum's family who live in Bristol, which I respect bare.

I don't forget to mention how easy it is to talk to her, that I like that she's studious and that she geeks out on Chelsea Football Club.

I finish, saying, 'It's gonna sound mad but she's got this kinda aura or energy where I feel safe talking to her. She accepts who I am and tries to understand me, even though she doesn't agree with some of the stuff I do.'

When I finish, Hals sips on her peppermint tea. Since when did we have peppermint tea in the house? It must be some weird liberal type thing she's learnt at university because all we drink here is Somali tea, which is filled with sugar and condensed milk.

'That's a lot. But it also sounds as though you really like this girl. For real. Not like those other Somali girls you used to fuck around with and break their hearts.' She loves to bring up my past.

'Yeah, because all those girls wanted to do up image. Life isn't every day posting on Instagram in shisha cafes with some Gucci bags. *Wallahi*, it gets too much sometimes.' It's like they copy and paste.

'You can't stereotype Somali girls into one box because you've had a bad experience with two girls. Literally only two girls,' she snorts. 'And you love your designer shit.'

But she's speaking facts. I can't be thinking like that of my own people. Also, Hals is a prime example. I bet she likes them punk boys with them hoops in their earlobes though.

'You're right still. Also yeah, I like *some* designer clothing but that's cos they're good investments and better quality. Not because I need to stunt on people.'

'OK.' She rolls her eyes. 'Anyways, does it bother you?'

'Does what bother me?'

'That not only is she mixed English and Jamaican, she's also not Muslim,' she points out before adding, 'Me, personally, you know I'm not bothered. But you *know* my sister, she will not let that run.'

'I swear the Quran says that I can marry a Jewish, Muslim or Christian girl. And she's kinda Christian so it will be halal.'

'You're thinking of marriage?' She raises her eyebrows.

'Fuck no. I mean, I was just tryna justify it being halal.'

'Yeah, yeah.'

'But seriously Hals, she knows a little bit about Islam and that. I think it's cos her best friend is Moroccan so she ain't clueless,' I defend Sabs.

'That's good. It sounds promising though. I really hope this thing with Sabrina goes well. She seems like a good person and if she can bring some goodness into your life, Ima support it! Not my sister though, good luck with that!'

'If you support it, that's all I need for now!' She's a fucking G. Hals is a fucking G.

She hugs me in a headlock. We both know we are different but it's good to know that we have each other's backs.

Buzz. I slide my vibrating phone out of my back pocket, hoping it's Sabrina. It's the +252 number again, who the fuck is it and where the hell are they calling me from?

'Who is belling you?' Hals asks.

'I don't fucking know. It's some spam number starting with +252.'

'That's back home you know.'

Fuck. Is it him? What does Abo want?

CHAPTER 10

SABRINA

Vapianos was the best date I've ever been on. To be honest, it is the only date that I have been on. I don't know if my 'ex-boyfriend' in year ten taking me to Nando's and telling me I can't spend more than ten pounds counts. I'd never let Jalaal know that though – that's an *L* I'm never willing to share. Especially because he'd take the piss out of me forever.

I sigh. Things are going well with Jalaal, but something inside me is trying to get out. I don't know, I'm afraid that catching real feelings for him will distract me from exams and getting out of the ends. I have so many aspirations and don't want me falling for some guy from ends to ruin that. There's so much at stake. I can't disappoint Dad. There's a lot riding for me and I've seen it when girls just give up everything for their man. I don't wanna be like that. I'm spiralling.

I text Jalaal to call me. I need to get this off my chest.

I close my bedroom door slowly; the last thing I need is Izzy and Tasha eavesdropping.

'Oh, a phone call yeah? Must be serious then,' his joking voice soothes me.

'Relax. It's not that deep. I just cba to type.' *Keep it cool, Sabs.*

'Why don't you say "can't be arsed" instead of abbreviating. You're actually bare lazy.'

'Don't make me hang up,' I joke.

'OK, OK, speak your truth.'

'Right, promise you'll be understanding? I know how you boys are,' I pre-empt.

'Speak up, Sabs.'

'I don't know, like, I'm really stressed about these exams, you know?'

'These exams, don't worry, they're going to be light work.'

'But there's more, Jalaal. There's bare pressure and I don't wanna disappoint my dad.'

'What do you mean? Your dad sounds like he's got your back.'

'I sometimes feel like I'm on auto-drive, like I'm doing too much. Taking care of my sisters, tryna be a good daughter, getting the best grades and tryna do something proper with my life.' I take a deep breath. 'Not gonna lie, don't judge me but sometimes, I feel kind of alone, I can't explain it. It's like nobody in my family *really* gets me. None of them have been to uni, like, not even my family in Bristol. So none of them get the pressure. I'm doing this all on my own. I'm going to be the one in my family to *make it*. Earn real money, buy a big house in a nice neighbourhood, go out to fancy dinners, drive a nice car and everything else like those rich white people that live in Notting Hill. It's just proper long, and I want to do well so I don't disappoint anyone.' I sigh. I've said too much.

'No word of a lie, it actually be like that sometimes. Sabs, you're actually lit – you know that? You're doing bare well and I don't think you realize how amazing you are. I'm not even lying; I wish I was like you. I'm here if you need me. Like if you want someone to gas you up to revise or you need a likkle break. I'm here. You got this. Trust me.'

'Likkle? You're so cringe.' But I can't ignore how my heart is legit melting at his kind words.

'Just telling the truth. Keep focused on where you wanna go and you'll make it. Like, I know you wanna go university, but after that, too.' He pauses. 'Like what are your dreams?'

I've never had someone ask me what my dreams are. This is really a different side to Jalaal. And not gonna lie, it's giving boyfriend material. *Sabs, how are you going from one extreme of being afraid of losing yourself, to him being boyfriend material?*

'I'm trying to get into Warwick, as you know.'

'That is quaaaaay.' There is a hint of something in his voice. 'Anyways, tell me more. What you tryna do when you leave the ends?'

I tell him almost everything. Obviously, I evade the mum situation as much as I can. *Sabs, be honest, a big part of moving away is to leave that pain she left.* Well, Jalaal only knows that she hasn't been in the picture for a couple years. I don't want to burden him with more.

There's also the whole 'living in the hood' thing which I explained to Jalaal. I don't know if I can call it being poor because I have a roof over my head, food on the table and a bed to sleep in. But I want something different. A different type of life. Jalaal really understands that. He says that him making money isn't for lifestyle purposes, it's for him to do something better for his family and himself. But it does make me wonder why he has a few designer items. I guess we can all treat ourselves here and there. I mean, I wouldn't be seen dead in Fila platform shoes, so I've had to fork out for the stuff I want. Also, working at JD gave me mad discounts. It's a shame I had to give up my weekend job because of A Level exams.

Jalaal asks what Warwick Uni is like, and I sheepishly tell him that I haven't visited because I've never been able to leave my sisters for a day *but* I know intuitively that that's the place for me. It sounds silly saying it aloud, but I genuinely mean it, I've done the online virtual 360 tour – it's perfect. Also, I'm being extra defensive because how can I justify wanting to move away from home for three years to a different city that I've never been to before?

'Sabs, I can't lie, I didn't clock how much you've got going on.'

Finally, somebody who understands my struggle.

Relief seeps into my body after hanging up. Someone actually understands. Or wants to understand. And they aren't questioning my intentions. *He's really starting to get you, Sabs.*

I go downstairs to the living room where Dad is watching TV and sipping on Sorrel, catching up on *EastEnders*. It's football off-season otherwise he would be watching *Match of the Day* or highlights from games. Dad's always exhausted from a night shift on a Friday, so even though it's only 8 p.m., it surprises me that he's still awake. Dad says all the 'youngsters' on the bus going into the city have lost their minds and that we should never drink excessively. Anyways, he doesn't even like *EastEnders* because it's too dramatic – but would tolerate it when Mum was around. Guess he's missing her tonight.

It's weird to think it's only been two years since Mum left us. Or chose to pick that life over her kids. We used to be a relatively normal family. Me, Mum, Dad, Izzy and Tasha. But when my grandma died, mum's alcohol problems got worse. Like stupidly bad. She started taking cocaine and within months, she was injecting heroin, and that was enough for dad. He said he couldn't have his daughters witnessing their mother slowly killing herself. So, he gave her an ultimatum. He told her to fix up and get help, or else leave the house. We haven't seen her since.

At the beginning, I hated Dad because I blamed him for her leaving. There was a period we didn't speak that much and all I wanted to do was just scream and shout at him. I eventually got support from the school counsellor and it proper helped. I kinda realized afterwards that Mum made the *choice* to go. Nobody actually forced her. It was easier to be angry at Dad than to accept the fact she *decided* to go. It's all fucked up. *Not worth thinking about her now, Sabs. You've got Dad, Tash and Izzy. Count your blessings.*

He seems content in his reclining sofa chair now. I wrap my arms around his head. 'I appreciate you Dad.'

He doesn't respond but I know he is smiling because his cheeks lift under my embrace. I unwind from him.

After my difficult phone call with Jalaal, it's time for another difficult chat with Dad. *Sabs, you're defo torturing yourself today.* I swallow my anxieties. 'So Dad, what do you know about Somalis?'

His laugh rumbles. 'Why would you ask me that?'

'Just curious.' I shrug my shoulders.

'They're insular people, they don't delve out of their culture. Some of them are crazy though – no morals, they will kill for stupidity. Back in the day, they were a laughing stock. Nowadays, different story, you don't mess with the Somalis. They're Muslims too. Different world.'

I don't know what I was expecting, but he's obviously being narrow-minded.

'Oh, but that's a stereotype right. Not *every* Somali is like that.' I stumble on my words.

'Maybe,' he says dismissively. *Won't be telling him about Jalaal any time soon.*

'Anyways.' Time to wrap this up. 'I'm going to the shops – does anyone want anything?' I yell out to the house, no consideration for my dad's ears.

'Sabrina, what did I tell you about shouting in the house?' My dad swings his head back at me.

'Sorry Dad, do you want anything?' I soften my voice.

'Nothing. Take Izzy with you.'

Babysitter duties again. *Stop trying to make out as if it's bad.* I don't mind taking Izzy, I love listening to her talk about the drama at her school. Literally has me in hysterics.

In her room, I find a disgruntled Tasha sitting on her bed scrolling through her phone. She glances at me for a split second before she focuses back on her screen. 'What do you want?'

'Didn't you hear me?'

'Of course I heard you, you were shouting like a madwoman. What do you want though? Like why you in my room?' She's in a mood.

'Where's Izzy?'

'She's in the garden playing with those rugrats.'

'Bit mean?' I can't help myself.

'Anyways . . .' she deflects. 'Can you buy some pads?'

OK, so now she wants to give me the time of day.

'Yes, I can indeed. Explains why you're being such a bitch.' I close the door before she has time to respond.

'There's ten pounds on the table for whatever you need. Get Izzy something – but not too much sugar,' Dad says.

You can tell who the favourite child is. I pick up the ten-pound note and scrunch it into my front jeans pocket. Although I'm tempted to put it in my back pocket, I have this weird paranoia that some weirdo will grope me and take the note out. Mum always told me to put cash in the front pocket.

The sun beams against the blue sky. Lucky there's a cool breeze. Izzy is in the front garden kicking a plastic football with the new kids from across the road.

I notice that all of them are wearing tatty clothing and look kinda dishevelled. Once navy-blue T-shirts are now a washed-out grey colour. They've got maroon-coloured dry food on the corners of their lips. I'm assuming baked beans or ketchup. They're all wearing sandals that are way too small so their little toes poke out. Maybe Tasha was right. But calling them rugrats was a bit much.

'Sabs. These are my new friends. Abdel, Khalid and Yousef.'

'Hey!'

They all stop and stare at me. I grin, showing all my teeth.

They look among each other before smiling approvingly. So adorable. They've got sandy-coloured skin; I reckon they could potentially be Arab. I wonder if they're Syrian. I've never seen them before.

'Right.' I lift my shoulders up and raise my voice. 'Let's all go to the shops then.' I smile at the kids. 'Are you guys coming?'

I don't think their parents will mind. They've already let them roam outside looking quite messy. Mum wouldn't let us out like this. *Stop being so judgy, Sabs.*

The three kids look at each other worriedly. I'm assuming they have no money.

'And I'm gonna get everyone sweeties.'

Izzy jumps in glee yelling, 'Yay!'

The kids take her happiness as reassurance and nod their heads towards me. The youngest of them, Yousef, with his big, sunken, brown eyes, reaches his hand towards me. I firmly hold on, letting him know I'm here. I reach out my other hand for Izzy, but she's squished herself in between Abdel and Khalid, engrossed in conversation that is incomprehensible to me.

I gently tug on Yousef to walk.

Nearing the corner shops, I feel someone staring at me from the park adjacent. Without making it obvious, I glance over to see whose eyes are burning through my soul.

It's a guy, stood alone, dressed head to toe in black, one hand in the messenger bag and one hand in their pocket. The fair complexion and unshaved beard catch me off guard. *Who the hell is this?*

I study him again and the recognition hits me like a ton of bricks. It's Jalaal's friend from Shanice's party. Shaah.

Shit, he obviously knows who you are, that's why he's staring at you. I don't know if I should smile or wave. I decide to make eye contact and mirror him.

Once our eyes meet, Shaah continues to stare into my soul. Not flinching at all. What the hell is his problem? *Weirdo.* I drag my eyes away and hurry the kids to the shops. Jalaal needs to pick better friends.

CHAPTER 11

JALAAL

I drag myself out of bed and throw on my work uniform. It's 6.30 a.m. and I've got a morning shift. I'm lucky to work at the Baker Street branch, it's a quick cycle. A ride down Old Marylebone through the empty streets early in the morning. No one is going to catch me slipping. No one from ends is going to make the effort to trek to a Sainsbury's when they can go to the corner shop.

I pull my worn-out Nike hoody over my uniform, put on my Beats headphones and get myself out the house. It's blitz outside but I'm sure by midday, it's going to be baking. That's usually when all the office people with their red, burnt skin come looking for their Kopparberg. *Wallahi*, them bottles are heavy to carry, and on hot days like this, I'm in and out of the stockroom constantly. If Habo Hani knew that part of my job included carrying crates of alcohol, I swear she would faint. Imagine if she caught me sipping on a Magnum. I wonder what would happen then.

I started working in Sainsbury's soon after I finished my GCSEs. That is when Halima had left for uni, and she bussed me with this job because she used to work here. She was sick at her job, mainly because she knows how to banter with white people, and they loved her. They probably assumed that I'd be the same by association. I'm all right though, I like focusing on doing tasks that are kind of mind-numbing. It feels safe to think at work.

Once I clock in, I check the duty rota to see if anyone decent is in. I don't really chat to anyone at work. Don't get me wrong, I'm calm with everyone, but I'm not on that chatty patty stuff. I see that Sohaib is on an 8 a.m.–4 p.m. shift. Thank God. Sohaib is one of the few people that I rate at work. He's eighteen years old and he's not from my ends. He's from North, like Camden area. Really blessed guy. Pakistani brother. Whenever he comes to work, we always buss jokes or have some deep convos about random stuff. I wouldn't say he's proper religious, but he doesn't smoke, drink, none of that stuff.

'All right there, mate,' my supervisor calls me.

He doesn't know how to pronounce my name, or he refuses to, so he calls me 'mate' or 'son', or some other word English people like to use.

'I'm good, how ya doing Steve?' I mirror his accent.

Halima told me this is called code-switching. It works though, these man will treat you differently once you start mimicking the way that they speak.

'Had a right ol' weekend, my Mrs decided she wanted me to clean out the garage and I've only just gone and cut me bloody arm. Jesus fucking Christ. Let me tell you something, son, make sure your Mrs is a quiet one. Then you won't have to deal with this nonsense. Bless my wife though, I love her to bits, but she can be a bit much sometimes.' He speaks too much.

'Note taken.' I give him a hearty laugh back. He doesn't realize that I'm taking the piss.

Small talk is dead. I don't understand why he thought I needed to know that information. *Wallahi*, it's like we come from different planets. If Sabrina asked me to clear the garage, a) I wouldn't be chatting shit about her and b) I wouldn't be dumb enough to cut myself. I can't ever imagine Sabrina asking me to clear our garage out though. She seems like a bit of a control freak, but I bet she likes to do things together. Hold up. Why am I thinking about Sabrina and me living together? With a garage? I don't even know if we can afford a house with a garage. I don't even know if we'll be together. Relax, Jalaal.

I walk to the break room and pull out my phone. It's 6.46 a.m., fourteen minutes to kill. I re-read my text exchanges with Sabrina. If the boys knew I was moving like this, they'd think I'm moist and roast me non-stop. Not gonna lie though, Sabs is special. It's mad that we're not even the same religion or culture and we get along so well. I love that she accepts me for who I am.

I like working at Sainsbury's. It keeps me focused. And I enjoy people-watching. Except the dickheads who talk to me like I'm some dumb kid. But the people that jar me the most, are those who pity me. A guy once told me he would tip me if he could. It does make me wonder how different life would be if I grew up with money. And married parents. A mum who is alive. It gets bare philosophical in my head sometimes.

Sohaib arrives to his shift ten minutes late, which is unlike him. When he walks in, I clock that his hair is scruffy, and his face looks dry. I stop restacking the water bottles and approach him.

'Yo bro, you good?' I place my hand on his shoulder.

'Nah fam, things are a bit peak at the moment, listen, I'll tell you later.' He avoids eye contact.

During our break, we go to the delivery van entrance on the back road. This is where Sohaib and I go to have our catch-ups. I'm sat on one of the empty crates and he's pacing back and forth, a cigarette in his hand. He only started smoking a few months ago and told me he 'needs it' for his 'stress'. He's studying Biomedical Science at King's College. I swear that's like a BTEC version of Medicine. I don't say that to him. But he *is* at a top university, so maybe he is stressed.

'It's my little sister,' he says.

'What about her exactly?'

'She's acting up, bro.' He inhales deeply.

'How?'

'She started wearing make-up, dressing like . . . you know . . . revealing clothes. She comes home late. Even her friends are done out here. She's only sixteen you know. And I don't know man. She's acting like a hoe.' His face flushes red with embarrassment.

'What does this have to do with you being late?' I need the full story.

'She tried leaving the house, the *panchod*, and I found balloon cannisters in her bag. It was a madness at home. But yeah, parents got involved and everything. Bro, she needs to go back home to Pakistan and fix up.'

I don't understand why he's so calmly calling his sister a hoe for carrying balloon cannisters. And why he's tryna send her to Pakistan.

'Bro, that's kinda mad, are you really tryna do all that?'

His eyes widen. I stay silent.

'It's cos she's moving like a hoe,' he blurts out.

'Fam, it's kinda brazy. I think maybe you're reaching, man.'

'Imagine if you had a sister that came home with cannisters in her bag?' he switches on me.

'Firstly, I'd understand because I, too, have done balloons. Like you, fam.' I know he's tried it. 'But if I had a sister, bro, I'd actually speak to her on the level and explain the dangers of doing balloons and it's something that she should stay away from.'

'So, you'd just talk to her?' He doesn't blink.

I never thought Sohaib, who's not even on road, would think so backwards. I know it's different for boys, but I imagine how I'd try to help Ibrahim in this situation.

'Yes bro. Deep what you're actually saying.' I get off the crate and walk towards him. I place my hands on his shoulders. 'Look *wallahi*, I ain't even tryna act like I'm some big man. But listen, as boys, men, whatever, it ain't our place to have a say on what women wear or do with their bodies. No one tells us what to do, so why should it be for them. Imagine if someone said you can't wear a *thobe* cos you might blow up something.'

'This is different, fam.' He shakes his head.

'And you're not a girl.'

'Let me think about it, bro. You're saying a lot.' He sits on the crate I just got off and lights another cigarette.

I sometimes feel like, am I the only guy who thinks like this? But I can't be. I blame Halima. She shows up at my house and now I'm preaching human rights. It all started when she told me about FGM. Female Genital Mutilation. It's a surgical practice that basically involves removing parts of or all of the female genitals. For no reason. It's not a medical thing. It's a cultural thing that's fucked up. Loads of the older women in my family have it. Habo even had it done.

Anyways, I was shook when Hals first explained it to me. I didn't even believe it. She told me to ask Habo and when I approached her, the look on her face said it all. She just told me it's not for boys to know. I don't know man, it had me feeling a certain type of way. When I actually deeped that loads of female bodies from my fucking cultural background got tortured like that for no reason, it made me think about how I see girls. I had to proper evaluate who I am. And Hals also forced me to listen to her long lectures about consent and boundaries. I haven't spoken about it to any of my other friends, not even Shaah.

'OK, I kinda get where you're coming from,' Sohaib says.

'Try chat to her still, maybe she'll listen you.' I don't know when I became a fucking Samaritan, but fuck.

'I don't know . . .' He shakes his head.

I raise my eyebrows at him.

'I'll think about it.' He holds his hand up, cigarette interlocked between his thumb and forefinger.

'When you gonna stop bleming?' I change the subject.

'Now you're overstepping the line, Jalaal.'

I raise my hands to surrender. 'OK, OK, forget that. But seriously fam, bless things with your sister, you only got one life and one family.'

He understands. He knows about my situation.

'*Alhamdulillah* to that,' he says.

I look at my watch. 'We got ten minutes.'

'Good.' He takes a puff of his cigarette. 'We got time to discuss what you doing with your life now,' he smiles.

'What are you chatting about?' I play dumb.

'Bro, don't make me say it out loud.' He exhales the smoke. 'Being on road and all that,' he whispers. As if saying those words is a criminal offence.

'I'm not on road.'

And it's true. I'm not on road. Yeah, I admit that I buy weed and sell it to people I know. But I'm not out here banking packs, running lines or involved in that gang shit. I'm not like the other guys.

'You selling weed though,' he accuses me.

'To people I know. I'm not some roadman that spends all my time selling drugs. I don't like how you're saying it, man. I'm here working right now.' The anger is fuelling up inside me.

'What do you want? Surely, it's not working at Sainsbury's and selling cannabis to your "friends".'

'I don't really know,' I lie.

'Anyways, you made any moves on that design course I told you 'bout? If you apply now, you can start in September.'

Not this again. Sohaib is the only one I've talked to about design. I've always been interested in starting my own clothing brand for the mandem. I got an A* in my graphic design GCSE and was taking the A Level course. Sohaib told me to apply for some courses and that he'd help but I don't know. I'm happy customizing my Air Force 1's.

'If that's what you wanna do, I'll help you do applications and shit. But you've gotta think about what you're doing. How is selling weed gonna help you?'

Before I even have time to answer his questions, I flinch in response to the fire exit door slamming open and seeing Steve's red face.

'You two. Back inside. Now,' he commands of us. 'You were meant to be back fifteen minutes ago,' he says monotonously.

I look at my watch again. Fuck. I read the time wrong. I walk towards the exit door, hanging my head in shame.

'We haven't finished this convo by the way,' Sohaib mutters.

CHAPTER 12

SABRINA

The exam hall is hot. Like really hot. I've taken off my hoody and am sat in my vest top. No time to be self-conscious about showing too much skin. I've got this long essay question on *The Great Gatsby* and *Wuthering Heights* to answer.

I stare at the half-empty Volvic bottle in front of me. No one would know it's Volvic because the label was removed and dashed into the bin by the invigilator. I mean, how could I possibly cheat through a water bottle label? It's not going to tell me how to answer the question.

'Women characters are portrayed mainly as those who endure suffering and pain.' By comparing two texts of choice, explore the extent to which you agree and/or disagree with this statement.

My eyes scan over the lined exam paper in front of me. I've written extensively about Cathy from *Wuthering Heights*. Probably more than the examiner needs to know. Now, *The Great Gatsby*. I gotta think about Daisy, Myrtle and Jordan. Like I said, potassium levels in the Volvic water bottle aren't going to help me with this.

My right hand aches, palms are dripping with sweat. Why the hell are my sweat glands like this? My finger joints are in pain and my hand is slipping off the pen. Reluctantly, I stop writing and harshly rub my palms against my jeans. I look at the big clock. 3.02 p.m. We have two hours and fifteen minutes for this exam and we started at 2 p.m. That means I'm good for time. *Come on Sabs, you got this.*

I take a minute to look around. It feels like an out-of-body experience. I dip my head, close my eyes for a moment and focus on my sense of sound. I hear the swishes of the papers flipping over, the deep breaths of my peers, the one scrape of a chair, two coughs, pens scribbling against paper, the footsteps of the invigilators walking up and down, my breathing, my inhalation, exhalation, the thumping of my heart, the white noise.

My eyes flash open, my hand instinctively grabs my pen and I begin writing. About that crazy bitch Daisy.

After the exam, I find Liyah sat on the sofas in the hallway, chewing her gum and babbling away to Amelia, our friend from English. Walking towards them, I overhear the others speaking about what they wrote. I tune out. Listening to their answers always makes me feel bad. Post-exam discussions are not for me.

'Hey guyssss.' I interrupt their conversation and slide on the sofa. 'I hope we aren't talking about the exam.'

'Don't worry, sis, we done talking about that,' Liyah says.

'Yeah, it's an issue for August results day,' Amelia chimes in.

'So, what's the plan?' I ask.

We usually grab something to eat before we head back home to submerge ourselves into more revision.

'That was actually my last exam,' Amelia says. 'My boyfriend said he's going to pick me up and take me out to celebrate.'

Amelia is dating some Lebanese guy who is three years older

than her. At first, I found it kind of weird because she's barely an adult, but they seem like a cute couple. I've met him once when we walked her to his car and he was super nice, offered to drop me and Liyah home too.

'You lucky bitch,' Liyah says. 'Sabs and I still have our Sociology exam left.'

'I know, I know. Even though getting hot wings and chips with you guys sounds tempting, I'd rather get spoilt by Khalil,' she jokes.

'OK we get it, you're getting an upgraded munch,' I add. 'Where do you think you'll go?'

'Probably some shisha lounge. I need to go home and get ready. You know how them places are, boujee for no reason.'

'I'm glad you said it before me,' Liyah says.

I've never been to a shisha lounge. To be honest, I always thought they were full of Arabs, Asians, Middle Easterns or even Somalis. It might be weird if they see me coming in, some random mixed-race girl, especially if I'm not dolled up with a full face of make-up. I don't think it's my vibe, but Liyah's cousin is opening a shisha spot soon and she says we are definitely going. I guess you don't know if you don't try.

'Anyways.' Amelia looks at her phone. 'My man is here, so I'm going to have to go. Listen though, let me know when your last exam is so we can all link up.'

'Of course,' I say.

She gives us both a quick hug and power-walks off.

'I wonder if we'll ever have boyfriends who act as our chauffeurs,' escapes my mouth.

'You're more likely to experience that than me.' Liyah wiggles her eyebrows.

*

I tear open my wings and chips box and place the lid on the side. I pick up the big bottle of mayo and squirt it on the flimsy cardboard paper. I then squeeze the chilli sauce on top. I pick up a chip, take a bite and allow the hot steam to roam my mouth while using the rest of the chip to mix my concoction.

'I still don't understand why you can't be a normal human being and use ketchup?' she comments.

'Don't knock it till you try it, sis.'

'Huh?' She scrunches her eyebrows.

'It's an expression.' I pause. 'That my dad says.'

'Are you sure it's not your mum's side of the family, cos that sounds bare white.'

'How does an expression make you sound like a race Liyah?' I sometimes can't believe some of the stuff that comes out of her mouth.

'You're right, I'm being regressive. Anyways, tell me about Jalaal. You barely mentioned anything since that day you ran off to Vapiano with him.'

I remain cool and chew on another chip, avoiding her eye contact. *You better answer her, Sabs, she's put you on the spot.*

'We had a nice time; the food was good.' I pray she doesn't pry.

'Did he pay?'

'Yes, he was adamant that I didn't.'

'What a gentleman,' she replies sarcastically.

She waits.

'OK, fine. We kissed.'

'Sabs! I love this for you. So . . . was it any good?'

'I can't believe you're asking me that, but yes, it was!' *Don't get ahead of yourself, Sabs.*

'Did anything else happen?' She raises her eyebrows.

My pulse races at the thought of sexual intimacy. It's not that I'm frigid or anything, but I haven't really done anything except kiss a guy. Well, only two guys, for the whole duration of my eighteen years on this earth. From the way he kissed me, I get the feeling that Jalaal is more experienced than me and I don't want to disappoint him. Or for him to think that I'm not good at . . . you know . . . pleasuring and stuff. *You're too much of a perfectionist, Sabs.*

'Oh no, no way, Liyah. This is the first date!'

'So, it's more than a link-up. OK, this guy is defo tryna be your boyfriend!'

She knows more about guys than I do. Liyah has dated a few guys – roadmen, university students, older guys, younger guys. Never long things. Either talking stages or situationships.

I want to believe her, but I don't want to get ahead of myself. Jalaal could potentially be my first *proper* relationship.

'You're thinking too far ahead.' I bite into my wings.

'You've got to though, as he's Muslim and Somali. Haven't you considered that?' Her tone is serious.

And the truth is, I don't want to think about it after what Dad said.

'Is it gonna be an issue?' I ask her genuinely.

'Obvs, I'm Muslim so I can speak on the faith part, but for real, it could be a barrier if things become serious. You don't even know if his family will accept you. Plus, Somalis ALWAYS stick together. How often do you hear about them dating outside their culture?'

I pause a moment to think.

'There was obviously Stormzy and Maya Jama, and they were

together for a long time,' she adds. 'But they're celebs so it's not *really* the same!'

There have been Somali guys that go out with other races, like Abdi who dated Casey (she's white) when we were in year eight and then Rashid who dated Fauzia (who is Pakistani) in year nine. Those were immature relationships though – they never lasted. I don't think she's right about the comment that Somalis stick together though.

'I think you're being a bit ignorant Liyah. There are Somalis who date outside their culture,' I reply.

'Maybe. But it's the fact that you haven't considered it. In our cultures, this kinda stuff is big you know – what happens if you have kids and he wants to raise them Muslim, what you gonna do?'

'Woah woah woah, what do you mean kids? I'm not thinking that far ahead. I'm literally just speaking to him.' Heat rushes to my face. 'Also, I'm hardly Christian, I do the bare minimum. Mass on Christmas and sometimes Sunday service, but that's about it. Honestly, I believe in God and know he's out there but I'm not super religious, you already know that.'

'I know, sis, but for the Muslim community, religion can be linked to culture. I think if you lots get serious, like marriage serious, you need to have this convo.'

'Marriage? Let's slow down please, Liyah.' My stomach knots.

Breathe, Sabs. I know she's right, but I can't believe we are discussing this stuff. I haven't stopped thinking about what Dad said. He will not be happy about this at all. We never talk about boys; I can't imagine having to one day tell him my boyfriend isn't Jamaican or Christian. I think he would be OK with one or the other. But neither? He'd bug out. Not that Dad is even remotely religious, and he didn't even marry a Jamaican! He doesn't have a leg to stand on if we are being honest, but this stuff runs so deep. My dad is so Jamaican. His friends, his values, his interests, how he speaks, his mannerisms, what he cooks, his house – no, our house. And I am connected to him. I can't help but feel like he would be let down and totally against me not being with someone of the same heritage. I'm mixed-race though, surely it makes things *different* for me.

'I don't think I'm knowledgeable about this stuff, I can't lie,' I confess.

'You need to pattern up and do some research.'

She's right. When I met with Jalaal at the chicken shop, he knew so much about my culture. Maybe more than me. *You're exaggerating, Sabs.* But he did know quite a bit. He told me that his cousin Hals shoves the information down his throat. He spoke about our cuisine and even speaks patois phrases, but then again, so does everyone else I know.

I don't know much about Somali culture. Apparently, they eat banana with their rice. And apparently, they all have big foreheads, too. This knowledge comes from dead jokes in high school and to be honest, they're not funny at all. Anyways, I couldn't tell you where Somaliland is on the map. I can't believe I'm admitting that. *Sabs, you're being kinda ignorant.* But Liyah is right.

I've learnt so much about Moroccan culture from her. Obviously, she always brings me gifts from her travels back home and I've learnt about the customs and traditions through her storytelling. Plus, her family always invite me for dinner, so I live it and see it. I love their lamb tagine. *Seriously, Sabs.* It's not even a 'I like this guy so I should know about his culture' thing, it's a respect thing.

'You're right, you're actually so right.' I instinctively smooth my finger against my cross necklace.

When was the last time you prayed to God? I haven't been to Sunday service in ages. I'm not even sure whether I can call myself Christian at this point. Just feels like I have had to focus on other parts of my life – I'm so close to achieving my dreams, which means I should probably be practising even more gratitude. That reminds me, I need to see Auntie Maureen, I haven't seen her in ages or been to the church to help her with the foodbank. If she knew about my love life, it definitely wouldn't align with her traditional views.

I make a mental note to visit her soon.

CHAPTER 13

JALAAL

'So, what's the update with the *iska dhal*?' Hals puffs her cigarette. I give her a dirty look. She knows her name.

'Kinda weird just calling her mixed-race,' I cringe. 'When did you start smoking anyways?'

'It's a phase,' she sighs.

'You've been hanging around those hipster Bristolians.'

She poses and points to the 'consent is sexy' slogan on her acid-washed T-shirt.

'Habo would freak out if she knew what your shirt meant.' I take a sip of my Boost drink.

'Well, she doesn't, so keep it that way. Anyways, answer me Jalaal-o.'

'I don't remember giving *you* consent to speak about my private life.'

'Speaking of consent, what do you know about it?'

I roll my eyes. 'Yes, I know what it means. How can I forget how you tortured me with bare lessons about consent the last time you came back to ends for Christmas. Allow it, bro.'

'I'm not your bro.' She flicks the burnt ash from her cigarette. 'Anyways, let's go help Habo with the cooking and cleaning.'

She throws her cigarette, crushes it with the heel of her sliders and scrapes it into the bush.

We exit the alleyway back home. If Habo knew that Hals smokes, then it'd be curtains. Habo warned me that if I smoke, I shouldn't do it in public cos it'll shame our family. I don't smoke cigarettes but it's mad that there are different rules for mandem and girls. I've heard stories of girls that get sent back to Somaliland or get kicked out of their homes for smoking cigarettes. The hypocrisy is mad. If I had a sister and she was smoking, I'd like to think it's her body and her choice. But obviously I'd try talk her out of it cos it's hella bad for you.

Ping. It's Shaah.

And another missed call from +252. I'm gonna have to answer his call at some point. Just not now.

I open the message from Shaah.

I'm in studio with some of the mandem. Nico is making a track and we're just chilling.

The studio is a ten-minute walk. It's not even a proper studio, some guy converted his garage, but it's a link-up spot for the mandem. Nico is two years older than us, and we went to school together. I'm certain that he gave me my first zoot as well. He raps, but his music hasn't popped off, so he just keeps recording. I rate the work ethic.

The mandem are Adnan, Michael and Jemal. These three got excluded before they sat their GCSEs though. They are cool people *wallahi*, but they're too into this gang shit now. Affiliating with St Mary's and getting into pointless beef. Not for me. That's what I hope, anyway.

There's no other motive this evening and Sabs is busy revising. I might as well join this motive.

Cool, on my way.

'Jalaaaaal. Broski. What you saying?' Jemal leaps up at me.

I tolerate him the most. He's not an instigator, more of a follower than anything. We used to chill back in school, and he was always talking about his homeland. He's from Ethiopia. *Xabesho*. That's what we call them in Somali. We got this unspoken allegiance among East Africans.

'Man like Jemal, it's been a hot minute.' I embrace him in a hug.

My nostrils are attacked by the smell of cigarettes.

'Last time I saw you was just before Shanice's birthday,' he says.

That wasn't too long ago, but since I got wrapped up in this Sabrina entanglement, I haven't really been chilling with the mandem besides Shaah. Not gonna lie, I'd rather be with Sabs.

Adnan and Michael come up to spud me, both their eyes bloodshot. I'm late to the party. Nico is midway spitting bars in his makeshift booth, so I don't disturb him. There's an empty space next to Shaah so I sit there, low-key at ease.

'You came through!' He grins hard.

'Always bro.' I pat him on the back.

'Wanna smoke?'

'Nah, I'm good.'

That's when I notice the three empty Magnum bottles next to him. He's waved.

'That nigga in the booth is going hard.' He laughs.

'Fam, it's not cool for you to say that. I told you before.' I straighten my back.

'Why you so sensitive? We all black, no?' he says with a

short giggle.

'You're not black. You're Afghan.'

There is something that jars me about Shaah feeling entitled to say that word.

'Fam, I'll say what I want. All the other mandem are OK with me saying it.' He turns towards Michael and Jemal, Ghanaian and Ethiopian boys. 'Can I say the word nigga?'

'Yeah bro, we allow you to say it. You're fam-lee,' Michael nods.

'As long as you ain't white, you can say it bro,' Jemal adds.

I expected more from Jemal. These mandem must be tapped because I'm shocked by what I'm hearing.

My anger freezes as I hear low vibrational banging. The others are too busy chatting shit to notice. My body turns still.

'Yo, guys, can you hear that?' I ask.

'Stop tryna change the subject.' Shaah begins to slur his words.

Bang. Bang.

'Yo, cut the music, now!' I shout at Jemal, who is sat by the master board.

His eyes widen and he cuts the music off with a screech.

'WHAT THE FUCK, MAN?' Nico shouts from the booth.

BANG. BANG. BANG.

It's the front door.

'POLICE, POLICE.'

We freeze. We have ten seconds before they'll get from the front door to the garage.

I'm the only sober one here.

'Anyone got anything on them?' I whisper in the silence. Jemal shakes his head. Michael shakes his head. Shaah shakes his head as he balls his two snap bags.

Footsteps are getting louder.

'Fuck.' Nico rushes out the booth, takes a large Rambo knife out from his Nike bag and hides it under the keyboard.

SLAM.

Ten police officers armed with tasers and batons come running in.

'POLICE, GET DOWN, SHOW ME YOUR HANDS.'

I place my hands behind my head like in the American movies and kneel. Rough hands grip my wrists and twist them awkwardly to my back. The cold metal of the handcuffs rubs against my skin and my wrist joints scream in pain.

'Ouch! It fucking hurts,' I say.

Somebody forcefully twists my hand, realigns it within the cuff and tightens it. The pain subsides but the discomfort remains. By the shaft of the handcuffs, I'm forced up to my feet and I see what's going on around me. The other three are in handcuffs, officers rummaging through their pockets. Nico has his face slammed against the garage door and has two officers patting him down aggressively. He's cussing them, telling them that they're pigs and that they smell of bacon. He's so dumb, he's got a Rambo knife the size of my arm stashed under his keyboard with his fingerprints all over it. I'm not trying to catch a case because of his stupidity.

'Jalaal Abdi.'

Who the fuck knows my name?

'Been a long time,' he smirks.

It's the fed who stopped me on the way to the pharmacy. You couldn't make this shit up. He must be tapped because I've got nothing on me except forty pounds . . . *oh shit*. And my brick phone. Fuck.

'Ain't you got anything better to do with your time?' I ask him.

'You don't have a warrant; you can't search this place without a warrant.'

It's the one thing I know to say. He places his hand in his back pocket and pulls out a piece of paper. Westminster Magistrates' Court. It has Nico's full name and address.

That must mean that the feds were watching us, because how the fuck would they know that I'd be here at this exact time?

'Do what you need to do officer, I'm innocent,' I lie through my teeth.

He slaps his blue latex gloves around his wrist. Fucking pathetic. He starts off with my hood, wandering his hands deep inside and shaking it so aggressively that it tugs on my neck. Has the dickhead forgotten that I need to breathe? He continues to pat down my chest, using the outer part of his hands, sliding them up and down my chest, feeling for something that clearly isn't there. I watch his head in front of me. I wonder what he's thinking. Probably that I'm just another body. Not a human. The sweat is trickling down his receding hairline. I can't focus on anything but his head.

The commotion of the others blurs in the background; all the sounds have merged into loud noise. All I focus on is this guy, the thumping of my heart and Ibrahim. I can't leave Ibrahim. I can't disappoint Hals and Habo. Not again. And what about Sabs? She would never chat to a guy in pen. He finishes patting my arms and seems disappointed. As he makes his way down to my trouser pockets, I tense up. He's about to find the burner. He can't arrest me for having a burner phone though. It's not illegal.

He fumbles through my pockets, removing the iPhone and placing it on the floor. Removing the two twenty-pound notes and placing them on the floor. And rummages deeper and whips out the burner. The corner of his lips perks up.

'What's this?'

'My phone.' I roll my eyes.

'What's that?' He points towards the iPhone.

'My phone?'

'Why do you have two phones?'

'Is it illegal to have two phones?' I spit back.

He places the burner phone to the side of my other items and continues digging through my pockets, but there's nothing else. All my stuff is scattered on the floor like puzzle pieces. I don't think he can bag me for this. And I think the dickhead realizes that too.

'We haven't finished searching yet,' he announces.

Jemal, Michael and Shaah are sat in different corners around the room. They each have an officer speaking to them, writing in their little notebooks. They better not take Shaah for a strip search otherwise he's fucked.

They've taken Nico into the booth now. He's with two other officers. It looks like they haven't found the shank. Nico's calm now, leaning against the wall and taking deep breaths. He wouldn't be looking so calm if they had found it. I can't hear anything.

Eventually, one of the two officers comes out of the booth and announces to everyone, 'There's nothing on him. And nothing in the booth. Have you all finished searching here?'

'We aren't finished yet,' the dickhead fed next to me declares.

The ugly fed rubs his hand against his chin. Allah, please don't let him find the knife. If you're listening, please. I'm begging you. It's not even about Nico. I have no loyalty to this brudda, but *wallahi*, I have this feeling in my gut that this dickhead officer will find a way to stick it on me if he finds the knife. Please Allah, just this one time, make a miracle happen.

He inspects the room, opening drawers and checking windowsills while asking his mates, 'Have you checked this?' They all respond with 'Yes sarge' to him.

He glides slowly towards the keyboard and an eerie silence fills the room. We all look at each other. Luckily, the feds don't clock.

The silence is disturbed by a ping and someone shouting through the police radio. The pigs look at each other. All of their radios are pinging red and there's a woman's voice shouting. Fear plasters on their faces. The shouting continues and you can hear someone else on the radio clearly shouting, 'come here you fuckin fed, stop running you pussyhole' against the panting of her breath. She manages to respond, 'running eastbound on Edgware Road'.

'It's Louise. She's pressed the emergency button. Fuck,' my opp fed says, his voice tight with worry.

'Right, Joseph, Dillan, you come with me in the unmarked vehicle. The rest of you finish up here.' Before I know it, he's running out the door with the other two dickheads pacing behind him.

We all stand in silence. Us mandem versus the feds. The silence is deafening.

One of the police officers fidgets with his belt.

The officer with Shaah breaks the silence. 'There's nothing here lads. Uncuff the boys and let's go.'

Allah is listening to my prayers. I let go of the breath I've been holding on to. My whole chest concaves.

CHAPTER 14

SABRINA

It's good to be home alone, to finally revise in silence. Dad is at work. Tasha and Izzy are at school. I sip on my instant coffee; Nescafé is going to get me through this exam period.

I promised my dad that I would pick Izzy up from after-school club and then I'll go see Auntie Maureen at the church. It's more fruitful to spend revision breaks out with family than mindlessly scrolling on Instagram. That's what I tell myself anyway.

I've just finished a practice paper, so I go down for a quick snack. Before I reach the kitchen, I stop at the china cabinet in the living room. It's basically ancient and I don't know why we have it here. Dad literally took it from our old home because it's a 'family staple'. It's filled with untouched dishes and some framed pictures. Photos of my grandparents and some of our immediate family. Those have Mum in them, too. It makes me think that Dad still holds on to the hope that Mum will come back and that everything will go back to normal. If I was him, I'd burn them all. Out of sight, out of mind.

I know I shouldn't dwell on memories of Mum when I'm alone. It hurts too deep. I want to reminisce though, feel her closer. I pull out the closest picture frame to me.

It's a photograph of all of us. Three years ago. A family holiday. We went to Bristol for the Balloon Fiesta. Mum and Dad wanted to show us their hometown – where they met. We were all so mesmerized by the different-coloured hot-air balloons flying against the sunset. It was such a beautiful view. Of course, we all were dying to go on a hot-air balloon, but there was no way we could afford it. We watched from below, starstruck at the beauty that was floating into the sky.

I can't remember the shops and places that Dad and Mum were pointing out, but I vividly remember the expressions on both their faces. They looked so in love, so immersed and engulfed in each other. I never thought Mum and Dad would ever separate. Or whatever the fuck is happening now.

My eyes start to sting. It's too much for me to think about right now. I lock up the memories and store them in that hidden part of my mind.

I carefully place the frame back in the exact position. Dad is so particular, he would notice if it's been moved, even by a millimetre. I slowly close the cabinet door and stare at the photo through the glass pane.

On my way to pick up Izzy, I notice a familiar silhouette across the road. He's walking with a carbon copy of himself. They're engrossed in a conversation that has them in hysterics.

Jalaal and Ibrahim. If I didn't recognize his body frame, I would never have believed that that giggle had come out of his mouth.

Ibrahim is in his school uniform and Jalaal is wearing his Spider-Man backpack. Jalaal's curls flop over his forehead as he crouches down to speak with his younger brother, and they do a weird handshake together. They're so fucking adorable. I didn't realize that Ibrahim and Izzy went to the same school.

It's so weird seeing someone who does illegal stuff being so kind and considerate towards others. *Sabs, you're being judgemental and stereotyping – bad actions don't make a bad person.* Maybe it's because I have the responsibility to look after my siblings and I'm low-key resentful that my peers don't have to. But I love my family; even though Tasha can be a pain in the arse, I'd die for both my sisters.

Jalaal and Ibrahim are about to turn the corner towards our estate.

'Jalaal!' I shout across the road.

His head snaps in my direction, and he uses his body to shield Ibrahim. Once his eyes meet mine, his posture softens, and his younger brother emerges from his shadow. Jalaal's apprehension turns to delight, and he shoots me a smile.

I might be catching feelings for this guy. Proper feelings. I know it deep down. 'Sabrina!' He waves us over.

'Who's that?' Izzy asks.

'He's my friend from school.'

'He's with my friend Ibby, is that his brother?'

'Oh? You're friends with Ibby? Yes, that's his brother.' I tug her hand. 'Come, let's go.'

Once we reach the duo, Jalaal embraces me in a warm hug. He bends down to Izzy's level and puts out his hand.

'Hey, I'm Jalaal, what's your name?'

Izzy shakes his hand. Before she can answer, Ibrahim interjects, proud, 'That's my friend Izzy from school.'

'Nice to meet you then, Izzy.'

They exchange smiles. *This is so friggin' cute.*

Jalaal stands to my level. 'How you doing, *sweet one*?' He whispers the last part.

My cheeks heat up, especially with the two miniatures watching silently.

'Good, just going home, obvs. How come I've never seen you outside their school before?'

'I don't always do this, but my aunt's knee isn't good,' he says. 'What you doing the rest of the day?'

'Dad's working so I've gotta cook dinner for my sisters. Then I gotta see my aunt. Probs do some revision after that. It's my life, eh.'

'What will you cook?' He tilts his head.

'Not sure, will see what's in the fridge.'

'Hmmm.' He rummages in his pocket before pulling out two twenty-pound notes and some random sweets. 'Use this to buy dinner.' He puts the money in my hands and closes my fingers around it.

'Jalaal, I can't.' I begin unclasping my hand, but he wraps his hand around it and holds it shut.

'Let me take care of you,' he says quietly, even though Ibby and Izzy are now fully immersed in whatever pre-ten-year-olds talk about.

'It's too much . . .'

'Nothing is too much for you. I beg you, take it,' he pleads. 'Saves you time. You can get more studying in.'

I can't say no. I don't want to say no. *You love this, Sab.* It feels good having Jalaal help me like this.

'OK,' I succumb, 'thank you.' I gaze deep into his eyes. *You're catching real feelings for this guy.*

'Come Ibby, let's go!' Jalaal says before handing Izzy a Chupa Chups lollipop.

'Nice to see you!' I wave goodbye to them both.

Once out of earshot, Izzy puts her hands on her hips. 'Is that your boyfriend then?'

'No sassy queen, he's my friend. Anyways, guess what? We are having Domino's pizza for dinner!'

That's enough to distract her.

By the time I get Izzy and the hot pizza back to the house, Tasha is already here. She's sat on the sofa in her sweated-out football kit with an ice lolly in her mouth, scrolling on her phone. *How is she so nonchalant? So different to me.*

'Did you get ice lollies for us, too?' I snap at her.

Her head slowly turns to me as she continues licking the ice lolly. 'Well, if you didn't come in here making wild assumptions, then you would've found out there's a pack in the freezer for ALL of us.'

I check and she's right. I give one to Izzy and take one for myself. 'I'm leaving, going to see Auntie Maureen,' I announce. 'There is Domino's pizza in the kitchen for everyone!' Minus the one slice I scoffed down on the way home.

'Watch when Dad finds out you've dropped babysitting duties on me. He's gonna be pissed,' Tasha says.

'Well, I'll be back in a few hours and it's not like I'm doing unproductive things with my time – like you.' I peer over her phone; she's on Twitter. 'Look who's going through dead tweets. Plus, I think you need to take a shower.'

I want to bolt out the door but I wait to hear some form of acknowledgement before I leave. I hear her grunt and take that as confirmation that she's heard what I've said, then I leave.

*

The route to church takes me through the uncles' quadrants. I call it that because a group of yardie uncles are always on the street, listening to music, engaging in chatter, drinking – a bit too much – and playing dominoes.

'You all right there, Sabrina?' Delroy shouts, one of Dad's friends from back in the day.

'Yeah, I'm good, you all right?' I yell back.

'Good as ever! You still playing football?' He grins.

'When I can!'

I admire how happy they are. I don't think I could ever see myself living on my estate, happy, in my adulthood, doing the same thing day after day. Don't get me wrong, I am grateful for my upbringing, but I know there is more for me in life than St Mary's. I'm not like Delroy, who can stay here forever and be happy. *Their happiness isn't your happiness, remember Sabs.*

The church has a distinctive old-people smell. I go upstairs to the holding room where they keep all the donation food. I didn't tell Auntie Maureen that I'd come over to help. She thinks I'm taking a break to study for exams, which I am technically. Thanks to Jalaal's help, I can come to church and still fit in more revision.

Auntie Maureen is Dad's older sister but she's like significantly older than him. Nobody knows her real age, but the grey hair and restricted mobility say it all. I really appreciate her, she's a bit old-school but she does spend all her time helping the community.

The foodbank is a good place to recalibrate from the shit going on in the outside world, and to remind myself that I can change the world, even in a small way. It takes me back to volunteering at the old people's home as part of my Duke of Edinburgh award. I'll never forget how happy they were to see me. And I was literally only there for two hours a week. I couldn't believe it. I'm only Sabs. *But destined to be more.*

But it made me realize that giving back to your community, and helping others, is important. And very healing. For others. And for me. Anyways, the foodbank at the church is my new sanctuary.

When I enter, the ladies are gathered in a circle, holding hands. They all turn to me when I creak the door open.

'Sabrina!' My Auntie Maureen rushes over to me. 'It's so good to see you. Are you helping us today?' She kisses my cheeks.

'Yeah Auntie!'

'Great, we were just about to start prayer. Please join us!' She pulls me into the circle.

The beautiful elderly Caribbean women smile at me, and we all close our eyes.

'Dear Lord,' my Auntie Maureen begins. 'We thank you for bringing us all here together as one to help the needy people of the community.'

'Amen.'

'We thank you for our good health.'

'Amen.'

'We thank you for bringing Sabrina to us today.'

'Amen.'

I smile.

Then we disperse into our sections. I'm managing the toiletries. Auntie Maureen is reading aloud the different items. Our hands move in unison, passing and distributing items into different bags, ready to be taken downstairs for collection.

It feels good to do this. No need to think or worry about exams. Right now, I am so much better. I am lighter.

Once I finish with the aunties, I have a catch-up with Auntie Maureen.

'I still can't believe your dad hasn't taken you girls to Jamaica yet. You would love it.' She gives a toothy smile.

'I know right, Auntie! To be fair, we were meant to go as a family but had to postpone that trip because of Mum . . .' I wish I didn't have to bring her up.

'Must be hard, mi dawling.' She rubs my back. 'Everything gonna be all right,' she adds, rolling her R.

'Hopefully Auntie, tell me about Jamaica though – I want to hear about it!' I change the subject.

'Where do I start? I really miss my mother's sweet and tangy tamarind balls. They were the *best* in our small town, the neighbours would always be begging her to make some. And our beautiful bungalow home. We were so lucky, we even had two mango trees and an avocado tree. You don't know how many days we spent shielding ourselves from sun under that avocado tree, playing cards. No place like home . . . but . . .' I listen to her reminisce about her holidays back home and all the things she misses. There is a strong part of me that yearns to immerse myself more in my Jamaican heritage and visit my hometown. Maybe when I have some security in my life, my own money. *You're getting there Sabs, you're gonna do it.* I hope so.

'Ahh, I've been rambling. Enough of that. So tell me, you got anybody special in your life?' She nudges me. 'Lord forgive me!'

'Nah, not really.' I shy away.

'Pwetty gyal like you don't hav a man. I don't believe it!' She raises her eyebrows. 'Don't worry, you don't hav to tell me nuffin. Just make sure you find yourself a good man who gon' take care of you. A GOD-FEARING man. Make sure he's grown up with the church too. Otherwise, he will have nuffin to fear. Ya heard me, Sabrina.' Her tone hardens.

I gulp. 'Yes Auntie.'

Jalaal is a God-fearing boy. Just a different faith.

I go downstairs to the church and sit by the altar alone. I consider praying to God but struggle to begin. So, I remain seated and silent.

CHAPTER 15

JALAAL

Hals and I are sitting in the living room watching *The Vampire Diaries*. Well, she's watching. I'm just killing time before I link up with Shaah. I don't want to think about him and all the shit that went down at Nico's yard right now though. I want to think about Sabrina, like the whipped guy I am.

Hal's long body spreads across the sofa while her feet hang limp. She's chewing on some strawberry laces, sugar settling on her Bristol University hoody. I respect that she embraces that part of her life; it makes me wanna create a brand so the mandem can rep the ends too.

'Don't you have essays or assignments to be doing over the holidays?' I ask.

'Don't you have a girlfriend?' She pauses. 'Oh wait, you don't.'

'She's actually got her last exam today.'

'And you haven't got anything planned?' She presses pause on the TV.

'What am I supposed to do?' I screw face.

'Plan a date or something. You said you liked her!'

'Yeah . . .' I say slowly as if she can't comprehend, 'so, what do I do?'

'What do you think she'd like to do?' She shrugs her shoulders. 'I don't know the girl.'

'I mean . . . there is something I've been thinking of, but we'd have to do it later. It's kinda moist though . . .'

'Speak up, Jalaal.'

I tell her my idea. She jumps from the sofa, sending sugar everywhere.

She's gonna help me make it happen. She is too fast sometimes.

I meet Shaah at the underpass by the tube station.

'Yo, what's up?'

I don't want to tell him I've spent an hour organizing a surprise for my babes Sabs with Hals. We go to the park, to our usual bench where we smoke and chill, but mainly talk shit.

'Look what I got.' He smiles at me, his silver incisor showing. He zips open his puffer jacket and jiggles his inner pockets. I hear the clank of glasses and already know he's got bottles of Magnum.

'You're actually tapped.'

'You're still gonna drink some though,' he smirks.

'True still.'

I suppress the guilt, I know it's wrong. I'm nowhere near the Muslim I'm meant to be. I'm sat in some park sipping on Magnum, doing fuck all with my life.

Shaah passes me over a bottle. I take a sip. It tastes disgusting but, in this moment, the thick liquid sliding down my throat feels good.

'So that day at Nico's. Madness right,' he chuckles.

'*Wallahi* bro, that wasn't funny.'

'What are you talking about?'

'We all could've got bagged. I'm not on getting into trouble again you know.'

'What does that mean?' His tone switches.

'It means I don't know if I'm about that life no more. I don't think I wanna be doing this for the rest of my life,' I confess.

'Nobody wants to trap for the rest of their life. But we have to do it until we get to a better place.'

I kiss my teeth. 'What you chatting about Shaah? Why do you actually need it? Your mum and dad got decent jobs and they give you P's whenever you want. I don't even understand why you're on road sometimes.'

'Fam.' He shifts to face me. 'We grew up in the trenches. We are brothers. All of us from the ends, we are family – it's a brotherhood. True, my family got P's, but they don't know about me, they don't care about me. Us man on the roads. That's my real family. Been here since day one.'

In his defence, Shaah has loads of friends, he's better connected than me. He's also got his boys from his Afghan community too, but something ain't right about him saying he has no other choice. I never really aspired to be shotting but Big H and the olders were looking after me back in the day. Then all of a sudden, I was shotting to the mandem and making P's. Habo wasn't complaining about the extra cash, even if she *believes* it's from Sainsbury's. And is it bad if I want to use the cash to buy clothes for myself? Am I selfish for wanting something for myself? I deeped that if my mum and dad were in the picture, I wouldn't be out here on the roads. I would be doing something proper with my life. It kinda jars me when I see Shaah's family, who are bare supportive, and he's taking things for granted. He's my boy but he ain't ready to hear it.

The convo switches; it's getting dark out and there's nobody in the park except us. Besides the slow bustling of the branches, the only sound is us chatting away. When I'm halfway through my second bottle of Magnum, Shaah starts pressing me.

'So, fam, tell me about you and the mixed-race girl. You ain't the same. And before you start moving mad, I ain't saying that's a bad thing.' His eyes say nothing.

'Seriously bro. I'm feeling her. Bare. She isn't no sideting, she could be wifey material.'

Shaah chuckles. 'Is that you broski? You're whipped.'

'How can I be whipped on someone I've known for two minutes?'

'You tell me – the way you're speaking fam. You might even have to marry the ting.'

I cringe at him referring to Sabs as a 'ting' but refrain from showing him how I really feel. 'Woah woah, no one said anything about marrying anyone. I'm just saying I like this girl and Ima take things seriously.'

I can feel the heat on my cheeks. I've never been so grateful to be dark-skinned in my life. Shaah would roast me for blushing.

'Bruv, do you even get girls?' I switch it on to him.

'Shut up, bruv.' His eyes narrow. 'But seriously fam, tell me more.'

'She's actually bare smart, and peng. But she's got her life together and wants to do things. I'm actually gonna take her out of ends.'

'Where?'

I don't feel like telling him where we are going.

'I haven't decided where yet,' I lie.

'Let me know bro, I might need a favour still if you're going OT.'

'What kinda favour do you need out of ends?'

'Drop off some white to a connect?' He holds my gaze.

I clench my fists and inhale deeply. 'Why would you ask me that? You know I'm not on that stuff.'

'Sorry fam, I just thought you might be near the spot OT. And I was gonna give you the P's for it too. But forget it, like you said, you ain't on it.' I sense judgement in his voice.

'It's calm bro. Say no more.'

'Do your ting, I respect it.' He spuds me.

Maybe I should do this drop-off. It's not even really that deep, and I could do with the P's as the surprise I'm planning for Sabs will low-key be a cash loss. On the flip side, I know that if I start on that stuff, it's only going to go one way for me.

Nah, I got morals, I don't need to do this.

CHAPTER 16

SABRINA

P*ing.*
 Good luck for your final exam Sabs, you're gonna smash it. Looking forward to seeing you in Bristol soon. Luv, Auntie Lisa xxxxx

I grin at my phone. I can't wait to see my mum's side of the family.

Omg thx! I can't wait, luv ya loads xx, I reply.

Right now, it's 8.37 a.m. and my hoe ass is in school. Actually, I'm not a hoe and I'm not gonna refer to myself as one. I know that I'll buss this Sociology exam. I'm just struggling to shake the nerves.

My lukewarm coffee keeps me company in the library along with this stupid librarian who keeps peeping over the shelves to watch me. I don't know why she keeps checking on me. I'm legit sat here alone with my multicoloured revision notes sprawled over the table. Green: things I'm certain about. Orange: things I need to re-read. Pink: I have no idea. As you can imagine, it's mostly green.

I bet Liyah is at home sleeping. She is the opposite of me – super chill when it comes to exams. I respect her for it, but it could never be me.

I re-read my notes about a nuclear family even though I know this topic inside-out; I always zone out because it makes me think about my family. I wonder how things would be different if Mum and

Dad stayed together. The life we'd have if she didn't end up having a drug addiction. If my grandmother was still alive, I don't think my mum would've spiralled. *You don't know for sure Sabs, nobody knows.*

Jalaal's only living parent is his dad, who he never sees. That must be tough. Even though Jalaal's life decisions are questionable, I can't blame him. What's important is that he's caring and attentive towards me, and always listens.

The hard thumping of heels against carpet catapults me out of my daydream. This can't be the librarian, she tiptoes silently. The stomping is accompanied with heavy breathing. There's only one person who walks with purpose like that. Ms Ross.

She plops herself on the far side of my table. Her mascara-smudged beady eyes staring at me. I can't help but focus on the excessive blush sat on her matte face. It's her iconic everyday make-up look.

'You're here early, Sabrina. Your exam isn't for another . . .' She looks at her Casio watch. 'Five hours or so.'

'I know Miss. I just needed a change of scenery because I couldn't focus at home,' I admit. My brain has been in overdrive.

'Is it that boy distracting you?' She narrows her eyes.

'What boy?'

'I saw him with you a few weeks ago, after one of your exams. He was outside. God did he stand out – his head swinging about. Then you walked off with him quickly.'

How does she know about Jalaal? 'How did you see? Were you watching us? That's kinda weird Miss . . .'

She interrupts me. 'No. Not at all. I was driving out of school when I noticed him. One of those Ubers I think.'

'Ahh,' I manage to get out of my mouth.

'So?'

'So what?' My muscles tense.

'Is that why you're tired? That boy.'

'Nah Miss, defo not that. It's just that exams can be stressful and I'm ready to be done with college and go to uni.'

'Good. Because that boy. He's not good news. You know he used to study here, right? I shouldn't be telling you this, but Sabrina, you're one of my brightest students and it would pain me to see you lose everything you've worked so hard for. He was, well, you know, getting into trouble with the law.'

'So?' My face goes blank.

'So?! You're much better than that. You don't need a boy like that dragging you down, do you?'

'It's not like that Miss. I know what he did was wrong but . . .'
Sabs, why you tryna prove yourself to this woman who doesn't even know a single thing about your situation?

'Then why are you still associating with him?' She shakes her head.

'Ummm, what?'

My head's getting hot, can't she just leave me alone?

'Sabrina,' she says slowly. 'I hope you know that I'm only trying to look out for you. This is coming from a place of genuine care.'

She's my teacher, not my mother. I wonder if I should tell her this. *Nah, forget it. Remember, she comes from a different world than you, Sabs.*

'All I'm suggesting is that you keep your goals and aspirations in the forefront of your mind. You have your whole life ahead of you, you have time to think about boys and love. Just make sure you put yourself first. That's all I'm saying.'

My body relaxes.

'I am, Miss.' I plead with her. 'I put my education first and he respects it, even supports me.' I feel the need to let her know. And defend his integrity.

She smiles. 'It's good you've done that. And be consistent with it.' She looks at her watch and sighs at the time. She lowers her voice so the librarian can't hear. 'Jalaal was always different to the rest. It's a shame what happened to him.' She squeezes my arm before walking off, her heels thumping on the carpet.

I completely forgot she knew Jalaal the whole time – she was his form tutor. And what the hell could she possibly mean by 'he's different'? And why is she acting like he's finished? He made mistakes but it doesn't mean his whole life is over. You're not meant to give up on people when things get hard. Especially if you're a teacher. But I do wonder if she gave Jalaal a lecture like this when he got in trouble. Maybe if she gave him the same energy then, he wouldn't have ended up in his current situation. *You don't know that Sabs, can't blame her for his actions*.

Anyway. I don't have the capacity for this drama right now, I got a bloody exam to prepare for.

'Sabs.'

My tired eyes peep to my left. None other than Liyah.

'What time is it?' I ask. My mind is foggy.

'Quarter past one. Exam's in forty-five minutes.'

'Shit.' I groan and bury my forehead into my palms.

Liyah's face softens as she sits down where Ms Ross was sat a few hours ago. 'What's wrong, sis?'

'Girl,' I grumble. 'I'm just tired. I've been sat here all day. From like 8 a.m. Think I might be bugging out a little bit.'

'Don't worry, I got you.' She rummages into her black Michael Kors handbag and fetches a cold can of Starbucks Doubleshot Espresso. She slides it over to me and without hesitation, I flip open the can and gulp down the liquid. The milky coffee swims down my throat, cooling me down.

'Thank you, you're literally a life saver.'

She grabs all my revision notes and books and dashes them into her bag.

'Now you're going to get up. Go to the canteen. Get some food. Go for a walk. And I'll see you outside the exam hall.'

I stare at her.

'What are you waiting for? Go!'

'I love you, man,' I say as I walk dazedly towards the library exit.

I hear Liyah from down the corridor, talking outside the exam hall. She's so loud sometimes. Always vibrant, telling everyone small snippets about her life. I make ways to her and wrap her in a big bear hug from behind.

'Now you've filled your belly, you want to show me love. Get off me *himar*,' she jokes.

I'm definitely not a donkey. I squeeze her tighter to show her my annoyance.

'OK, OK, I get it, you love me, now get off me,' she laughs.

I unwrap myself from her. 'Are you ready to buss this exam?'

'Ready? I was born ready.' She mocks a power stance. 'Last exam sis, we got this.'

'Who's ready to say goodbye to W&A college?' I say to the rest of the girls. 'Cos I sure as hell am.'

'I can't wait to get out of here,' Fatima comments. She's one of the two hijabi twins in our class. Her sister Ayan nods in agreement.

The door opens, and the lead invigilator yells, 'Right, year thirteens. Please enter the examination hall.'

I grab hold of Liyah's hand, and she squeezes mine in return. We got this. *You got this.*

CHAPTER 17

JALAAL

Not gonna lie, it vexed me a bit that Shaah would ask me that favour. I know he's my boy, but he has been moving kinda off recently. Maybe he has issues with me chatting to Sabrina cos he can't really draw gyal like that. I'm not entirely sure but maybe I should do it. I could do with the extra cash. But then . . . I don't wanna be one of the mandem who get sucked into selling Class A, cos then you're in too deep. There is a part of me that wants to stop all this fuckery anyway. There's bare shit going on in my head.

I press the home button on my phone. It's 5.07 p.m. Sabrina would've finished her exam by now. I don't know if I should wait to hear from her. Fuck it. I actually need to speak to someone in my life who means me well.

Congrats, finally free. Do I get to see your peng face today?

I backspace, that's too eager.

Hey Sabs, how was your final exam?

I sound like I wanna be in the friendzone.

I exit the chat and close my iPhone.

Ping. Sabs.

Weirdly missed speaking to you.

My fingers are typing before I know it.

Same. How was the exam? What u doing rn? I reply.

Sabs

Just got home. Gonna burn my books and shower.

I miss her weird sense of humour.

Lol. Wanna chill after?

She doesn't respond immediately. I'm never this nervous when waiting for someone to reply. She's got me moving mad, staring at this screen like an idiot. She replies.

Sabs

OK but local and not for too long.

Calm. Meet outside chicken cottage at 8?

Sabs

All right, see you then.

I smile. I'm gassed to see Sabs. I know she likes to smoke so maybe we could bill a zoot. I'll take some with me. We could also go to the park. There's actually bare stuff we can do but I don't even care. I just wanna see her.

I've been waiting outside the chicken shop for five minutes and Sabs isn't here. I hope she doesn't think I look like a bum. I'm dressed in my black Nike Tech jumper and joggers, matched with my red and black Air Jordan 1's.

Sab walks over to me, grinning. She looks pretty in her oversized Nike T-shirt and black Nike leggings. Her hair is slicked back in a low bun, and she has a bottle of Volvic water in her hand. I make a mental note to remember that she likes Volvic water. I bet she's one of them picky ones that don't even drink tap water.

'Heyyy.' She stretches her arms out.

I pull her into my embrace. She smells like cotton sheets and baby oil.

'OK, I'm gonna be a control freak and tell you what we are doing. Let's go to Paddington Basin.'

Her confidence rattles me. It's sexy though.

'Where's that?'

'You know that nice area with the canal, near the station?'

Oh, them boujee ends. I knew I was right about Sabs being boujee.

'Oh yeah, say nothing. This is your day anyway, we doing whatever you wanna do.'

'Hmmm, OK.' She squints her eyes, looks at me suspiciously.

She begins walking in the other direction and I rush to catch up to her, matching her stride.

'So how do you feel now that you're officially done with college?'

'Happy. Let's not talk about it though. How have *you* been? What have *you* been up to?'

'Just been working really.' I have seen more of Sohaib than my actual family.

'Working?'

'Sainsbury's?' I raise an eyebrow.

'Oh yeah. I thought you were talking about . . .' She stops herself.

It jars me that she thinks that low of me. Imagine if she knew what my boys were doing, then she'd be shook. Talking about boys, I don't know if I should mention the whole police incident at Nico's yard. Probably best not to disclose it.

'Nah, you think I'm some hoodrat don't you?' I joke. Even though I'm praying that she tells me I'm wrong.

'If you were just a hoodrat, I wouldn't be with you right now, trust me.'

I take a second to deep the back-handed compliment.

'Anyways.' She steps ahead of me and turns the corner by the Hilton Paddington. 'Here we are!'

Fuck. It's actually bare scenic. The canal is decorated with colourful fairy lights beaming on to the nearby offices and new-build flats. The restaurants and bars are quiet, and a few people are sat outside sipping on orange drinks in fat wine glasses. You wouldn't think you were anywhere near the ends. It's kinda peaceful.

'It's like you're in a different London.' The reflective lights twinkle in her eyes.

'Yeah, you wouldn't think you're on Edgware Road.'

I follow Sab's wandering eyes and imagine that I'm not on the block. I pretend that I'm someone who can afford to eat endlessly and drink from the fat wine glasses. And live in these expensive brand-new flats. And own nice cars. I glance at her and guiltily imagine living in this world with her. I want to give that to her. I want to provide for Sabs. I want her to achieve her dreams. She's gonna be doing bits with her social justice shit and then I'll be taking her on dates like this every night, dressing up in the freshest clothes, and eating expensive food. Not having to worry about money or being G-checked in the wrong ends. Safe. Happy.

I softly take her hand and pull her towards me. I look around us to make sure nobody is watching. I interlock our fingers with one hand and wrap my other arm around her waist. I bring her into an embrace and quickly drop our locked fingers to kiss her.

As our lips press, I close my eyes; I imagine myself in a peaceful world. One where I don't have to look over my shoulder. One where

I don't have to worry about the police stopping me. One where I don't have to worry about Shaah getting into trouble. One where I can be certain that Ibrahim will grow up in a safe environment. One where our whole families are supportive of us.

Just as I'm about to step back from Sabrina, she dips her tongue in my mouth and thrusts herself towards my groin area. I part open my lips and let her tongue slither in my mouth – only the tip of it before I cheekily take a nibble at her lip. I slowly dip my hands from her waist and towards her bum. I go at a slow pace so if she wants me to stop, she can signal it. She doesn't. I move my hands down and cup one of her cheeks. I give it a soft squeeze as it jiggles in my hand. She moans in my mouth, and I feel my dick starting to harden. I think she feels it too because she's now fully pressed her hips into mine.

Before anything else happens, she steps back and giggles. She is so fucking sexy. She's got me all horny and shit, and now she's backing off.

'You're jarring, you know that, right?'

'Sorry not sorry,' she grins.

I pull her in for another embrace. My head arches over hers and I bend over to snuggle myself in the crook of her neck. I plant kisses down her cheeks and tell her she's so adorable.

'OK, OK, enough of being mushy.'

She steps away, grabbing hold of my hand and pulling me along with her. I laugh as I allow her to lead me on.

CHAPTER 18

SABRINA

If someone had told me three months ago that I'd be celebrating the end of my exams with Jalaal – I'd laugh in their face. I'd tell them there is no chance that could ever happen. But it's happening. Here I am. And to be honest, there's no one else I'd rather be with. *Except Mum, if she was around.*

It's official, I like Jalaal. During my exam period, he has been on my mind. It sounds cringe, but with him, I can be myself. I am comfortable in my own skin. And he genuinely makes me feel like I'm the only girl in the world. *Sabs, you are whipped!* He always asks the specifics of my day and really tries to get to know the real me. I recently read something online about 'active listening' and it reminds me of Jalaal, because he's always engaged in our conversations and remembers the little details about me.

Also, he's peng. Like he's actually peng. He's six foot and got them beautiful curls. It's a bonus that he always smells nice. I hate to admit it, but when I'm with him, I forget that he's kinda on road or doing something illegal. Part of me believes that I can make him pattern up. I know it sounds messed up, but if things get serious between us, I need to let him know that selling weed is not gonna run. My dad would never accept it. Auntie Maureen would never accept it. I would never accept it.

Sabs, you're thinking too far ahead. I don't even know what is happening right now but all I want to do is spend time with him.

We sit at Paddington Basin on the steps by the water fountain. There are always little kids running through the water but it's empty right now. I sometimes bring Izzy here and Dad always bugs out when she comes home drenched.

'There's something that's bothering me that I need to ask you about.' He places my hands in his palms. 'Actually, wait, let me ask you something first,' I say.

He nods.

'What's this?' I point my finger between me and him. 'Like what's going on between us? Because you know I'm not some "beat and delete" girl and I'm also not some sideting.' It comes out more confident than it feels.

'Hmm.' He looks up at the sky. 'I don't really know how to speak about my feelings, and this is proper weird for me, ya know. You're not a sideting or anything that you said. Put some respect on your name please. Look . . . I do like you. I like spending time with you. I don't know what else to say but I got a good feeling about this.'

My stomach is doing backflips. I feel it too, in my gut.

'I'm the same. Like, it feels right to me. And I do respect myself! You respect that I respect myself please!'

He rolls his eyes.

I playfully punch him in the chest, and he grabs on to my hands and interlocks his fingers with mine. Our heads move closer towards each other until they are millimetres apart. Before I know it, he quickly taps his lips on mine.

'What was the original question now? Tell me babes.'

He's getting proper comfortable with this 'babe' thing now.

I take a deep breath. 'Are you umm . . . a proper roadman?'

He sighs. 'I knew this was gonna come up at some point. OK, I'll tell you.'

'OK . . .'

'I don't know if roadman is the right word. Yeah, I sell weed. I have been doing so for about a year. I did do deets for a bit – that was a long time ago.' He hushes his tone and looks behind his shoulder. 'I chill with mandem who are on that gang shit but I'm not actively part of that. *Wallahi*, I only chill with them.' He holds his hands up in innocence. 'I don't have opps against me, but my boys have opps and that means if I'm caught lacking – I don't know what'll happen. But nah, don't call me a roadman. I just make P's by selling weed.'

'Have you ever sold other stuff? Do you carry weapons? Have you, you know, hurt other people?' The questions fly out of my mouth. *You're such an idiot Sabs, why do you speak without thinking sometimes? He's going to think you're some weirdo right now. You sound like a fed. Like Ms Ross.*

'Woah woah woah. Sabs. I'm not on a madness now. You know that I work at Sainsbury's too. And the plan is to go legit, at some point. But I just don't know what I wanna do with my life, how to get there . . .'

I reverse his grasp on my hands and squeeze them hard until he focuses his attention on me.

'I can help you figure it out if you need it, but like no pressure.' I smile. It's good to hear that Jalaal actually does have a desire to leave this road life. Now I feel more confident about our future.

'Thanks Sabs, I mean it. But not gonna lie, this is something I think I need to do for myself. Anyway, I been meaning to ask you this, but you always talk about your sisters and your dad, but I don't know much about your mum,' Jalaal says as he strokes my fingers.

She's still locked away in the back of my mind.

'It's a long story,' I sigh.

'I wanna hear it . . . if you're comfortable. Like, it's calm, I won't judge you or anything.'

Sabs, maybe you should let him in. He might be able to help. Maybe it is time to open the gate and let the flood come out.

'Umm,' I gulp, gathering the strength to revisit those memories. *He makes you feel safe though.* 'Promise not to judge me or anything like that.' I search his eyes for trust.

You know it's already there.

'I ain't like that, I'll never judge you.' He holds my gaze.

I fumble with my fingers. *You can do this Sabs, just be honest and tell him the truth.*

I must've been like fifteen. I never understood the hold cocaine had on Mum. I can't believe it made her forget about us. Her family. During that time where she disappeared for a week – I went through her drawers looking for anything that would help me figure out where she went. Mum always liked to write things on notepads, so I thought I could find a contact number or address. At the bottom of her drawer, in her jewellery box, is where I found it.

White powder. A small baggie. There wasn't that much left. Maybe like a quarter of a teaspoon. Less than the amount of sugar you would put in your tea.

I don't know what came over me in that moment, but I felt the urge to try it. I knew it was cocaine but I just wanted to understand why she was addicted to something so evil.

My body succumbed to a toxic feeling of nerves and adrenaline.

You know that feeling when you know you're doing something wrong – like when you're cheating on an exam, and it overtakes your body, down to your bones. I ignored those knots in my stomach that told me otherwise. My fingers were shaking as I opened the baggie. I dipped my index finger into the bag, swirled it around until the powder rested on my finger.

I spent like two minutes staring at my finger, having an argument in my mind. I knew that Dad was downstairs so if something bad happened, at least he'd be here to save me.

I snorted it.

I placed my finger under my right nostril and inhaled deep. I sat on my parents' bed waiting for something to happen. Just anything. There was nothing. I genuinely thought that I was immune to cocaine. It hit me five minutes later.

First, my heart rate sped up. It was like I could see it thumping from my chest. A heat flushed over my body. I was wide awake; I'd never been so alert in my life. My eyes were darting from side to side in the room, analysing anything and everything. I ran to the mirror and saw that my pupils were huge. *Fuck*. My dad would realize that I'd taken something and probably kill me. That's when I started to panic. I went to the bedroom door and kept unlocking and locking it. I was paranoid. A different level of paranoia to weed.

Because it was so silent in the room, all I could focus on was my thumping heartbeat and the itching hotness of my body. I rested my back against the door and slid down to the floor. I placed my hands on my head, closed my eyes and waited for the trip to finish, hoping that my mind would stop rushing a million miles an hour.

It all stopped after like thirty minutes. I ran to my bed. I slept for like two hours and woke up groggy. I don't think anyone ever realized. Nobody knows. Not even Liyah.

Jalaal stares at me, his eyes wide with something I can't place.

'I don't know what came over me, I was so curious to try this evil thing. It was only one time. I've never told anyone about it.' I start defending myself, afraid that he thinks the worst of me. 'Please, don't think less of me, please, I hate this secret, I hate it, I just want to do well—'

'Sabs, Sabs, stop. Of course I don't think less of you . . . trust me, I get what it's like. It's like the roads. You kinda do something mad for no real reason. But you don't have to hide anything from me.'

He moves closer and squeezes my hand. I tear up. He gets it. He doesn't judge me for it. *Sabs, this is your man.* We sit for a moment in silence before he says, 'Do you think she'll ever come back?'

'I don't know.'

I take in a deep breath and Jalaal squeezes my hand.

'Like, I miss her so much. That's my mum, you know. And it fucking hurts that she doesn't care about us any more and it scares me to death that she could be dead somewhere. I hate the fact my sisters are growing up without a mum and it hurts my dad so much.' I remember the photos in the china cabinet. 'I think he still is waiting for her to come back.'

'Ahh, Sabs. I'm sorry to bring back these bad feelings but I swear, it's good to let it all out. Whatever your mum decided to do, that was her choice you know. It's nothin' to do with you. Sometimes parents fuck up and it's got nothin' to do with the kids. Don't stress yourself about it. *Wallahi*, I can promise you that it's nothing to do with you.'

At this point, my face is slobbering with snot and tears. I've gone through about a million emotions today. *Why is this happening to me?*

I cling on to Jalaal and smother my face into his jumper.

'Thank you . . . for listening to me and allowing me to be a complete mess.'

He pulls us apart and looks at me. 'I gotchu. I'm always here for you, you know that.'

I nod as he pulls me back into his arms and I gaze up, the sky bursting with hues of purple, red and orange. I arch my neck back and notice his eyes are welling up with tears.

'Hey, what's wrong?' I beg for his eyes to meet mine.

'I miss my mum too.'

The tears don't fall.

'You don't really speak much about her, either,' I tread carefully.

'Yeah . . .' He pauses. 'I told you that she passed away, right?'

'How?' I bite my lip.

Fuck, here I am talking about my mum problems and Jalaal's one isn't even alive. *Sabs, you're so inconsiderate.* 'It happened a long time ago. Eight years ago. And she passed away during childbirth. With Ibrahim.' He pulls his chest up.

My heart sinks. Ibrahim grew up with no mum whatsoever. It's like Izzy growing up without Mum. I can only imagine what Jalaal is going through. All this time, I've been judging him, not knowing that he was carrying this heaviness.

'And my dad . . .' He pauses. 'He ain't around either. Left us after Mumzy passed away. Kinda fucked off back to Somaliland, so my aunt basically raised us. It's not fully "absent black dad" but close enough. It's this shit thing where some Somali dads return back home and miraculously have another family. So yeah, kinda peak.' His shoulders relax.

'I'm so sorry, I had no idea.'

'Sabs.' He forces a smile. 'Stop apologizing. It happened a long time ago. Just you chatting 'bout your mum reminded me about my mum. Actually, it feels kinda good to say everything out loud. My life is mad complicated Sabs, I won't lie to you. Almost as complicated as yours. Makes me think that we are more compatible than you think.' He nudges me.

'Haha. Trauma bonding and suddenly we are compatible. Relax.'

'OK then,' he mimics my voice.

'Who's being jarring now then?' I fake flick my hair.

Jalaal bursts into laughter. 'You're bare annoying, don't ever change. But on a real note though.' He pauses. 'Do you believe in God?'

The bun on my head suddenly feels tighter. *You knew this conversation was gonna come at some point.* All these deep convos are a lot. I take a moment to think, letting the sound of the fountain and people laughing wash over me.

'I am Christian, but not proper religious. But yeah, I do believe in God. Why?'

'That's good to hear, cos you should have faith that God has your back and whatever happens in life, it was meant to be.'

'Is that an Islamic saying?'

He shakes his head. 'No, it's not. It's just a "me saying". Did you know that Christians, Jews and Muslims all believe in the same God?'

'Uhm, no?' I reply honestly.

Liyah was right, I should have made the effort to do some more research. *Fuck Sabs, you're actually clueless sometimes.*

Jalaal spends the next ten minutes giving me a crash course on Islam. He keeps repeating that this is his interpretation and understanding of it. He speaks about the five pillars of Islam, which I sheepishly tell him I remembered learning in RE GCSE but completely forgot what they stood for. I know about Ramadan because Liyah fasts during that month, and we don't really go to the chicken shop together. I also tell Jalaal that I know women can't fast if they're on their period and how Liyah still doesn't go to the chicken shop during Ramadan because people in the community will judge her. Jalaal chuckles and rolls his eyes. He says, 'People need to mind their fucking business.'

'I like that you have such great conviction in your faith.'

'Yeah, I guess.' He bites his lip. 'But sometimes Sabs, I ain't *really* feel "religious" because I don't pray or fast. That's the BARE minimum you know. Not gonna lie, nothing about me distinguishes me as Muslim apart from this "great conviction" of my faith you're chatting about.' His shoulders slump.

'Trust me Jalaal, I know how you feel.'

I really connected with Jalaal. I know that there is some entity out there, God, but I'm unsure about religion. It all seems very overwhelming for me, but luckily, I don't have the pressure from family to practise a religion. I know loads of Jamaicans are sort of religious, just not my family, except for Auntie Maureen really.

'It jars me that Somalis mix culture and religion together. Everyday some auntie is calling me *gaalo*, saying that I'm a non-believer. I don't know, it's mad. It makes me bare angry, but also guilty at the same time. It's fucked and gets me emotional when I think about it,' he confesses.

Sabs, you gotta comfort him. Say something!

'You said something about your belief in Allah?' I know I just butchered God's name. 'That keeps you sane or whatever. And I think you should hold on to that. Plus, you're only like seventeen so don't stress yourself, you got a whole lifetime to figure it out.'

'I hope so, man.'

Does he think I'm one of his boys?

He notices my facial reaction because he corrects himself. 'I mean, babes?' he jokes. 'Nah seriously, I even feel bare guilty after I'm drinking or smoking cos these things are *haram*.'

Haram is one of the first things that Liyah taught me, so I know this.

'I understand. But you can always stop if you want to. And plus, we all make mistakes. God is all-forgiving, all-merciful right?' I repeat what he explained to me earlier.

I didn't know he had such knowledge on his faith. He's so different to me. I don't think about religion to this level. It's kinda inspiring. *Sabs, maybe you should have listened to Dad and Liyah's apprehensions.* I'm sure we'll be all right. I hope we will.

'Yeah. He is,' Jalaal says, voice heavy.

'Don't beat yourself up about it, babes,' I mock him.

Jalaal smirks at me. 'Babes, yeah?'

Before I know it, he's tickling my underarms. My body jolts and I can't stop laughing.

'Jalaal.' I manage to speak. 'I'M TICKLISH!'

He pauses momentarily. 'I know.'

The feeling of his fingertips squeezing into the crevice of my underarms keeps me laughing.

We stop when we're both out of breath.

He relaxes. 'Sabs . . .'

'Yeah,' I whisper.

'Make sure you keep next Tuesday free. The whole day.'

'Why?'

'Just keep it free. It's a surprise.'

'Whatever you say, *babes*.'

CHAPTER 19

JALAAL

At home, my aunt halts me at the corridor. '*WARYAA*.'
I wonder what crime I've committed now. I fling my trainers off before she starts on me.

'Wait one minute, I need to speak with you.' Her eyes plead with me.

Hals emerges behind her, nodding. Her face serious.

'What's up.' I narrow my eyes.

'It's your dad . . .'

'What about him?'

'Maybe you should sit down . . .'

My heart plummets, but I keep a straight face.

'What has he done now?' I roll my eyes.

'He's sick.' Habo's front tooth catches her bottom lip. 'Very unwell.'

My insides twist. I guess this is why he was trying to call me.

'So?'

She sighs deeply.

I wait.

'Don't you think you should talk to him?' Hals interjects.

'I don't have anything left to say to him. I hope he gets better.' I grab my Yeezy slides, turn around and leave straight through the door I just came in.

*

How the fuck am I supposed to feel? *Wallahi*, I don't know what the fuck is going on. I want to punch the wall and cry at the same fucking time.

I pull out a half-smoked zoot from my pocket and light it up. After a few inhalations, everything subsides. Abo. He's not well. But it doesn't sound like he's gonna die, otherwise Habo Hani would've said something. At the same time, it must've been serious enough for him to keep belling my line. I don't get it. He fucked off to Somaliland to live his best life and now he's calling when he feels a bit sick. What am I supposed to do? He's the reason I'm in this shit situation. Selling weed and making small profits. For what reason? It's all his fault. Everything. I might as well just get deeper into this thing if he's not gonna be around. Like what's the fucking point.

I swipe open my phone, load up Shaah's message and type.

I'll do it.

My fingers are pulsating.

My boy, I'll drop it off to you later, Shaah responds.

I rest against the brick wall and finish my zoot.

Today is the day. I'm taking Sabs out of London for a surprise. And for my little side quest as well. All that shit with Abo, I smoked it away. He's not my problem any more. I've got packs under my waistband that need to travel across the country. What's me stressing about him gonna do? Nothing. I need to do this drop, then focus on making this day as special as possible for Sabs. She deserves everything.

I text her.

> Im gna meet you at Marylebone stn at 11.45
> or I can pick you up and we make ways together?

Sabs

Hmmmmmm.

                                             Make up your mind bbs

Sabs

Ugh. I'll meet you there . . . where are we goin?

She's so stubborn sometimes.

                                                   11.45. Don't b late.

I click my phone shut.

I wonder if I'm doing too much for this girl. I've never done anything like this for any girl. Especially someone who I've only known for a month. Not gonna lie, this connection is like nothing that I've ever felt in my life. It's mad that I feel safe enough to open up, that's something special.

I look at myself in the reflection of Habo's mirror. Her chest of drawers are decorated with strong-scented perfumes and oud.

My black jeans and white shirt look smart. And with my Clarks, I look like such a neek. It's my outfit from 'interview day' back in year eleven. I'm surprised that I can still fit into it. I can't be travelling OT looking like some roadman. If the mandem saw me now, I bet they would be roasting me. I feel good though. Like I'm about to accomplish something. I wonder what Sabs will think of the fit.

The house is quiet and it's probably cos Hals is out. I try to sneak out but am surprised to see Habo Hani sat at the kitchen table helping Ibrahim with his homework. She ain't really teaching him, Ibby is mad smart. It's more like supervising him so he doesn't get distracted.

Habo stares at me and Ibrahim whips his head around, mouth wide open.

'What?' My voice cracks.

'You look . . . smart?'

'And?' It comes out ruder than I expected.

His face turns sad.

'And do I look good or what?' I feel Habo's eyes burning.

'You look kind,' he smiles. 'Can you wear that when you pick me up from school next time?'

Habo smirks.

'Whatever you want, lil bro.' I can't say no to him.

'Where are you going?' Habo tilts her head. But before I can even answer she's already in there again. 'Maybe speak to your dad when you get a moment.'

I ignore her comment, head outside to my Uber and make my way to the station.

I wait for Sabs next to Hotel Chocolat. The sun is beaming today, but it's not too hot. I thought about buying her some chocolate, but I'll be real, the price is unnecessarily expensive. Plus, I don't know which one of these chocolates she'd like. I spent bare money already on the train tickets. My bread is running low. Thank God for this drop-off as I'm gonna need those extra P's. Maybe I'll buy her some on the way back.

Sabrina's swaying head grabs my attention. It's the first time I've seen her hair out natural. She's got beautiful curls. She's wearing a white-and-pink sundress with Birkenstocks, and her skin is glowing. She is a goddess, for real.

'Marylebone Station yeah, where are we going today?' She

scrunches her eyebrows and gives me a side hug.

'I don't know if I should tell you the surprise or we just make ways.'

'I'm itching to know. I don't like surprises.'

'Fine.' I can't wait to see her reaction. 'We are going to . . . Warwick.'

'Why?' She breaks into a grin.

'Because you rattled me when you told me that you've only ever seen your university on the computer.' I never feel nervous like this, but the way my heart is pulsing right now is mad.

'Yeah, I get that. But why have you decided for *us* to go together?' She points her fingers between us.

Does she like the surprise or not? I don't get it. Am I doing too much?

'So I know where I'm going when I come to visit you,' I half joke. It's the only thing I can respond without bugging out.

I dunno why she's fighting back her smile. I can see how happy she is from the way her eyes are shining, how much they're creasing. She is gassed.

'Jalaal Abdi, you have set the bar very high.'

'I know,' I wink.

'I'm going to the toilet, one sec.' She leaves her bag with me before running off.

Being with Sabrina must clear my head or something, because it's while she's in the station toilet that I clock that I've fucked up. Sabs would kill me if she knew that I had cocaine on me. It's the same shit that took her mum away from her, and here I am, standing on platform two waiting for a train with a shitload. I've actually fucked up. She can never know about this if I'm ever gonna keep this girl. She would cut me off forever if she knew. I consider calling

Shaah to change my mind and give him back the coke, I consider flushing it down the toilet and just not seeing it through, but it's too fucking late now. I have to follow through the plan.

We finally make it on the train and sit opposite each other. My heart is thumping, but then the sun catches Sabs's hair, she smiles at me and I deep it. It's her. This is the girl that I can see spending the rest of my life with.

Shaah said the yute I'm dropping off to is going meet me in the station toilets when the train arrives in Coventry. I have my burner on me, but it's on silent. Sabs can't know what's running on her special day.

'So, shall we watch some TikToks on my iPad since you're always complaining that I need to get on the app.' I pass it to her before she can decline.

'Aww, look at you, so considerate. What did I do to deserve you?'

'Go on, continue being sarcastic and I'll take it back.'

She sticks her tongue out. 'What's the passcode?'

'6217.'

She types in the passcode and immediately her eyes bulge in shock.

What the fuck did I leave on that iPad? Fuck. Fuck.

'These are sick.' She flips the iPad around and cracks a grin. 'You didn't tell me you were this friggin' creative.'

It's the clothes designs I was illustrating on Adobe Illustrator.

'Ayy, don't gas me. It's just some things I'm messing about with.'

'Are these going on trainers too? You're so talented Jalaal, you should do something.'

'Yeah, hmmm, we will see . . .'

'Seriously though Jalaal, you could—'

'Allow it, Sabs,' I cut her off. That's not possible for someone like me. Deep it, I'm here with wraps of cocaine stuffed down my pants. I'm far from what she expects from me.

'Oh, sorry!'

'Just show me the TikToks, we can talk about design stuff another time.' I try to make her feel better.

She forces a smile. 'Yeah, sure.'

CHAPTER 20

SABRINA

I'm literally shook that Jalaal has surprised me with this trip to Warwick University. Like I'm shook. Now Ms Ross can't chat shit about him any more. No one can say he's a wasteman. He literally made the effort to take me to my dream university.

Getting off the train, the air hits me immediately. I kid you not, it's cleaner than whatever shit we breathe in London. Jalaal's been in the bathroom for a hot sec, he mentioned eating some dodgy food last night. There was some sketchy kid in dirty tracksuits who went in after him. It's probably nothing, Jalaal can handle himself. But . . . *Something feels off, Sabs?*

'Doesn't the air feel clean to you?' I ask Jalaal when he comes out of the toilet. He seems more relaxed so . . . I don't think I have anything to worry about. I shrug off the doubt.

He looks at me and laughs. 'You're bugging out, the air is the same.'

'Nah seriously, doesn't it feel easier to breathe in?' I need him to co-sign.

'Nah Sabs,' he chuckles. 'It feels the same. Anyways, let's grab a taxi to the university. We ain't got time to wait for the bus.'

'Do we have to?' I whine.

'Yes, we do,' he mimics my whine.

*

The cab drops us off at the students' union on the university campus. I have no idea where to go or what to do, but Jalaal does. He leads me to a meeting point in the students' union reception. It feels super weird not being in charge or like, responsible, for the day.

'Hello,' he says. 'We have a campus tour. Umm, are we at the right place?' He shuffles awkwardly with his hands in his pockets. Jalaal can be really cute sometimes.

'Yeah, you are, what's the name it's booked under?' the chirpy boy asks.

'It's Jalaal Abdi, I'll spell that for you. J-A-L-A-A-L.'

'Oh right, yes I've found you,' the boy interrupts as he looks closer at the screen and then, 'Perfect! Now, follow me and I'll show you . . .'

Everybody on the tour looks super middle-class. Their accents are so posh, and they enunciate their words prim and proper. I can't help but feel out of place. I'm sure some of the parents are side-eyeing me and Jalaal up, probably wondering why we don't have any parents tagging along with us. We are also the only non-white people here, unless you want to count half of me. *Relax, Sabs, you have every right to be here.*

'So, this is the piazza,' our tour guide tells us, pointing towards the amphitheatre-style seats outside the students' union. There are a few older-looking students sat drinking beer. I'm surprised there are even students here, I swear it's meant to be the summer holiday.

'This is the heart of campus; during the summer term, there are loads of us just chilling here. And we sometimes have live music and food stalls. It's a proper good vibe!' Our quirky guide continues waffling, using his arms very expressively. I wonder if he studies drama or he's just super dramatic on purpose.

I catch Jalaal smirking, holding in his laugh.

'All right, let's go back into the students' union, the main hub of everything.'

We walk back into the building which we started at. God, it looks so cool. Two black girls smile at Jalaal and me as they wait for us to walk through the door. *OK, so it's not completely white.*

'Jalaal,' I whisper, 'except the two girls we just saw, don't you think this place is super white and why is everyone on the tour watching us like some tramps?'

He places both hands on my shoulders and slowly rubs. 'Stop bugging, nobody is watching us like that. Listen, this place is a vibe and you're gonna find your "tribe", don't worry. Didn't the guy say there are like almost thirty thousand students here? Plus, those girls at the door were grinning for days. Don't stress Sabs!'

My shoulders ease into his palms. *He's right Sabs, you're overthinking. Focus back on the tour. This is going to be your new home.*

The union has an enormous amount of open space. Our guide shows us the different shops and explains it transforms into a club at night. I'm impressed with the pool tables in the common area that are free for everyone to use. Free! Jalaal slides his hand across the table as we walk past and gives me a nod of approval. I knew he would like it.

My favourite part of the student union is the bread oven cafe. It is such a homey vibe and I love chilling out in coffee shops. I mean, I don't think I've ever done it, but I imagine being *that* girl chilling in the coffee shop with my laptop. I'm envisioning it already.

'This is one of many cafes on campus,' he tells us.

There are more?! I legit cannot contain the excitement. *I wish Mum was here to experience this with me.* No. This day is about my future, not my past. I take a deep breath and let her escape my thoughts as quickly as she entered them.

'So, this is one of our accommodation halls – Cryfield Apartments.' He points at a modern building, and we all go inside.

I compare it to my room at home and I can already tell it's bigger. And it's got a floor-length window directly in front of the bed. I love natural light. I don't know why I was expecting hospital beds. The room also has a huge desk and some shelves. The bathroom is simple. At least it's en suite. I don't think I could be sharing a toilet with others – I'm not *that* girl. The kitchen area is super modern, maybe even more modern than mine at home. It's got a bar-type table with stools. This whole place is a vibe.

I pull out my phone and take photos to show Dad. *Cryfield Apartments*. What a weird name. Everything outside of London is weird.

'I guess this is where I'm going to come visit you?' Jalaal whispers to me as he squeezes my hip.

'Maybe, or maybe you'll be staying here with your own room too?' I raise my eyebrows.

'Me?' He points towards himself. 'A student at uni? They ain't gonna let me in with just GCSEs,' he laughs.

I laugh too and roll my eyes.

'But . . . you know you could try . . . you could study design and get loads of opportunities. I saw what you did on the iPad.'

'Yeah but . . . I know what I'm doing. I don't wanna talk about this now. Trust me, Sabs. I know what I'm doing.'

'Do you? Cos there are some things you gotta stop doing first.' It slips out without thinking.

'Soon,' he mutters and pulls away from me.

'Are you OK? You seem a bit off . . . kinda distracted.'

He perks up. 'Seriously?' He must think he's hid it well.

'Kinda, has something happened?' I inch closer to him. 'Are you OK being here?'

'I'll tell you when we are alone.' He quickly glances across the room. 'It's nothing that you need to worry about.'

During our walk back to the train station, Jalaal finally opens up. 'It's Abo. My dad. He's sick.'

Now I get why he's been acting so off. I can't believe he's been holding on to this, all this time. I know what it's like to be worried about one of your parents.

I can't help but feel that this is unchartered territory with Jalaal; he hasn't really opened up to me like this and I'm not sure what to say. I really don't want to deal with the silence that may follow. *Be brave, Sabs, give him the space to share.*

'How did he sound?' I probe.

'Uhhh . . . not gonna lie, I haven't spoken to him. My aunt told me.'

'Ohhhh.'

Silence. *Bite the bullet, Sabs.*

'Why don't you call him . . .' I suggest.

'Are you crazy?'

'No . . . let me ask you this though. It might sound kinda mad. If your dad died tomorrow, would you regret not talking to him? And actually deep it before you answer me. No ego.'

Jalaal pauses, mouthing 'no ego'.

'When you say it like that Sabs . . . then of course I'm gonna regret it, he is my dad, but I don't think . . .'

'Then that's it, there's no further discussion. I know it's not the same, but I'd jump at any chance to speak to my mum . . .'

'Your situation is kinda different. No disrespect. I ain't sure 'bout calling him. I don't know if I wanna chat to him.' He shrugs his shoulders.

How can he not see that reconnecting with his dad is the right thing to do? I don't know Jalaal's full boundaries yet and I don't want to push him further from his dad. Even though I want to shake him, I bite my lip this time. *Take it easy.*

'Whenever you're ready.' I snuggle closer to him.

Our train isn't due for another fifteen minutes. Jalaal and I sit at the platform bench. I've got a cup of tea in one hand, and his fingers interlocked with my other.

'Jalaal, thank you for today. Like thank you so much. It was the best thing you could have ever done for me and . . . *wallahi* . . . I appreciate it so much.' I use his lingo.

'Of course, I'd do anything for you Sabs. Don't tell no one though, but you got me acting like a simp,' he chuckles.

I smile, my lips ever so slightly quivering.

'You're cold still! Let me give you my hoody.' He swings off his backpack and fumbles around.

'No, it's OK, we're gonna be on the train soon and I'll be warm. I don't want you to think I'm being *that* girl taking your hoody home.'

He laughs to himself as he softly takes the tea out of my hand and pulls the grey hoody over my head.

'What's mine is yours, don't be stupid. Ain't no chance I'm ever gonna allow you to be cold.' He gives me a quick peck on the lips before handing me back my cup of tea.

'Sometimes, I wish we could just hang out like this in my house or something. Just chill, eat food, cuddle, watch TV, do you get what I mean? Obviously, I could never bring you home – my dad would never allow it. He's even strict about what friends can come over.'

'Yeah, I get it, trust me. I could never bring a girl home, even if it was just a friend,' he chuckles. 'At least that's something our families will agree on.'

'But seriously.' I'm surprised by my forwardness. 'Even if it was just one day that we had our own space to do that, it would be so amazing!'

'We'll have Cryfield Apartments.'

'You're so annoying!' I fake punch him.

'I'm joking, but one day, it'll be like that, trust me.' He gives me another peck.

I'm starting to love this. Jalaal is becoming everything.

CHAPTER 21

JALAAL

Hanging out with Sabrina is the best thing to happen since she finished her exams. Since our trip to Warwick, I've only become more infatuated with the girl. And yes, I learnt that word from her.

It's bare obvious that she fell in love with Warwick, and it gassed me that I could do that for her. It's a mad feeling because part of me is happy and the other part is pained. Like I'm letting a big part of me leave. I feel so selfish about it. I like spending time with this girl too much. But I know that she is destined for something better than the ends.

We've linked a few times since Warwick, like the other day we went to Nando's to get munch. I can't believe she whacked off that *extra-hot* Sunset Burger meal. She was roasting me for only taking lemon and herb. But *wallahi*, I ain't tryna burn my tongue, I wanna enjoy my food. We also went to central again and took the Boris bikes around Hyde Park. We've hung out in the park to chill and talk. We have lipsed and stuff, but it's not as scatty as it sounds because Sabs is bare classy. We haven't had sex and I'm not gonna lie, it's getting harder and harder. But I like the pace we are going at, and I'm being bare respectful of what Sabrina wants.

*

My phone vibrates. It's Ahmed from W&A college. Another drop-off.

Give me 3 mins fam.

I'm playing *Fortnite* with Ibrahim, but money is money. Now I gotta figure out how to get the weed from under the bed without Ibrahim clocking. I haven't had the time to put it inside the brush. He can't see where I hide my food.

'Ibby!'

'Yeah,' he says, his eyes still focusing on the game.

'Can you get me a can of Coke from the fridge please, *walaalo*?'

'No! Get it yourself. I'm playing,' he moans.

'I'll let you have one as well.' He isn't allowed to drink fizzy drinks, but I'm desperate.

He leaps up and dashes out of my room.

He's quick, but I need to be quicker. I immediately throw my mattress upwards, pull up the wooden panel and take out the big, clear plastic bag that is wrapped in cling film. I don't think I'll have time to unwrap it all, so I chuck it in my messenger bag. I know there's a small baggie that I weighed beforehand inside. I put the mattress back into the bed frame and Ibrahim kicks my door open with two cans of Coke in his hands.

I take a can and walk towards the door.

'Don't get any Coke on my controller *waryaa*, I know how sticky your hands get,' I warn him.

'OK, but where are you going? Are you coming back to play?'

'Yeah, one sec, I just need to drop something off to Shaah, then I'm coming back,' I lie.

I silently creep down the stairs. Hals is out tonight, probably at a shisha spot or something. Habo has a leg up and is busy watching Nollywood sitcoms in the living room, she doesn't notice me. I put on my slides and leave the house.

The cool air soothes my face. I slap open the Coke can and take a huge gulp.

I meet Ahmed in the alleyway where he is standing awkwardly under the dim lamp. It's a bit of a sticky one for me to be carrying all this food on me. I pray none of the feds are out tonight, otherwise, I'm fucked.

'You good bro?' he asks me.

'Yeah blessed.' I spud him.

He's with a friend I don't recognize. I side-eye him and give him a cautious nod. He nods back. It's jarring when people bring randoms with them. I convince myself that he doesn't look like the kinda guy to rob me.

I fumble in my bag with the cling film. I turn away so he can't see while I dig for the small baggie.

I finally exchange it with Ahmed. His friend is still silent.

As we part ways, Ahmed calls me, 'Yo Jalaal.'

'Yeah . . .'

'You and Sabrina, yeah? You clarting?' He laughs to himself.

The blood drops to my feet.

'No, what the fuck you on?'

'Nah nah, nothing fam,' he retreats. 'I was gonna say if you're tapping that, then I rate it. She's leng.' He laughs awkwardly.

What a fucking piece of shit, talking about my girl like some sideting that's out here for everyone.

'You're disgusting, man. You need to pattern up.' I ain't tryna draw too much attention to myself but *wallahi*, if it was a different day, trust me this guy wouldn't be standing right now. He must be mad to think he can disrespect Sabrina like that.

'And don't come to me no more for your shit.' I spit at him, throw my Coke can on the floor and leave. Fucking pussyhole.

Fuck. The blue lights flash in my peripheral vision a bit too late. *Fuck*. Not today. Not now. The fed car drives slowly down the road. My yard is thirty metres away. *Allah please don't do this to me. Not right now.*

My fingers fiddle in my bag and I think about throwing the weed into the bush. Time is ticking too fast, and I can't analyse the pros and cons. I continue walking and slowly take my fingers out of my bag. I guess the weed is staying with me. Whatever happens, happens. It's out of my hands. *Allah, please protect me*.

Just as I approach my block, the police car stops and the windows wind down. It's a female officer who I don't recognize. She's pale with dark eyebrows and slicked-back hair.

I stop and we watch each other.

'You all right there mate?' she asks me.

I find it booky that all these feds like to call me 'mate' but at the same time are looking for a reason to lock me up.

'Yes, officer.'

'Where are you off to at this time?'

'I'm just going home, officer.' I point to my house.

'Oh OK, stay safe,' she says.

She doesn't drive away. She waits for me to get my key out, unlock the door and walk inside. I don't even bother to turn back. I hear the wheels on the car screech after I close the door. I rest my back against it and inhale deeply.

Thank you, Allah. For protecting me.

'Jalaal,' my aunt yells. 'Is that you back in the house?' She snaps me out of my moment.

'Yes, Habo.'

My hands are clammy. There's sweat on my forehead. That was too close.

'JALAAAAAAAL,' Ibrahim shouts. 'Come play, I'm bored.'

He's staring at me from the top of the staircase.

'OK, OK, then you are going bed *waryaa*, it's almost ten,' I say before kicking off my slides.

I run up the stairs and chase Ibrahim into my room.

Spending quality time with Ibby is unmatched, but I soon clock that I'm distracting myself from deeping the situation. Running away from my thoughts.

When I finally get bored of playing *Fortnite* with my bro, I lock myself in my room and I stare up at the ceiling. What is the right thing to do? What would Allah want me to do? I'm sorry for not being a good Muslim and not keeping God at the forefront of my mind. But life has been fucking hard and I'm bare confused.

I had a weird fucking day today and I feel like everything is coming undone. I don't know how much more shitty news I can take. Sabs said I should call Abo. I'm not too sure 'bout that, but if there was one thing she was right about, it's that I would regret it if something bad had happened to him.

It's 12 a.m. in ends so must be like 3 a.m. in Hargeisa. Maybe he'll be asleep. Hopefully. Not hopefully. Whatever. I have to call now.

I open WhatsApp and ring back the +252 number that's been harassing me. He answers immediately.

'Jalaal.' His voice is hoarse.

'Abo.'

He whimpers, 'Thank you for calling me.' His breaths are deep.

'Are you OK?' I force the monotone.

'I feel OK abo, but I'm sick.'

'Is it bad?'

'I'm not sure, it's in Allah's hands now but *inshallah* I will be fine.' He takes a long breath. 'Do you think you can come visit me?'

'Why?'

'Just in case, I need to see you and Ibrahim.'

My stomach knots. Fuck. Is he gonna die?

'Don't say that to him!' I hear a womanly voice in the background.

My knuckles tense.

'Who is that?'

'Who?'

'The woman in the background, don't be dumb.'

'That's Salma . . .'

'And who the hell is Salma?' I raise my voice.

'I didn't want you to find out like this . . . she's my wife and . . .'

I hang up.

I fucking knew it. Fucking loser. I hope he fucking dies with that bitch.

CHAPTER 22

SABRINA

My relationship with Jalaal is really starting to blossom. I'm kind of unsure of our label because we aren't officially together. But there is no way we are 'just linking', because that sounds like we are having casual sex. We definitely haven't had sex. Not yet anyway. We haven't even talked about it. I kind of feel like I'm ready to explore sexual stuff more but it's all very new. I want to take my time and hope Jalaal isn't getting bored of me.

Besides Liyah, Jalaal is the first person that I've spoken to about Mum. He's the only one who knows about me trying the cocaine though. And even though I bawled my eyes out, I felt *really* heard. *For the first time in forever.*

It sounds kinda messed up, but I think that speaking about our family problems brought us closer together. Hearing Jalaal talk about losing his mother really touched me. And the fact that he has to deal with his dad not being here too. I can understand why Jalaal is the way he is now. I'm surprised he's not more fucked up. Not to say that he's fucked up, but you get what I mean. Some people in his situation would've just gone proper off the rails and ended up in a coffin or prison cell. I'm proud of him.

I do wish that Jalaal would find his drive. He needs tangible, positive aspirations. *Sabs, has it never occurred to you that maybe he just hasn't told you*? I wonder why he'd hide it from me though; he got so cagey when I brought up the design course. *Sabs, it's not your job to change people. He has to do it himself, just be patient.*

'Sabrina,' my dad yells from downstairs.

'Yes Dad.'

He is not a patient man.

'Can you come down and help me?'

We both know that I don't have a choice.

I do love it when Dad's home at decent hours though. It means he does the cooking. A little bit like when Mum used to be here. They used to alternate and we all used to complain that Mum's cooking wasn't as good as Dad's. But she learnt. Sometimes, her chicken was dry though. Doesn't matter now. Dad is the best cook. Ackee and saltfish. Banging. Dumplings. Banging. Ginger cake. Banging. Curry goat. Banging. He told me that while growing up in Bristol, his parents encouraged him to cook to make sure he didn't forget his culture.

By the time I reach the kitchen, the smell has infiltrated my nose. I know what he's made without even having to look. It's his famous brown stew chicken with sweet potatoes and coleslaw. He makes mash for Izzy because she doesn't like sweet potatoes. I was like that at her age, but I think it's a thing that you grow to like.

'Can you take the coleslaw out of the fridge and set the table please, Sabs?'

He's got his gloves on and is beating mash in the bowl.

I can't help but comment, 'We haven't had a proper sit-down since Mum . . .'

'It's about time this family starts spending time together, especially with you moving out soon.' He doesn't address the Mum part.

'Are you afraid of me moving out?'

'What is there to be afraid of? You're going to be studying at a prestigious university. You're going to be the first one in the family to get a degree. There is so much to celebrate and be proud of.'

Dad's food was so good. Like so bloody good. You can tell when someone makes food with love. He promised that he'll make it again before I leave for Warwick. Apparently, I will have to teach my 'white' flatmates how to cook. He's so discriminatory sometimes, like does he forget he's married to a white woman? But him saying that did make me worry. Being the only person of colour in my accommodation fills the depths of my stomach with anxiety. I don't want to be the odd one out.

Dad and I sit in the garden drinking ginger tea and playing dominoes. The sun is beaming, and my heart feels comforted while yearning for more. Days like these are why I love London, but they also keep me wondering, is there more out there for me? *Sabs, you love to romanticize your life*. My life is romantic, so I'm allowed to. I'm meeting Jalaal soon to watch a movie in the cinema, which in my opinion, is sooo romantic. I can't wait to see him, to cuddle with him and feel his lips on mine . . . I do think about us being together more often now.

'Sabs,' my dad pulls me out of my daydream, 'it's your turn now.'

'Dad, I'm gonna miss this when I go.' I place a domino piece against his.

'That's normal, it's a new chapter of your life. But I need you to know how proud I am of you,' he smiles.

I accept his pride – who knows what he'll say if he finds out about Jalaal.

'Feels scary though, so much pressure. Why didn't you or Mum go to university?' It feels weird bringing her up, not knowing how he'll react.

'Well, back in the day, it was easier to get a job without a degree, so it didn't really appeal to me. I'm more of a hands-on type of man so have no idea what I would've studied. As for your mum, I never really asked her. She was . . . is . . . a driven, intelligent woman so I didn't want to undermine her.' He smiles sadly.

'Ahh, I see. So . . .' I tread carefully. 'Do you think she'll come back?' I avoid his eyes.

He sighs deeply.

'Please answer, and don't shut me out. Please, Dad.'

'I pray to the Lord that she will. I believe in my heart that she will. But I have to protect you girls, and I can't control the future, I don't know what will happen. Life moves on, we have to move on. She is still my wife, and I am loyal to her. I love her. There is nothing else on that matter. You need to live your life, Sabrina; things will happen as they were meant to. I'm sorry you have to go through this.' He reaches out his hands and clasps mine.

The tears fall effortlessly down my face.

'I will always be here for you, even when you're in Warwick, I will be here – no matter what.'

I get out of my chair and fumble over to my dad, scattering the dominoes on my way there. He embraces me in a big hug, and I allow this burden to seep into his shirt.

CHAPTER 23

JALAAL

I thought I'd be angrier when finding out about this Salma. I was expecting to go on some kinda madness, but I didn't. I only feel disappointment. Maybe it's cos I always knew, deep down, this was the truth. Not gonna lie, I kinda accepted it a long time ago. Still, the way things happened ain't right, *wallahi*.

I tell Sabs to meet me outside her college, and once again, I arrive before her. She's going to Bristol in a few days and I'm tryna spend the most amount of time with her. I know if Shaah saw me right now, he'd say that I was looking for trouble, because I'm at a bait spot. Ever since I started chatting to Sabs, my sixth sense has gone out the window. I guess this is what it is to be whipped on somebody.

I sit on the steps outside the courtyard, rest my elbows on the floor and arch my neck back. I gaze up into the sky and look at the burst of pinks and oranges above.

'Uh uh, hmm.' I hear her cough before I see her.

'Man like Sabs.' I prop myself up.

'Man like Jalaal.'

Sabrina places herself on the steps next to me. Her natural hair is out again. She looks peng as fuck when she styles her hair like that.

'Why are you staring at my hair like that for?' She pulls her hood up.

I carefully pull it down. I feel a sudden desire to brush my fingers through her hair, but by the way she just reacted, I don't think I should. It's better for me to ask her. I'm getting flashbacks of Hals's lectures on microaggressions.

'You've got bags under your eyes, are you not sleeping well?' she interrupts and softly touches the skin under my eye.

How the fuck is she able to notice when things aren't OK?

'Kinda.' I hope she changes the subject, I don't wanna kill the vibe.

'What's wrong?' She snuggles closer.

I face her properly and take everything in. She has this intense look of worry on her face, you'd think she just received the worst news in the world. There's no point lying to her. And after what she told me about her marj, I should be open. She's the one who suggested I call Abo, so she's gonna ask how that went anyway.

'I decided to call my dad.'

'Oh.' She momentarily moves back before inching closer and tracing her fingers against my hand, waiting for me to talk.

My heart swells. She doesn't understand the impact she has on me. I relay to her what happened. Salma.

'This is kinda fucked up so don't judge me, yeah,' I say.

'You know I never do.'

'I don't know if you know but basically, there's this thing that Somali dads go back home and just have another secret family. It's kinda fucked up.'

'Did you always suspect this though?'

'Yeah . . . but I was hoping it wasn't true.'

'Maybe . . . it's not the worst thing in the world.'

'It's not the best either. I hate that he's made me into one of those guys whose dad left. I'm angry you know, being stuck where I am, doing the same shit every day, it's all his fault. I'm no different to other mandem in the ends. I'm never leaving the ends.' I sigh. 'But . . . I am bare worried about him and I'm not gonna lie about it.' It's hard for me to admit, but it's the truth. That's my *waalid* and at the end of the day, I have to accept the fact I wouldn't be on this earth if it wasn't for him. 'I just don't think I'm ready to even chat to him.'

'That's normal. You can always send him a message, that way you do it on your terms and your boundaries.' She whips out my phone for me. Not the trap line. 'Just message him now.'

'What am I gonna say even?'

'What is it that you want him to know?' she pushes. 'Do you love him?'

'Umm . . . yeah . . . I do.' It's bare weird admitting it.

'Tell him.'

The weight of the pressure is real, but Sabs has a point. Even when I called him, which she encouraged me to do, it felt good to hear Abo's voice even though I heard the witch's voice too. Sabs don't even have her mum around; I should listen to her.

I scramble my fingers to the phone, send Abo a message just telling him that I love him. While I'm still on the app, the ticks turn blue immediately and I close it. My phone pings a WhatsApp message from him saying he loves me too, followed by a call. I'm not ready for that. I put my phone on silent and tuck it in my pocket. *My own terms.*

Sabrina smiles and I pull her into my arms. 'Look Jalaal, I like you and I've caught feelings. I ain't ashamed to say it.'

'I caught feelings a long time ago. The minute I took you to Warwick, it was game over,' I say.

'Really?' She looks me dead in the eye.

'Yeah, I do like you. A lot,' I smile.

I move in closer to Sabrina and firmly press my lips on to hers. She kisses me back and places her soft hands on the crook of my neck. She parts open her mouth, which surprises me, and slowly slides her tongue into my mouth, skimming my teeth. She lifts her leg up and thrusts herself on to my lap. I won't lie, she's a bit heavy on my skinny legs but damn, she's fucking sexy.

She cradles me and my eyes open and meet hers. She smiles at me before closing her eyes and coming in for another kiss. I could fucking get used to this. My dick is hard, and she knows this because she has her hands touching my crotch area. I can feel her, the fabric of my tracksuit bottoms isn't that thick.

She's stroking me above my tracksuit waistband and that alone sends electricity down my body.

'I like this side of you.'

She moves back and I see a hunger in her eyes that I've never seen before.

'I want you, Jalaal.' She doesn't blink.

I want her too. She reaches her fingers to stroke her necklace but then drops her hand after touching the cross.

'Let's just continue kissing,' I say.

'I want us to have more privacy, I wish it was easy and we could hang out at each other's yard,' she says before crooking her neck around, looking, as if there is some other alternative place nearby.

'I know, but this is fine, I'm enjoying myself.' I rub my thumb against her finger.

'Can we go to the cinema now?' She looks at me sheepishly. 'I know it's earlier than we planned.'

Swear down? It's like that. 'Sure, whatever you want.' I give her a peck on the lips and we leave.

I pay for our new cinema tickets. I'll happily spend whatever money I can afford on Sabs.

She takes the lead, and we make our way to the back row, in the far corner. It is fucking blitz in here. It's confusing how it's colder inside the cinema than outside. Even though there's barely anyone in the seats, I turn off my phone cos I hate it when they go off in the cinema. Sabs holds my hand and snuggles close to me. This isn't my usual vibe but I'm happy to be here with her.

After watching the movie for thirty minutes, and as I'm getting quite into it, Sabs's hands start roaming around. I quickly glance around to make sure that nobody is watching but the nearest people are in the middle of the cinema.

Sabs uses her fingers and slowly pulls at the elastic waistband. I'm kinda surprised at this because her pace has been slow all this time. I respect it though, always have. I really like Sabs, and I proper care about her, so I'm ready to do things whenever she is ready. I just didn't expect it right now.

'Can I put my hand inside?' she whispers so sweetly.

She was so confident in the park, and now this? I try and catch her face to check her mood but I can't lie, the electricity is back in my body and I'm so excited that I put my head back on the seat.

'Sabs, you can do whatever you want.' At this point, I surrender.

Her hands are warm and soft. She wraps her hands around the shaft of my dick and my body responds in delight. She's going super slow, and I don't know if it's because she's teasing me or because she doesn't know what to do. Within twenty seconds she's found herself a rhythm and is nibbling on my ear simultaneously. I can't stop my eyes from rolling back in pleasure. The fact that I like her so fucking much makes this that more enjoyable.

After about a minute, she abruptly stops. I open my eyes and look at her.

'Are you OK, Sabrina?'

She looks weirdly worried. I haven't seen this expression on her face before.

'I don't know, this feels a bit scatty.' Her lips begin to tremble.

'Let's stop,' I gently push her hand away. Not gonna lie, that's one of the hardest things I've done, but that look on her face has sobered me the fuck up. 'And you're not scatty, don't ever think that.'

'I don't know what came over me, this isn't like me.' The cinema screen shines in her eyes, and I see they're watering. 'I wanted to but . . . I just thought this is how you'd like to, honestly, I don't know Jalaal . . .' She shifts away, holding on to herself.

I grab on to her arms and focus her attention on me. I don't want her to cry. I thought she was doing it because she wanted to, not for me. 'It's fine. You were feeling it in the moment and now you're not. That's calm. And you don't need to do this stuff *for me*. It's a two-way thing. There's no rush and there's no pressure. Don't stress yourself,' I try to calm her down.

'Really? You don't think I'm some hoe?' She doesn't blink.

I can't believe she's fucking asking this.

'Don't ever say that – there's no fucking way that makes you a hoe.' I pull her into a hug.

'Are you sure?'

I sigh. 'Don't ever let this come out of your mouth again. I'm one hundred per cent sure.'

Wallahi, I don't even think of her sideways. If anything, her whole idea of doing this made me see her in an adventurous light. I know I'm lucky to have Sabs.

We both get up. I take a hold of her hand, interlock our fingers and we walk out of the cinema.

12 a.m.

When I get to the yard hours later, Habo is stood at the door already. She's got an unusual expression on her face. It's hollow and worrying. Hals is swaying side-to-side behind her. Ibrahim is sat on the staircase, frozen. I can't handle any more fucked-up news. Not today. My heartbeat pounds in my ears, drumming against the deep breaths I'm taking.

'Why didn't you answer your phone?' Habo asks.

'What's happened? Why do you all look like that?' I side-eye them all.

'Sit down Jalaal, please,' Hals tells me softly.

It's strange that she's not being sassy.

I drag myself over to the staircase next to Ibby. He doesn't even look at me. I don't bother taking my shoes off and Habo hasn't realized. Something must be wrong.

'It's Abo.' Her lips tremble as she struggles for the words.

'What about him?' I ask.

'He . . . he . . . passed away.'

Everything stops. My body comes to a halt. A pain stabs my heart. I can't control it. I'm wheezing and weeping on the floor.

Abo. He's gone.

'How . . . did it happen?' I ask.

Ibby breaks down after I do. I embrace Ibrahim in my arms,

rocking him back and forth as he cries into my chest. I have never felt as close to my brother as I do right now.

'You know the doctors in Hargeisa, they aren't that good, they weren't able to tell. They're saying probably pneumonia. But they don't know for sure,' Hals speaks up.

Habo is now hysterical, she's shouting while reciting prayers to Allah. Her palms placed next to each other; she's making *dua*.

'What, I don't understand, I messaged him like five hours ago, what the fuck!' I should have answered his fucking call.

Hals swoops her arm around my shoulders and holds us.

'Hals.' My voice breaks. My salty tears mix with the snot running down my face and into the crevices of my lips.

Hals pulls me into her embrace. 'It was written. This is what Allah wrote to happen.'

How could Allah want to take my dad away from me? From Ibrahim? Especially when we are so young. What did I do to deserve this? First Hooyo, now Abo. This is fucked up. It's my fault. I made stupid fucking choices and so I deserve this. But not Ibby. He's only eight and now he's got no mum and dad, what the fuck. He doesn't deserve this.

'Why me? Why Ibrahim?' I bang my head against her chest.

She grips me tighter.

'I'm sorry.' Hals's voice breaks too. 'We all have our time, it's fucked up, but it happens.'

I squeeze my eyes hard and clench my fists. Trying hard to force out this pain – but it doesn't work. Good memories bombard my head. I remember when he would take me to the park to play football. Abo bringing Hooyo her favourite flowers home after he finished work. Him FaceTiming Ibrahim and then me listening to

Ibrahim tell me about his FaceTime sessions with Abo. He pissed me off when he left. But he did try.

I wish I tried. I wish I didn't let my ego and pain push him away. Now, he's gone. I fucking hate myself. I'm the only one to blame now for not having a dad.

'Let it all out,' Hals whispers to me.

I escape her arms and march towards the kitchen. I need to smash something. Just anything. I need to get this heavy feeling out of my body. My eyes dart around the kitchen, searching for something to mash up. Cupboards. No. Plates. No. Table. No. Chairs. No. It infuriates me. I march back towards the landing area and straight out the door.

'Jalaal, where are you going?' I hear my aunt shout.

'Let him go,' Hals's voice responds.

My vision is blurred from the tears. The first thing I notice is the communal bins. Before I am even able to focus on them, my arms are swinging towards the hard plastic. Pow. Pow. Pow. Pow. I groan and shout. The physical pain is almost unnoticeable in comparison to the pain that my heart is carrying.

I continue to plough my fists at the bin until there are blood streaks on my knuckles. My knees fall weak, and I drop to the hard gravel. I let go. Of everything.

I don't recall how I end up back at the kitchen table with a lukewarm cup of Somali tea in front of me. But here I am. Habo and Hals are sat with me. I don't know where Ibrahim is. My hands are washed clean with bandages over my cuts.

'I need space.' I walk off.

Even though every inch of me wants to bolt outside and scream,

I hold it in. I go up the stairs and when I reach the top, I see Ibby's door is slightly ajar. I silently peer inside and I watch him lying on the bed staring blankly at the ceiling. I can't tell if he's making sounds or mumbling words. I lie next to him. His small bed shuffles against my weight. He barely notices my presence. I lie back and stare up at the ceiling. It's a different pattern to my room. My brain can't form shapes. So, I close my eyes and let the darkness take over.

1.30 a.m.

I wake up to a nudging feeling in my ribcage.

'Jalaal, you keep talking in your sleep.'

I'm confused to hear my brother's voice. I use the back of my hands to rub my eyes open. I'm not in my bed. I look to my right at Ibby.

'Jalaal.'

'Yeah.' I turn to face my innocent little brother.

'I heard Habo Hani and Hals say that you have to go to Hargeisa.' His eyes begin to well up.

Now I remember everything I just escaped. I want to shout. I want to scream. I want to cry. It ain't fair to let it all out at Ibby so I bite my tongue.

'I'm not,' I say.

'They said you have to.'

'I'm not going.' I raise my voice.

He looks scared.

'I can't go,' I say.

'OK.'

We both look at each other.

Once Ibrahim falls asleep, I get out of his bed and leave the yard.

CHAPTER 24

SABRINA

It's nearly 2 a.m. I want to forget about what happened with Jalaal yesterday. Something came over me that I can't explain. This brewing desire for Jalaal just overtook me and I didn't know how to channel it, so I tried to embody this sexy Sabrina from an alternate universe because that's what I thought he wanted. I swear down, I had no idea what I was doing. I wanted to, but I didn't know how. I thought *experimenting* in the cinema is how *he* wanted to do things. I've heard some of my friends doing bits with their man in the cinema and thought I'd be on that vibe, too. But I just couldn't follow through – it's not me. That's not how I want to explore with Jalaal. Not in a public cinema.

I assumed Jalaal would be ready to tell me to fuck off then and there. I was surprised at how he was chill about the whole thing, he didn't even care. *Sabs, just be yourself. Jalaal likes you for you.* My heart does feel for him though, his dad being sick and their complicated relationship. I can't even imagine what I'd do if something happened to Dad.

Confusion fogs my mind. I don't know what to do or feel. I'm not sure who to talk to about this. Maybe I should pray to God or something, for everything. Me. Mum. Dad. Izzy and Tasha. Jalaal. Even though I never really pray, I believe in the power of prayer. I've seen what it can do. Know what it can do. I smooth my fingers over my cross necklace and inhale deeply. I kneel by the end of the bed, rest my elbows and clasp my hands. I close my eyes.

Dear God,

It's me, Sabrina. Well, of course you know it's me, you're God. You know everything.

Please forgive me for being absent. I'm sorry I haven't spoken to you in forever and I haven't been going to church.

Things have just got really hard since Mum left us and now, I feel like my life is going one hundred miles an hour.

Anyways, I hope you can and will accept my prayers because I do genuinely mean it and do really believe in you. Well, firstly, I was hoping that you could help Mum so she can return to us, and we can go back to how things were before. There is nothing more that I'd like in this world.

Secondly, can you make sure that Dad and the girls are OK when I go to uni? I'm scared that once I'm gone, they won't be able to manage, and I'll just be worrying the whole time or have to transfer to a London university to take care of them. I don't know, I feel kinda guilty, but I want to do this.

And then Lord, can you help Jalaal out? I know he's not Christian, but we still believe in the same God and I'm praying that he is able to leave this road life, and I pray that his dad gets better. I do really care about Jalaal, and I think he has a kind soul but is just being led astray. So yeah, I'm praying for Jalaal.

And for me, I don't know, I'm just happy to be alive and I guess if everybody else is OK and those prayers are answered, then I'll be fine.

Thank you for listening to me and I promise I'll go to church more often.

Amen.

*

I already feel lighter after completing my prayer. *Sabs, you actually forgot how warm it feels to pray.*

Ping. A message from Jalaal. This day is only getting better!

He's dead.

I drop the phone. It hits my foot.

The pain shocks me into action. I grab it.

I call him. No answer.

Call again. No answer.

What the fuck was the point of praying if God is dismantling my prayers within minutes of me making them.

Jalaal's dad is dead. What the fuck.

iMessage: Jalaal, I'm so sorry to hear this, call me!

No answer.

WhatsApp: Not sure if you got my message, but I'm here for you, if you don't want to speak on the phone, that's OK. Just let me know if you need anything.

No answer.

Instagram: Getting a bit worried, can you just let me know if you're OK? Haven't got any response from you.

No answer.

Snap: Jalaal.

No answer.

CHAPTER 25

JALAAL

After leaving the house for a zoot, I didn't expect to be on my way to an apartment party. My family friend, Yoonis, belled me to share his condolences before suggesting we celebrate my dad's life. He said it'll be a good distraction. I don't even fucking know how he knew or why I agreed to this but my life is a fucking joke, I don't fucking care any more.

Yoonis is a calm guy. Our families are from the same tribe, which is why we have this weird affinity towards each other. I know he's on stuff. I think he bangs F, but I don't ask too much about it. I don't wanna know about fraud.

2.30 a.m.

I meet him in a blacked-out Ford Focus at the end of my road. It's a new plate. Rental car.

He's giggling while he's got a blue balloon in his hand. I walk towards the car, and he unwinds the window.

There's a Somali guy that I don't recognize sat beside Yoonis.

I fling myself into the car. It's cramped and it stinks of weed. Beside me are two Somali boys that I have never seen in my life.

One's got braids and the other has an afro. They both got balloons in their mouths. I don't think they deep how stupid they look.

Yoonis turns to face me, one hand firmly gripped on the steering wheel.

'This is Hussein and Hassan, my cousins from Leicester.'

'Family, yeah.' I reach out my fist to spud them.

'What you saying, you good fam?' the braided one says with a thick Midlands accent.

'I'm good *alhamdulillah*,' I lie to cut the talk short.

The Somali brudda sat in front of me turns to face me. He's lighter in complexion and I clock his bloodshot eyes immediately. There's no balloon in his hand, only a burnt-out joint in between his fingers.

'And this is Abdul. Everyone, this is my boy Jalaal.' Yoonis completes his introductions before revving the engines and accelerating out the estate, blasting Lil Durk on the speakers.

We're in South London, parked outside a tall building of apartment flats. We stumble out the car and Yoonis wraps his arm around my shoulder, guiding me towards the building.

'Jalaal-o.' He sounds like my aunt.

He picks out a small bottle of Magnum from his pocket.

'I'm sorry about your dad, *wallahi*, life is too short. You guys weren't that close but it's calm. I got you. This is where you need to be. With your people. *Wallahi*, I'm so gassed that you're outchea. And *wallahi*, these Somali girls. If you see the backs on them. And you, they're gonna be on to you. Just let yourself go. You deserve it fam.'

'You always gas everything too much,' I say.

'Bro, what is this I'm hearing about you doing a ting with some mixed girl? Some *gaalo* girl?' He jumps from one topic to another.

'What you talkin' about fam? What you on?'

'I heard from one of my boys that you been chirpsing some *iska dhal* girl, you know you ain't ever gonna cuff her, right?' He looks me dead in the eye.

I can hear the others' footsteps getting louder as we approach the communal door.

I just want him off my case, so I say what I know he wants to hear. What any incel roadman would say. 'Look, at the end of the day *walaalo*, pussy is pussy. I'm not denying I'm chilling with this girl, but not some serious ting. Respect me.' I regret saying these words as soon as they're out of my mouth.

Yoonis grins; his full set of teeth come out. 'Is that you yeah, getting pussy everywhere. *Wallahi*, I have to respect it. And the fact you know that the only pussy you taking home is Somali.' He slaps me on the back.

I laugh hard, trying to force down the guilt. I know that I'm fucked for talking about Sabs like that. Especially on a day when my dad fucking died. I'm so fucked up in the head. I've caught deep feelings for her and now I'm at some AP disrespecting her. I don't think Hooyo or Abo would be proud of the way I'm acting. Well they're both dead anyway. It's too fucking late now.

The party is low-key tapped. The living area is dark but lit up with red LED lights. It's hot and stuffy. My ears are ringing against the thumping bass of bashment music. I can't properly make out any faces of the people, but I clock the bodies dancing. Wines on skinny legs.

Yoonis is already across the room greeting the other guys. His cousins linger awkwardly behind him. Abdul, still dazed, ushers me over to the kitchen area. Red cups and bottles of Wray and

Hennessy scattered everywhere. It's peak for whoever rented out this Airbnb.

Abdul hands me over a Magnum, while he mixes himself some Hennessey and Coke. I let the tonic wine burn my throat. I swear this small bottle can do so much damage. I'm already starting to feel a bit light-headed.

'You see anything you like?' Abdul grins.

'Huh?' Is there meant to be food somewhere?

'The girls,' he states as if it's obvious.

'Nah man.' I turn away.

I pick up another three bottles of Magnum and open the baggie I brought with me. It's time to roll another zoot. But first, I put my phone on 'Do Not Disturb' and slide it into my back pocket.

A girl walks over me. I think her name is Nasra. I'm not sure, my head is spinning. There's no doubt she's the lengest girl here. *Wallahi*, she looks so fucking good. She's in a deep-cut V-neck dress that has a split down her breasts. They're so big and perky. And somehow, they're shimmering too. The curls of her hair are beautiful. I know I sound moist, but I can appreciate beautiful hair. Sabrina has sexy hair.

I'm slouched on the sofa, my head leaning back, and my legs spread apart.

She sits on my knee. 'Hey Jalaal.'

I can't tell if she's moaning my name or if I'm bugging out. The music is loud. The bass penetrating through walls. It's way too hot in here.

'Hey Nasra,' I say softly.

'You good yeah?' She rubs my leg.

'Yeah, I'm good.' It comes out as a mumble.

I don't think I can carry on conversation. I pat on my leg, the closest part to my crotch, signalling for her to come closer. I need to look at her properly. She smiles at the invitation and slides closer to me. I can feel her warmth and weight now.

I look up at her face. She's pretty. Big brown eyes and long lashes. I can't tell if they're real and I don't care, my dick is hard.

'Shall we go somewhere more private to talk?' she whispers into my ear, slowly moving her lips across to my face.

'Yeah,' I groan. 'That sounds like a good idea.'

She gets up and intertwines her hand in mine, tugging on me to stand up. I get up and make sure my bulge isn't on show. My head feels slightly dizzy, but Nasra pulls me towards the room on the left and smiles smugly. I feel the others close by staring. I look back at them and see Yoonis grinning at me.

'Do your ting, bro!'

The others whistle over the music. Nasra blushes and I can't help but feel gassed.

We move into the bedroom and leave the door slightly ajar. The room is dark, but I can make out a double bed. I throw my head back and lie flat on the bed. I allow the light-headed feeling to momentarily absorb me. It's quieter here, the thumping music nothing but a blur. My mind wanders. I want to share a bed with Sabrina. I can feel her as she climbs on to me and cradles me by the hips, the warmth radiating from her below. She leans towards me, rubbing her arms up and down my chest. She feels so good. Sabrina. Just as I allow myself to enjoy her, I open my eyes and realize it's Nasra smirking at me.

My body freezes. It starts at the pit of my stomach and rises. I feel like being sick. Guilt hits me from nowhere.

She notices the shift.

'What's wrong?' Her tone slightly accusing.

'Nothing.' I hoist myself on to my elbows, narrowing the space between us.

Something feels wrong. Abo is dead. I'm disrespecting Sabrina. This is wrong.

'Wait. Are you a virgin?' She looks at me with disgust.

'The fuck. No, I'm not.'

'What's wrong then?' She crosses her arms.

The haze I'm in is starting to fade and I feel my dick soften.

'I know what it is,' she answers herself. 'It's that mixed-race girl.'

The shock sobers me.

'You need to relax.' I try to play it cool.

'What's wrong with Somali girls? You think you're too good for them? What business do you have with a *iska dhal* AND *gaalo* girl anyway?' She glares at me.

I cannot believe what I am hearing. I don't understand how this entitled girl thinks she can speak about Sabs like that. How did she even know? People talk too much.

'You're so done out here. You don't even hang around with your own people. Some tapped wannabe hood nigga that's not even part of us. Why the fuck you even here?'

The anger begins to boil. Just where the guilt was sat before. She needs to get off me now. I don't wanna touch her though.

'Please can you get off me?' I say through my gritted teeth.

She sees the anger in my eyes and moves off me. Thank God the door is still open. I want to cuss her out so fucking bad, but I bite my tongue because I know this ain't the time or place. I sit on the side of the bed and face her.

'Look Nasra, I don't need to explain my *Somali-ness* to you. And fuck, I don't need to explain anything about me to you. You're a peng girl, but I'm just not on it.' I hold my breath; I know she won't understand.

She looks me up and down with repulsion. I can tell what's coming and I brace myself.

'You know what you are? Somali *bila dhiig*.' She gets up, swings the door wide open and struts out of here.

I'm not even looking at her bunda. I'm looking to see who is watching through the door. Only a few people have noticed. Nasra's gone straight to the bathroom, probably to go speak with the other girls. I don't care. I get up and walk towards the balcony.

Yoonis shouts at me, 'That was quick bro.'

I ignore him.

There's only one other person on the balcony. Abdul. This time he has a Magnum in one hand and a joint in the other. This guy is a fucking superhuman.

'So, you're back.' He chuckles to himself. 'She didn't do it for you?'

'Shut up, bruv.'

'Chill *wallahi*, it's not that deep. It's not your fault that you ain't feeling the girls here. Fuck. Even I ain't feeling the girls here. I'm just here for the vibe.' He takes a deep drag.

I don't even know why I came here. I don't know why I listened to Yoonis. I don't know why I let Nasra pull me to the bedroom.

My head is spinning. This is just who I am. This is all I'm meant to be in this life. Some fucked-up loser that has bad things happen to them. Am I any different to Abo? Even if I tried to be better, this shit will just happen to me, because that's how it's meant to be. I've accepted it. The tears stream down my face and I slam my fists against my head.

CHAPTER 26

SABRINA

Ring Ring. Ring Ring. Ring Ring.
Jalaal is calling. Finally. I've been waiting since he told me his dad passed yesterday. I sit on my bed, trying to calm myself. One night not hearing from him has filled me with anxiety. I'm just relieved that he's OK and reaching out.

'Hello,' I hesitate.

'Hey.' He's monotonous.

'I'm so sorry about your dad, Jalaal,' I immediately burst out. 'Are you OK? What can I do for you? What do you need? I want to help you so much. I'm so sorry.'

'Stop, Sabrina,' he interjects. 'There's something that I need to tell you.'

Silence. My stomach knots. *This is where the penny is gonna drop, Sabs.*

'Umm can you hear me?'

'Yeah, what is it?' My voice trembles.

He inhales deeply before scrambling his words.

'Last night, after I texted you, I went to an AP. A link-up of mainly 'Malis. I smoked and drank, so I don't remember much. Anyway, there was this girl. She was proper trying it on with man. She was on to me.'

He pauses and I stay silent. My heart is in my mouth and my fingers automatically grab the necklace sat on my neck, which suddenly feels heavy.

'So, she kinda sat on my lap and rubbed my legs. I was so out of it, and I went into the bedroom with her. I lay on the bed and she sat on top of me, but nothing happened. *Wallahi*, I stopped anything from happening.' He corrects himself. 'I told her to get off me and that I didn't wanna do anything. And that's it. Nothing else happened. I'm telling you cos I fucked up. I'm fucked up. My dad fucked this up. He's not even alive. Sabs, I'm sorry. You don't deserve this.'

A sob escapes my lips. So I'm crying then. *How the hell am I meant to feel?*

'Sabs, can you hear me? Are you there?'

I cut the line.

I'm still trembling from shock. I'm pacing my room. I'm spiralling. He cheated on me. *Technically, he didn't cheat on you because you aren't in a relationship.* I knew it was too good to be true. I wonder if he took this other girl to visit her future university too. This is so messed up. He told me that the girl is Somali too. Does he expect me to compete with that? They are literally from the same culture and religion and everything. It's not like I'd ever be accepted in his family anyway. Is this because I haven't had sex with him? He had to go elsewhere?

Sabs, his dad just died, give him a fucking rest. He was already troubled enough so this was the icing on the cake.

I knew that I should have never gotten involved with a roadman. Ms Ross was right. I'm sure that stuff like this only happens with them.

Don't act above it, Sabs. You have your own issues, be compassionate.

He hurt me. Jalaal hurt me.

He's hurting, too. More than ever.

My heart has plummeted to the pit of my stomach. It's empty and I can feel the acid swishing about.

I sit on my bed with tears and snot dribbling down my face. The guy I've caught feelings for is out there doing the most with other girls. I'm so dumb for doing those things with him in the cinema. I'm so stupid for letting some dickhead come into my life and then mug me off.

I look at my iPhone. Message after message after message. Why the hell did I even save his name as J with a green heart? Fucking prick.

I call Liyah.

She answers in two rings.

'Ay, bestie,' she sings.

I can't even respond with words; all that escapes my mouth is an ugly cry.

'Wait, what Sabs, are you OK? What the fuck happened? Are you OK, sis?'

'It's him,' I cry. 'He fucked things up.'

'Take your time Sabs, what happened? I'm here to listen to you.'

'Well . . . he called me this morning to tell me that . . .' I gulp at the fact I have to repeat this again. 'That he "fucked up". And he was at some party. A Somali party where they were moving mad . . .' I tell her everything, the girl, his dad, everything.

When I finish speaking, she lets out a breath. 'How are you feeling?'

Why does this question feel so difficult to answer?

I swallow my sadness for a moment.

'How . . . do . . . I . . . feel?' I try to register it in my brain.

She doesn't respond. She always does this. When she asks me a deep question and wants me to think properly. Some stupid deep reflection technique.

How do you feel Sabs?

'Well, ob-vious-ly I feel like shit. I feel terrible that his dad passed away and I can understand how things happened. But this is about me, and how could someone that I care about so much go and do bits with another girl because he's upset. I don't know how to explain but it feels like . . . I don't know . . . yeah, I feel a bit jealous mainly because she's Somali and I know she's better for him and . . .'

'Woah woah woah. Put some respect on your name, sis. Yes, this girl is Somali but don't ever put yourself down. Also, Jalaal said that he wasn't feeling it and his head ain't right.'

I don't understand why she's defending him.

'But why did he get himself into that situation to begin with? Was he not thinking about me before?' I spit back.

'These are questions for him, Sabs.'

'You're right. But Liyah, I don't need to go to some party and have mandem move to me to know that I like Jalaal. I don't get it.' My tears won't stop.

'I know, I know. And it must feel like shit. I'm so sorry Sabs. I did warn you he's a roadman and you should be careful. But . . . I'm kinda surprised that he came and told you immediately. Them kinda guys usually try burying that stuff.' She pauses. 'I think he cares about you, you know. Any other guy our age would never tell you all those details. Think about it. You don't know any of those Somali people, you would've never found out. So, he could've gotten away with it. But he didn't pussy out. He came to you. I know it seems like

I'm defending him but *wallahi* I'm not. You know how much I've been tryna talk you out of it before. I keep it real.'

'You do,' I mutter.

'You're feeling hurt and you should be. Just think about how the situation with your mum messed you up – he's probably going through the same thing. Trust me, things will work out as they are meant to be. Whatever that is.'

I don't think my heart can take any more.

CHAPTER 27

JALAAL

Too many things have happened in one day and it's not even fucking over yet. Lost my dad in the early morning. Went to an AP and got into a madness. Probably lost the only person who I've ever cared about outside my family, Sabs. And when I check the time, it's just gone past midday. The last fifteen hours have been mad.

I sobered myself up as much as I could after that AP. I went and got McDonald's. Just sat there. I have no recollection of what I ate. I just shoved shit down my throat and drank water. I sat there for what felt like ages, staring ahead — blindly thinking. It was when I was walking home that I decided to call Sabs just to get this guilt off my chest. And it wasn't just the AP, I wanted to tell her about the Warwick drop-off too. She deserves to know what I am. I was still reeling from the effects of the drugs and alcohol, so there was bravery in me to open up and tell her the truth. There was no chance of doing that sober. She deserves to know that I am a fuck-up. And yeah, she hung up on me before I could even tell her everything. I deserve it.

When I finally get back to the yard, no one talks to me. I slump into my room, consider taking a shower, but decide against it, strip down to my boxers, and collapse on my bed. No need to gaze at the uneven ceiling, I allow myself to succumb to the darkness of my mind.

*

My door creaks open and I wake up in the same position I fell asleep in. I slowly turn my head and see Hals standing at the door, her body firmly stood in between the door and wall.

'What?' my voice croaks.

'You're going to Somaliland.'

'No.'

'You need to go to the funeral and see your dad for the last time. Also, you need to manage and collect whatever he's left you. You know they have to bury the body within three days. Time is against you.'

'No.'

'Jalaal, please.' Her voice softens. 'There's a flight really late tonight that you can get on, you don't have to worry about the Ps, and you'll be able to make it on time. Think about it.'

'Hals, get the fuck out of my room,' I say in a calm tone.

She abides and slowly closes the door.

No fucking way I'm going to that shithole.

CHAPTER 28

SABRINA

Ping. Instagram.

Halstheactivist wants to send you a message.

I have no idea who the hell this is. I click on her profile. She looks super edgy with her piercings and protest posts. We only have one mutual follower. Jalaal.

Her bio says Bristol Uni. Must be Jalaal's cousin that he's always talking about, Hals. I wonder what she wants.

Halstheactivist Hey Sabrina, sorry to intrude on you like this. I'm Hals, Jalaal's cousin (not sure if he mentioned me before). I know this is a bit awkward cos we haven't met yet, but I need your help. Idk if he told you but his dad passed away and we need him to go to Somaliland for the funeral ASAP but he's not taking this well. He's also the main beneficiary. Trust me, I know this is bare forward. If you could, I'd appreciate it if you could reach out to him, I think you're the only voice of reason for him and he cares about you deeply. He won't listen to any of us. No pressure though, do whatever feels right xx

I stare at this message from Hals. Does she even know what happened? Jalaal has broken my heart and now I'm in this predicament. Am I really his *voice of reason*? I don't know if I believe her.

Why would she lie though? If he had never met me, I'm sure somebody else could be his voice of reason. I don't know what to do. He betrayed me, he hurt me. I don't want to speak to him ever again. But my gut is telling me that I should support him – irrespective of this AP thing, he needs to go see his dad. Family is more important than anything. I don't know what to do. I want to pray again, but will that give me answers? There's only one person who will.

I go downstairs and find my dad sat in the living room watching the reggae music channels.

'Uhm, Dad, I have a hypothetical question for you,' I stutter.

'Yes . . .' He mutes the TV and turns to face me.

'Well, hypothetically, say for example your *friend* experiences something really traumatic but then you have a falling out with that *friend* because they did kinda a big thing. It's repairable.' *Is it really repairable?* 'Should you be there to support *her* with the traumatic thing she went through, even though you haven't yet sorted out the problem you had with *her*?'

He pauses. The anticipation is killing me.

'The answer you are looking for is in the question. Repairable.'

'So, I should be there for him. I mean *her*.' I stumble on my words.

He ignores my mistake. 'Could you live with yourself for not being there for them? If so, that's not the kind of daughter that I raised. Help them first. Then deal with your fallout after.'

'I understand.'

With that, he presses play on the TV remote and returns to his tranquillity of reggae music.

I dial Jalaal's number.

'Sabs?'

'Yes.'

'Hello.' His voice cracks.

'You OK?' *Of course he isn't OK Sabs, ask him something else.*

'I'm sorry, Sabs.' He breaks down immediately.

I pause; it's difficult to be compassionate on the phone because all I can think about is what he told me the last time we were on a call.

He sniffles.

'Meet me in thirty minutes, the corner of your block.'

I hang up.

I wait for Jalaal at the meeting spot. He really doesn't live that far from me. *Sabs, this won't be your home for that long.* I'm fuming for what he did at that party, and I don't even know if it's something that I'm willing to move forward from. *Why are you even here?* Jalaal is hurting right now, and I must be there for him. He was there for me when I needed him.

I hate to admit that I feel at ease when I see him turn the corner. His head is hanging low, he doesn't even raise it to look at me. My feet thrust me forward and I feel myself pressed against his chest. I raise my head to look at his sunken eyes. I can't explain the pang of pain I feel. I squeeze on to him tightly, letting his heart thump against my head.

'Let's go,' he whispers into my ear before unwrapping himself from me.

We walk ten minutes in deafening silence before making it to the corner shop. I have never seen Jalaal so broken. He's always got mad jokes for me but today, he can't even speak. If I could do anything to take this pain away from him and get him to be his normal cheeky self, I would.

We sit on the brick wall by the shops.

'Thank you,' he mumbles.

'Don't thank me. I haven't done anything.'

'I'm sorry about fucking up, Sabs.'

I can't believe this is the first proper thing he's saying to me.

'Look, don't worry about that now, we can figure that out when you come back from Somaliland,' I say matter-of-factly.

He raises his eyebrows.

'Hals told me,' I say.

'She shouldn't have because I'm not going.'

'And why's that?'

He slumps into his shoulders.

'Your dad, Jalaal. One last time to see him. Make things right in your heart so you're at peace. What's actually stopping you from going?' I step closer to him.

'I'm shook.' His eyes are big. 'I'm shook that I'll go there and meet his wife, and it'll remind me of what a fuck-up he is.'

'I get it.' I trail my fingers along the lines of his palm. 'You don't want to experience the potential anger or pain. But Jalaal, imagine living with the fact that you had the opportunity to see him one more time and you never did. Imagine what Ibrahim would think of you. And you're your dad's main beneficiary so you need to go. I know it's hard but it's the right thing to do. And you know it.'

'Why are you even here, Sabs?' His voice turns cold.

'Because I love you.' It comes out of my mouth before I even know it.

Sabs did you actually just drop the L-bomb. You're not meant to say it first. It's meant to be the guy. It's meant to be Jalaal.

'Did you say you love me?'

You have to own it now. There's no going back.

'Yes, I did.' I look at him pleadingly.

I hope he feels the same otherwise that's going to be so awks.

'I love you too, Sabs. But fuck, I wanted to say it first.' His dimple emerges.

As quickly as he smiles, his face sinks. He stares into the empty street. Only the faint sound of the wind blowing and cars on the road fill the space between us.

'What's this really about?' I ask.

'You don't understand. I'm a fuck-up. There's something else that I need to tell you . . . You know that time we went to Warwick . . . I did a drop-off for Shaah. Cocaine.' A tear falls down his face. 'It was such a fucked-up thing to do and inexcusable. I was angry cos of Abo. I'm still angry, Sabs. I don't understand, why does this shit always happen to me?' Tears stream down his face now.

How the hell am I supposed to manage Jalaal's feelings as well as mine? He delivered cocaine while he took me to Warwick, what the actual fuck?

He reads my expression. 'It was only the one time and I regret it.'

I remember the scruffy kid at the station. My intuition was right. *Sabs, you knew it.*

I want to crumble. Finally let loose everything in my life that's been bottling up inside of me. Things that aren't even related to Jalaal. Just the pressure of existing.

I try my best to put my feelings aside. I think of Hals pleading with me to get Jalaal to go to his dad's funeral. I think of Dad telling me to be the daughter he raised. I think of how much I love Jalaal's smile, of how much he understands me, never judging. I inhale deeply.

'Just go to Somaliland, Jalaal. Do something right for once.' My speech comes out slow.

'You're just going to ignore what I said. You know I fucked up but I'm so sorry . . .' His eyes glaze with tears.

'I don't have the capacity right now,' I cut him off. 'If you want any chance of making things right with us, you need to make it right with your dad first.'

He nods. His tears dry now.

I turn around and go home, wondering how I've gotten from expressing my love to Jalaal to leaving on terms that I'm not sure are repairable.

When I get home, I play slow jams music while packing for my Bristol trip tomorrow. Dad agreed to send Tasha and Izzy to Auntie Lisa in the Christmas holidays. He said I need to enjoy quality time with Auntie Lisa and the rest of the family without worrying about my sisters, especially before moving to Warwick. He's taken some time off work to spend quality time with the girls.

There's something comforting about listening to Aaliyah while letting my thoughts roam freely. If I'm being honest with myself, I'm not surprised about Jalaal having done a drop-off of cocaine for Shaah, but I am disappointed. I never thought he would do this to me, especially after I opened up to him about Mum. *Maybe he didn't even consider that. He's not in the right head space, Sabs.* He should've thought of me.

Despite all of this, I have fallen in love with him. It's all a mess.

I don't know where I stand with him. The whole AP. His dad. The drugs. It's too much for me. I can't explain – I am so depleted emotionally, nothing will faze me any more. That's why I'm looking forward to going to Bristol, because at least I can get away from it all there.

There's a sudden knock on the door.

'Come in.' I practise composure.

I expect Izzy or Dad but am surprised to see Tasha walking in.

She immediately notices something is off. 'You all right sis?'

'Yeah, what's up?' I fight the sadness.

'I was gonna ask if I can borrow your Ray-Bans, but . . . you don't look like your normal self. You OK?' She steps closer.

I step back slightly. 'Yeah, I'm fine, you can take the Ray-Bans, they're on the dresser.' I avoid eye contact.

She glares at me while grabbing the sunglasses. I stay silent.

'Not going to put up a fight? Thanks,' she says. She stands at the door like she wants to say more but can't. 'You sure you're OK?'

I can't share this with her, so I just nod in response.

'Well, if you need me, I'm here,' she says. I look at her. We just stare at each other for a moment. We've both been through so much, it's like some unspoken thing that no matter how much we argue, we still love each other. I feel it now. 'Anyway, I hope you have a good time in Bristol.'

My eyes fill with water. 'Thanks, Tasha.'

She gently closes the door and my heart bursts.

CHAPTER 29

JALAAL

Abo is gone.

Part of me feels like a mug for going to Hargeisa. But Sabrina is somehow making me see this a different way. I need to do this. No, I *have* to do this.

I don't deserve her.

I am numb. I have fucked up. Not only with Sabs, but with Abo. I can't help but feel like I should've answered that last call. I should've broken through the cement of anger built inside of me. He abandoned us though. If he wanted to be a proper abo, then he would've been living with us. Raising us. Taking care of us.

It's my first time to the homeland and I got no idea what to expect. I'm sat at the back of this Emirates A380. I'm grateful it's not the last row.

I'm wearing my favourite navy-blue Adidas tracksuit, and this dead backpack Habo Hani gave me. She also gave me three bags in cash to give to someone in Hargeisa. Not gonna lie, I'm low-key surprised that I didn't get stopped by security.

I know the road life is not it for me. Imagine if I died on this plane right now, I'd be going straight to hell. I need to fix the fuck up.

When I come back from Hargeisa *inshallah*, I'm gonna be done with this life. I'm going back to college to pattern this design course and actually make my family proud. No more drinking and smoking. I need to focus on my *deen*.

The plane begins to lift, thrusting itself forward with less noise than I expected. I put Lil Durk on pause on my headphones. I close my eyes and recite my *shahadah*.

I'm going to Hargeisa to meet my dad's new wife. My stepmum. I know there's no formal papers to say I've inherited his wealth, but the tradition is that Ibby and I will get majority. I wonder what my stepmum is expecting. She must be one brave woman to be reaching out to us.

I feel the unease starting to creep up my body. Seven hours is a long time *wallahi*. And then I've got to catch another plane when I get to Dubai. This is too long for man.

I open my phone to re-read the last text message Sabs sent me.

Jalaal, I hope you have a safe flight and **inshallah** everything will sort itself out in Somaliland. I know things are messy with us, but we can deal with that later. Focus on your family . . . Sabs x

This weird tingling feeling in my stomach is making me feel bare emotional. After the way we left things, I don't deserve this. I miss her so fucking much. Let's not lie, she's been here for me when she didn't need to be. I would do anything for this girl.

Hargeisa is a desert.

I step off the plane and am welcomed by a warm rush of air. Not like the humidifying heat in the ends, but a calmer heat. There's no tarmac on the floor. Just dust. Sand. Rubble. They don't lie when they say this is a third world country.

I'm not sure who I'm staying with, but I think it's my adeero who I haven't met. I never remember him hanging out with Abo back in the day, I don't think that they were close. Habo Hani also warned me about him; he's not the nicest person, allegedly.

I recognize him because he looks exactly like my dad. There is no mistaking that they are brothers. His fashion sense is tapped though. He's wearing one of them old-people hats. The farmer ones. In this Hargeisa heat. There's something wrong with him.

Behind the plane, there is only sand and thin branches against blue skies. The airport is a bland white building, smaller than the block I live in and this FlyDubai plane is the only one at the airport.

'*Waryaa*, move.' Some rude dickhead barges past me.

Before I'm even able to swing for the prick, my adeero calls me. '*War ninyahow!*'

The husk in his voice sounds just like Abo. I'm just baffled as to how he's on the runway.

In my periphery, I see the cargo door of the aeroplane being unlocked and suitcases being unloaded on to the dusty floor. A few of the passengers ahead of me grab their suitcases and walk off. Before I can even register what's going on, an arm wraps itself around my neck and encloses me over their shoulder.

'*Waryaa! Maad ilowdey sida af soomaali lagu hadlo?*' Adeero jokes as he ushers me towards the suitcases.

'No, Adeero.' I reassure him that I haven't forgotten how to speak Somali.

Without warning, my uncle lugs my suitcase in front of me and I quickly huddle behind him like a dog, following him into the building. He stops at a desk, and I place myself awkwardly behind him.

'*Waryaa*, do you have your visa money?'

'Visa money?'

He mutters something under his breath before digging into his pocket, pulling out his wallet and throwing American dollars at the man behind the desk.

'Thank you, Adeero,' I mumble under my breath.

Adeero is playing Somali music in his 4x4 land cruiser, and he's got *khaat* hanging out his mouth. His cheap sunglasses are sat on his nose, one hand on the wheel and the other arm lounging on the windowsill.

It's a straight road from the airport into the city and we stop at a few checkpoints along the way. Adeero is sometimes handing out money to the police officers. It's mad intimidating how they're just chilling around with rifles in their hands.

I look outside the window. It's the same light-brown dust and sparse trees. The further we travel into the city, the more houses and shops I see. It's hot outside but the breezy wind blasting in from the windows is keeping me cool.

'*Haye, waryaa.*' He disturbs my daze.

He needs to stop calling me *waryaa*. It's jarring now.

His eyes are still focusing straight ahead on the road. 'I'm taking you to see Salma.'

This is the first time that he has mentioned what's happening.

'Who is that?' I pretend to not know.

'Your dad's widow.' He tilts his face towards me, smiling. 'You know that all of the house doesn't have to go to her.'

Habo Hani and Hals already told me that majority of Abo's things would come to me: money, land, belongings and property. Not gonna lie, I don't need a house in a country that I don't even live in. And I'm not gonna kick a woman out to the street to keep a house empty.

I force a smile and look out the window. There's something off about my adeero.

CHAPTER 30

SABRINA

Being at Paddington Station reminds me of my first date with Jalaal, and how confused we were. *Don't think about him now Sabs, focus on the family quality time.*

I sit myself at a window seat on this rammed train and plug my phone into the charging socket underneath my seat. Obviously, my broke ass doesn't have an Apple charger because Tasha broke the head off the wire. So now, I'm sat with an Apple plug and a fluorescent pink wire that I got from Flying Tiger. I must look so cheap in comparison to all these other people on the train. It's mainly filled with old white people wearing sunglasses and sun hats. They must wonder why I'm so trampy. I don't know, I'm always conscious of how these posh people perceive me.

This adorable old man saw me struggling earlier and picked up my worn-out Tripp suitcase and threw it at the back of the rack. I mumbled a 'thank you' while I ran back to my seat, embarrassed.

I keep double-checking my ticket against the seat number. It is genuinely my worst nightmare having someone tell me that I am sat on their seat, and then having to deal with the awkwardness of getting up and moving elsewhere.

My mind naturally drifts to Jalaal. I'm not too sure where we stand and that unsettles me quite a bit. What makes matters worse is that I'm not even sure what I want. I've had time to sit with the situation and when everything is put into context, like in my literature exams, Jalaal's actions aren't that bad. I'm not gonna lie, I felt betrayed specifically because of the whole situation with Mum. It's like he completely ignored that whole part of me, something I don't open up to anyone about. At the same time, I know how your mind can get clouded when traumatic shit happens to you. If I was crazy enough to try coke, is it really that crazy for him to do a drop-off, just the once? *You're being too kind, Sabs.* I think I'm being understanding. Something still needs to be mended inside of me. Anyways, supporting him to go to Hargeisa was the right thing to do and he seemed apologetic and remorseful when we met up. *Sabs, don't stress about him. Just focus on spending time with your family.* Yeah, that's right.

I haven't seen my Bristol family in ages. I'm here to see them before uni and that's what I should be focusing on. And to be honest, this trip is just what I need. Recalibration. Plus, I'm gonna need some chill-out time before Notting Hill Carnival, that's gonna be so lit. I make a mental note to sort out my outfit.

I'm pretty sure that I'll be expected to entertain my little cousins. I wish Tasha and Izzy were coming with me. It's time for Tasha to take responsibility at home. I've had my fair share of doing up 'mum runs', it's her time to pattern up.

I'm sure it's usually the dad's side of the family that are *different*. But for me, it's undeniably my mum's side. Sometimes, they say things that are way out of pocket. I don't want to use their whiteness as an excuse, but I'm sure they don't mean it in a malicious way. Back in the day, they used to call me 'half-caste' until I corrected them, and now they don't say it. Sometimes people just don't know.

*

After what feels like forever, my train arrives at Bristol Temple Meads. I fight to get my suitcase out of the luggage rack. I quickly go to use the toilet. The thought of my pee flying around on a train makes me sick. At least at the station, I can properly squat on the seat.

As I wash my hands, I can't help but think of Jalaal doing the drop-off at the station toilet. *Stop thinking about that, Sabs.*

I pull out my phone and text my dad.

Just got off the train station in Bristol, will let you know when I'm with Auntie Lisa.

By the time I make my way out of the station, it's practically empty. I'm the only one shuffling about looking for my ticket. The man in the Great Western Railway uniform sees me struggling and opens the barrier for me, ushering me to go through.

'Thank you!'

As soon as I make it through the gates past WHSmith, I hear my aunt's voice.

'SABRINA!'

Auntie Lisa emerges from the outside and engulfs me in a big embrace. She's put on a bit of weight since I last saw her, but other than that, she looks the same. Tight bun, tank top and jeans. On brand for Auntie Lisa. It's so strange because she genuinely does not look anything like my mother. They have completely different body types. I'd say Mum has a fuller figure with hips and curves, which I've luckily inherited.

'You've gone so big.' She squeezes my arms before stepping back to look at me. 'God, you look gorgeous, don't ya.'

'Thanks Auntie Lisa, you look great too.'

'Right, the kids are waiting in the car, let's quickly get in there before the ticket man comes.' We hurry out. 'It's such a shame that Tash and Izzy couldn't come.'

She swings to the left and whacks open the passenger door of her Renault Clio for me. I plump myself inside and place my bag on the floor. I quickly turn my head to see my two younger cousins there.

'SABREEEEEEENA,' they sing in unison.

My favourite Bristolian cousins: Charlotte, six years old, and Connor, nine years old. They have different dads – and I've never met either of them.

'How are my two favourite cousins?'

They both giggle in response.

Connor has a smirk on his face. He's a little rascal, but genuinely the sweetest kid ever.

'Connor, why are you pulling that face?' I raise my eyebrows.

'Because . . .' He crosses his arms.

'Because, what?'

'Because you got a big head.' He bursts out laughing.

I think he's alluding to my large forehead. He clearly doesn't know that big foreheads are currently in trend.

'And you know what?' I lean closer to him. 'So do you!' I lightly flick my finger on to his forehead.

We all burst out laughing.

After a wholesome evening of entertaining Connor and Charlotte, baking gingerbread and soaking up the sun while playing football in the park, I can't help but rejoice in the joy that's filling up my soul.

It is refreshing to be away from the bullshit bad vibes in London. And not gonna lie, I do feel somewhat more content in my decision to move to Warwick. A fresh clean slate.

Auntie Lisa and I are sat in the back garden sipping on Aperol Spritz and chatting away. Like ever, I'm not the biggest drinker, but she poured me a glass and I know better than to refuse. *Just admit you low-key want to set your mind free with a drink.*

'So, tell me.' Auntie Lisa grins at me. 'You're definitely old enough, do you have a boyfriend?' She wriggles her eyebrows. 'Of course you have a boyfriend.'

Oh, here we go. Couldn't escape him for that long.

'Auntie!' I shake my head. She's always been like this. Low-key like a big sister to me. Mum's not here for this, and I can't talk about this stuff with Auntie Maureen, so I may as well try with Auntie Lisa. 'I don't have a boyfriend . . . but there is a situation,' I confess.

'Oh oh, what's the situation honey?' She scoots closer to me.

'I'll tell you, but you can't tell Dad . . .' I don't know if it's the couple of sips that I've had or Auntie Lisa's warm nature or the Bristol sun or a combination of everything, but I spill it all out. Jalaal. The weed. Warwick. His religion. My religion. His dad. Our love. Everything but the cinema and the cocaine.

'WOW!' Auntie Lisa sighs. 'That's a lot for you to be going through. It makes me sad that you've held on to all this alone. But first, it's good to know that this boy wants to move away from selling weed, otherwise this conversation would've gone somewhere completely different. But let me tell you Sabs, this does sound like a proper love story. Romeo and Juliet. It reminds me of the beginning of your mum and dad's relationship. Both our families were slightly against it, but they did their own thing. And they have three beautiful, amazing daughters.'

My heart drops at the mention of Mum. I didn't want to speak about her. Not today, anyway.

'OK but Auntie, I didn't mention this but when he took me to Warwick, he legit was carrying . . .' I quieten my voice, 'cocaine. It was for his best friend though,' I quickly add. 'He proper regretted it and promised me that it was a one-off.' *Surely she has to see this can't work – it's cocaine, Sabs!*

'Oh no.' She shifts in her seat, pulling a poker face.

'Yeah . . . he kinda cried when he told me about it. It was emotional. I do believe that he regrets it and that he'll never do it again.' *You truly do believe it, Sabs.*

'That's unacceptable *but* . . .' She inhales. 'And this is a big *but*, he was honest about it and told you it was a one-off. That's different. And I'm talking from experience here. The thing is Sabs, I can't tell you what you can and can't do. All I know is that we all make mistakes, and I think you know this, otherwise you wouldn't have come to me. I can validate your feelings, but you're going to have to confront them. How do you feel? What do you want?'

Why does she suddenly speak so much sense, Sabs? She's got us.

'I really like him. A lot. He takes care of me and he kinda just, fills my heart with love. I don't know. We come from different worlds.' I look into her eyes.

'So your dad doesn't know? Auntie Maureen?'

'No. He's already been firm about how Somalis are so different to us culturally and religiously. So, yeah. And Auntie Maureen, well, she doesn't know either. She's a churchgoer. She won't get it.' I shrug my shoulders.

'I understand your hesitation in telling them, but they're gonna find out anyway. Religion. Culture. They're beautiful things that can be challenging, but they can also be the bonds that bring you closer together, Sabs. And my thoughts? Trust your gut. He needs to heal. And only consider him if he's done with the dealing. Anyways, this trip away for him might be exactly what he needs.' She squeezes my hand. 'Work at it together. And listen, if it doesn't work, then don't forget you're only seventeen anyway, you have a whole lifetime to fall in love, as many times as you want. Don't stress about it. Everything happens as it's supposed to.'

CHAPTER 31

JALAAL

My uncle parks his beat-up 4x4 outside a massive concrete, gated building. The tall gates hide most of it. But fuck, I can just about see the second floor of the grey house with its huge windows. It's basically a mansion. Is this the house my dad left us? It's better than that shithole in the ends.

'Get out then!' my uncle barks.

'Aren't you coming with me?' Panic streams down my body.

'Absolutely not. We don't get along. Anyway, whatever she asks for, just say no.' He leans his arm over me, pulls the handle of my door and flings it open. He honks the car and places his head outside.

'*Waryaa*, open the gate,' he shouts at the watchman.

The watchman peers through the gap in the gate and gives my uncle a nod of recognition before opening the grand gates. I push myself out of the car and on to the rocky floor. Without saying anything, my uncle zooms off, sending sand all over my face and body. Prick.

The watchman is a skinny boy, probably the same age as me. He could also be thirty years old. You can't tell with Somali people.

The way he's staring at me, he knows I'm not from here.

I walk past him, my sliders trying to find balance in the ground, his eyes burning into my back.

The brown-tinted windows with bars stare at me. I can't help but imagine Abo coming out of the house, smiling at me, and hugging me tightly. Maybe I could've had that, been part of his life. Now, he's fucking dead, it won't ever happen. There's nothing I can do about it. I'm numb on the inside. Frozen on the outside.

A young woman wearing a brown *shiid* with flower petals and a matching turban comes out the house. She has dark henna painted against the lighter complexion of her hands. She walks towards me, her flip-flops slapping against the white marble of her patio. She stops by the steps, reaches out her arms with a wide smile on her face. This must be Habo Salma.

'Jalaal-o.' She calls my name.

I take two steps towards her, and she engulfs me into a hug and I allow her to wrap herself around me. I can't believe that I'm hugging my dad's wife. This is bare weird. I can feel her beginning to sob as she whispers some *dua*s that I don't understand.

She unravels from me and we take each other in, not saying a thing. I don't know how to explain it, but we exchange a knowing look. There's an energy radiating from her. It feels calm. It feels like Abo is with us.

She ushers me into her home. I follow her through the brown-tinted glass door and remove my shoes as soon as I get in. I glance around the house. You can feel Abo is missing. Habo Salma takes me through two glass French doors into a room with a big dining table. She points towards the table, and I pull out a chair to sit down. She places herself opposite me. I was expecting loads of people at the house for the *tacsi* but my uncle told me they're doing it at their childhood home.

'Khadra will bring you something to eat, I hope you are hungry,' she says in Somali.

I assume Khadra's the maid. I can't believe maids are a thing here.

'Oh, Habo Salma, that's OK, I'm not hungry.' I know it's rude to decline, but man's nerves are too much right now.

'Don't be silly, a big boy like you needs to eat.'

I smile awkwardly.

'You know Jalaal.' She pauses. 'When your dad told me about you, he never mentioned how much you look alike. Such a handsome boy you are, *mashallah*.'

I notice how her eyes glow when she mentions him.

Khadra brings us both a huge plate of *bariis iyo hilib* with a banana on the side. I thank her for the rice and lamb before she rushes back out of the room.

Not gonna lie, I have no idea what to say. I'm deeping the fact that this is the woman who has been with my dad for the past eight years. I don't even know what Abo looks . . . looked like any more. The throbbing, empty feeling in my heart starts to creep up again.

I start forcing down the food in front of me, trying to fill the void. It takes every grain of self-control to keep myself from crying.

Habo Salma senses my hesitation and carries on speaking.

'You know, your dad loved you very much. He would always speak about you. But there was a pain in his heart. He knew what he did was wrong. Leaving you and your brother in England. I tried to get him to do more with you both, but he felt that he had already lost you.'

I continue chewing, avoiding eye contact.

'I loved him, too,' I sputter out before washing down the food with fresh juice.

From the corner of my eye, I clock a child peering by the doors. I immediately notice her big brown eyes and irregular triangle-shaped face. Her hair is styled in cornrows, and she's dressed in a purple *shiid*. She looks the same age as Ibrahim . . .

'Shukri, come inside, stop being shy,' Habo Salma says while she sucks the bone marrow residue off her fingers.

I watch Shukri linger at the door.

'Come say hello to your brother.' Habo Salma raises her voice.

Wait, what, brother?

'Yes Hooyo,' Shukri replies.

Mum?

Habo Salma is her mum.

It takes a hot second for me to deep that this is my little sister that is stood opposite me. *Wallahi*, part of me ain't even shocked cos I always knew this at the back of my mind. I'm just fucking vex that my uncle never told me.

'Oh, Jalaal.' Habo Salma notices my surprise. 'They didn't tell you.' She sighs. 'I'm not surprised.'

I smile at my sister. Feels fucking weird thinking that.

She slowly walks towards me, not breaking eye contact.

'Shukri.' I assume she doesn't speak English. 'I'm your brother Jalaal, how are you?'

'Why do you speak funny?' She raises her eyebrows. 'And where have you been all this time if you're my brother?' She puts her hands on her hips.

I have no idea how the fuck I'm supposed to answer this question. I look to Habo Salma for help.

'*Naayaahee*, Jalaal only found out right now he has a sister. *Xishoo*.' Habo Salma saves me.

'How old are you, Shukri?'

'Six.' She smiles. 'I'm a big girl.'

I got no clue what else to say to her.

But she knows what to say to me. 'Can I show you the *bisado* outside?'

I don't even have time to answer, because she tugs on my hand and pulls me outside to the porch to show me the cats.

The mention of the word *bisad* got me thinking 'bout the ends. I can't believe that back in London we call crackheads cats in Somali. But then the heat outside reminds me that I'm far away from that life.

Shukri shows me the actual cats near the hut where Khadra cooks the food. It's not too far from the watchman's hut, who I can feel is watching us intently. Shukri bends over and starts stroking them, telling me their names. I reach down to her level, my curls swooping over my eyes. Damn, I wish I had time to get a haircut before I came here. Shukri explains all about the cats to me. I'm finding it hard to keep up with her. I'm embarrassed that I'm struggling this much with Somali. But she's bright and smart and patient. Like Ibby.

After playing with the cats for a while, and Shukri asking me a million questions about London, Habo Salma calls me over. I rush over to the courtyard. It's scaring me how easily they're accepting me into their home. In a good way though.

Habo Salma is stood with two light-skinned Somali guys. It's bait they're brothers because they have the same head shape. Their skin complexion is lighter than mine, and they're both dressed in khaki shorts and Nike T-shirts.

'Jalaal, these are my nephews Ali and Ayub. They're from Denmark and here for holiday. They will take you around Hargeisa and *inshallah* get you a haircut.'

'Thanks, Habo.' I smile at her.

'Yo bro, you good?' The older-looking one with the weird American-European accent says, 'I'm Ayub.' He pulls me into one of those half spud, half hugs.

'I'm good. *Alhamdulillah*.' I turn towards the other one. 'You're Ali then?'

He nods his head.

'All right, let's go.' Ayub walks towards the 4x4 Land Rover in front of the house.

You wouldn't know the car is black from the brown tint of dust thickly layered on it.

I learn a lot about them during the drive into the city. Ayub is twenty-three and Ali is seventeen, like me. They're from Aarhus. Ayub works as a youth worker for troubled kids in immigrant communities. It low-key sounds like the youth club in my estate, so I'm guessing that his job is to get mandem off road. I don't tell them that I'm shotting.

'Jalaal, what do you do back in London?' Ayub glances back at me from the driver's seat.

'Ah me? I work in the supermarket. Just tryna figure my shit out. Yeah.' I pray he doesn't ask more.

Ali looks at me and scoffs, as if he knows something.

'That's sick, bro.' Ayub doesn't notice. 'Talk some sense into my little brother. He got in trouble back in Aarhus and now he's here to pattern up. A soft *dhaqan celis*.' Somalis' take on rehabilitation.

Ali side-eyes his older brother.

'Oh, is it?' I look to Ali. 'I'll chat to you later, bro.' I awkwardly laugh. I never thought I was gonna be the person to give someone else advice to stay off road. Some weird 180 shit.

They show me all the spots around the city. Not gonna lie, I was kind of impressed when they started playing UK music in the car, specifically M Huncho and D-Block Europe. Even though I don't really listen to their music, it got me feeling nostalgic.

After eating munch and praying *maghrib*, we go to a shisha spot. Hargeisa is lit you know. It's not too different to those shisha spots on Coronation Road in Park Royal. Ayub and Ali were telling me how there are low-key parties where you can drink and smoke. It's mad how parents think they are sending their children 'back home' for rehab, but they're drinking and smoking. The guys invited me to a motive tonight. My dad died, I ain't tryna get lit. Especially after I fucked up the last time that I got waved. I was expecting them to pressure me into it – like the mandem back home – but they were bare calm about it. Didn't even ask me twice.

Ayub pays the bill for the shisha and tea. I tell him thanks.

'Bro, is it cool if I drop you back to Habo Salma's house?' he asks me.

'Yeah, that's calm.'

'Thanks, I'm gonna go to the bathroom, give me a sec.' Ayub nods towards his brother, signalling me to chat to him.

'What you saying?' I ask Ali once his brother is out of earshot.

'Nothing, fam. I know you're on stuff. My brother must be the worst youth worker cos he ain't clock shit.' He shakes his head.

'I'm not involved in anything, well, not any more.' It rolls off my tongue easily. Because it's what I want. 'Why did your mum send you here?'

'One of the opps got deaded off. I was there but I didn't do it. My mum sent me here before anything could happen.' He is monotonous.

This brudda is rolling with mandem who be out here killing people. In comparison to me shotting a bit of weed here and there, that's mad.

'Ahhh,' I manage to get out.

'Don't worry fam. I'm calm in Hargeisa. I kinda like it here. I'm just baking off.'

I'm not sure how to respond to him. Before I can string together a shit reply, Ayub emerges. I sigh relief.

I wasn't too sure about the whole sleeping situation, but it seems that Habo Salma and Shukri want me to stay over. And cos I haven't heard from my adeero, who I'm meant to be staying with, I'm cool with going somewhere I'm wanted.

'Shall we go?' Ayub asks.

'Yeah, course fam, Habo Salma is expecting me init,' I seek reassurance from him.

'Yeah. Even if she wasn't, she's blessed and would have you as a guest forever, if she could,' he says.

'Calm, say no more.'

It's pitch back when I get back to the house. Khadra opens the door for me and directs me to the guest room, which thankfully isn't Abo's old room. Somebody brought my suitcase here.

I'm not tired yet. Ain't gonna lie, I'm starting to like Hargeisa, and I want to tell Sabs about it. I wonder if she even wants to chat to me. Before I'm able to connect to the Wi-Fi, I hear shuffling.

'Jalaal, come here,' a voice whispers.

I peer into the dark and see Shukri waving me over. I tiptoe towards her.

'Do you wanna see something cool?' her eyes are filled with excitement.

'Yes.'

'Follow me.' She turns around and I follow her further into the dark.

We turn into a passageway with a steep staircase and Shukri instructs me to be careful. I take slow steps as I make my way upwards. There's an attic door which Shukri squeaks open. I can tell she's done this before. As soon as it opens, I see the dark sky and stars glitzing down on us.

She pushes herself upwards and I copy her.

As soon as I get up, I'm mesmerized by the view. The sky is clear, and the stars seem so close. The honking of cars and chatter of people below calms me. I stand and look around in amazement. Hargeisa is beautiful.

'Jalaal.' Shukri snaps me out of my trance.

I look down at her. Her eyes are forcefully wide.

'Thank you for showing me this Shukri, *wallahi*. I'm happy you're my sister,' I say in Somali.

'I love you, Jalaal.' She pulls me into a big hug.

I actually thank Allah for bringing me here. Finding out that I have a little sister is the best thing that could've happened to me *alhamdulillah*.

As we split apart from our embrace, Shukri hands me over an envelope and her faces softens.

'Jalaal, this is a letter from Abo. Hooyo told me to bring it up to you. I haven't opened it.' She presses her lips in a straight line.

The envelope is unsigned, but sealed closed.

'We need to pray *fajr* soon, so you can stay up here. I'm going now.' She dashes down the stairs.

I look between the attic door and the envelope multiple times before finally walking towards the ledge of the roof. I sit down on the edge and allow my feet to dangle in the cool air.

Without hesitation, I open the letter and begin to read.

My dearest son,

I don't know the circumstances under which you are reading this letter, but I must not be around. I am sorry. I am sorry for being absent for the most part of eight years. There are no excuses, but you must know that the death of your mother did something to me. It completely tore me apart to the core, until I felt nothing. I became numb. Your mother was the glue that was holding me together and when she passed, I became nothing. When I should have been taking care of my sons, I ran to Somaliland thinking that my problems would be solved or even erased. I thought that returning to my birthplace would make me feel better. But I was only distracting myself from the pain that I was too cowardly to face. What kind of man leaves his newborn and first son with his sister-in-law in a different country?

A weak man. Me. I have had to make peace with the fact I have been a terrible father to you. I tried to maintain contact, but my stupidity drove you away. I'm not angry with you for refusing my calls and invitations to visit. Don't beat yourself up about it. The fact that you even spoke to me for a while shows that you're nothing like me. You have the kindness and integrity of your mother.

I'm assuming you have met Salma and your sweet baby sister, Shukri. Salma helped me deal with the passing of your mother and has been a wonderful wife to me, completely different to your mother, but both amazing women in their own ways. Shukri came along soon after I came here and married Salma. Your sister is the most precious girl with the biggest heart to give and I hope you can be the loving big brother that she needs and deserves. She is innocent in my wrongdoings.

Jalaal, there is no hiding the fact that I have failed you and your mother. But the person who I have failed the most is Ibrahim. It has pained me every day of my life, but it is something I have had to deal with. When I speak to your Habo Hani at home, she always tells me how wonderful Ibrahim is, but she's worried about you. She's concerned that you might be getting up to no good and that your head isn't screwed on. And this scares me Jalaal, this scares me to my core. You are an intelligent man. Life hasn't been easy for you, but don't give up for no reason. Or give it up for uselessness. You are worth so much more and I believe in you.

As my sons, Islamically, you and Ibrahim will both receive thirty-five per cent of everything I own. Shukri will receive seventeen and a half per cent and Salma twelve and a half per cent. This is in relation to money, land and belongings. The house was gifted to Salma as part of Nazar many years ago; nobody except her is aware of this. Jalaal, I trust you to do what is right by your heart. Salma will take care of you in whatever way that you need. She loves you like her own.

Jalaal, I only ask one thing of you. It is a big thing, but it is the only thing that I want from you – even though I do not deserve it. I wish for you to forgive me. I wish for you to forgive me for how I have wronged you in this life. If there is any resentment in your heart, please let it go and use that space to feel love and experience the goodness from it. It is a big thing to ask, but it will make things one hundred per cent easier. Your mother taught me that. Jalaal, I love you and will love you forever.

إنه ليغان على قلبي، وإني لأستغفر الله في اليوم مائة مرة

'Sometimes I perceive a veil over my heart, and I supplicate Allah for forgiveness a hundred times in a day.'

CHAPTER 32

SABRINA

I didn't realize how much I miss my family. We've done so many fun things around Bristol. We took Connor and Charlotte to the science museum and the funfair nearby. We went to the suspension bridge and had a mini picnic there. They are true Bristolians. Even though I've lived in London my whole life, I don't think I could call myself a 'Londoner' because all I know is the ends. *Not for long*. My favourite day was when we went to Harbourside and watched the hot-air balloons soar up into the sky. They were so pretty against the purple sunset. It felt like déjà vu of when we went as a family. In a weird way, it made me feel closer to Mum.

We are all sat down watching reruns of *Take Me Out* on Auntie Lisa's sixty-inch TV. It's proper trash TV but these guys love it, so I can't even complain. Even Connor and Charlotte are watching it. I know Dad would flip out if Izzy was watching this show, probably even if Tasha was, too.

'That Paddy McGuinness, he's well fit ain't he?' Auntie Lisa nudges me.

'He's all right.'

'He's definitely not your mum's type, that's for sure.' She lowers her voice.

'What's that supposed to mean?' I clock my head towards her.

'She doesn't like white guys,' she says bluntly.

I'm low-key stunned. I can't figure out if I should respect her audacity or look deeper into her comment. *Not that deep, Sabs*.

'Do you miss her?' Her voice softens.

She has caught me off guard. Of course I miss my mum, that's my mum. I can't erase what she did and how she abandoned us though.

I stay quiet.

'I miss her.' She twiddles her fingers.

'Hopefully, she'll come back soon.' I try to comfort her. *Isn't it meant to be the other way around?*

'You know . . .' She pauses. 'Connor and Charlotte.'

They both turn around in unison.

'Can you guys go upstairs and get ready for bed please?'

'OK Mummy,' Charlotte says as Connor holds her hand and leads her upstairs.

After the kids go upstairs and out of sight, Auntie Lisa lowers the TV volume and faces me.

'There's something I have to tell you.'

Oh shit, Sabs. I hope she isn't going to say Mum died or has ended up in some ditch somewhere. No more bad news.

'What?' My heart is in my mouth. I stroke my necklace intuitively; feeling the shape of the cross always offers me comfort.

'I saw your mum a couple of months ago. Before you assume the worst, it's not what you think. She was in a bad state. And she didn't come to me. I went looking for her. I just couldn't deal with not knowing where she was.' She begins to cry.

I wait for her to continue. *What the hell is going on?*

'She's still using. And she's not in a good place. I tried to get through to her. Remind her of everything: you, Tash and Izzy, as well as your dad. But all she focuses on is the loss of our mum. Well, your grandma. But Sabrina, I lost my mother, too! You don't see me abandoning everyone. It doesn't make sense. I just don't understand. She said she will come back when the "time is right" but I wouldn't hold your breath. I don't want to get your hopes up for nothing. I felt it was important to share this with you.'

'Why didn't you tell me when you found her? I would've wanted to come with you. You didn't even ask us!' My fingers start to tremble.

I don't think Auntie Lisa comprehends how much we need our mum. This was selfish of her to do. And the nerve to only tell me now! *Why are the people closest to me hurting me the most?*

'It wasn't right. You should never see your mother like that. It would've messed you up for good.' Her lips quiver.

'Well, it's not anything I haven't seen before. If I'm old enough to look after my family and do everything else, I'm old enough to know where she is.' I begin to sob.

Auntie Lisa immediately tries to embrace me, but I shrug her off.

'Sabs, I never meant to hurt you. I only wanted to protect you. I hope you understand. I thought knowing that she was alive would put your mind at ease. I'm really sorry, sweetheart. I only wanted to help.' She puts her head in her hands and begins to weep.

This is all so fucking confusing. I want to punch something, but also want to lie on the floor and cry. This is how Jalaal must have felt. *Deep breaths Sabs – you can handle this.* Auntie Lisa looks wrecked. I don't think she was intentionally trying to hurt me.

'I know, I know,' I mumble. 'It just hurts.'

I let out an ugly cry. Auntie Lisa embraces me again and this time I let her.

'Do you think that she'll ever come back?' I whisper.

'I hope so sweetie, I hope so,' she says as she rocks me back and forth.

Jalaal said he wants to FaceTime me. I'm a bit nervous. It's just that discomfort of when you've had a falling out with someone and there's that awkward period of 'going back to normal'. It fills me with anxiety.

Speaking with Auntie Lisa and having time away from London has really forced me to take a step back and look at things from a different perspective. Without having to worry about my sisters and Dad, I've just focused on myself. And I know it sounds so cringey, but it gave me the clarity I needed. I love Jalaal. Despite my brain fighting my heart, I've accepted that I want him. I miss him so much and I won't deny the feelings that I have. I'm always putting other people before me, including Jalaal. But what do I want? I want love. I want to be loved by Jalaal. *And to love him back*.

I have forgiven him, because my heart has guided me to the conclusion that he made a genuine mistake, and he was honest about it. When I opened up to him about the coke thing with Mum, he refrained from judging me and just accepted that I'm not perfect. I want to uphold the same level of understanding and compassion.

Ring Ring. Ring Ring. Ring Ring.

I answer on the third ring and Jalaal's face pops up on my screen. My heart warms.

We look at each other, a nervous but eager silence growing.

'How are you?' I break the ice. *His father just died, how the hell do you think he's doing, Sabrina?*

'Things are all right, a lot has happened,' he says. 'How are you feeling?'

'Well . . . We didn't leave things on the best note . . .' He leaves me to finish.

I avoid looking at the screen. 'But being in Bristol with family made me realize what is important to me, and that's you,' I confess, now looking straight at him.

'Sabs, that makes me bare happy to hear . . . but . . . I should have never put you through all that. If I could take it all back, I would,' he says, his face pondering on my screen.

'I believe you,' is all that I can reply.

The silence ensues again.

'Can I tell you something about being here?' I feel his eagerness to share.

I wish I wanted to air him, but I don't. *Sabs, follow your heart.*

'What happened?'

'One, I got a little sister. Two, my dad left me a letter.' He bites his lip.

My eyes widen. 'A sister?'

His small smile emerges. 'She's six years old and so loving – reminds me of Izzy. But look, my dad left me a letter before he died. And he apologized for everything. And wait, it's not like I forgive him or anything yet. But it was good to finally understand where he was coming from, ya know? When I was reading this letter, I was bare emotional, just bawling non-stop. And it made me clock that I would've hated myself if I never came here. My stepmum and sister are kind. Their family is so nice. They've been taking care of me. *Wallahi.*'

'Wow Jalaal, that's a lot to digest.'

'I know, and I also wanna say that I love you bare and thank you for pushing me to come to these ends. *Wallahi*, you don't understand how much I appreciate it.'

'You already knew it was the right thing to do. You just needed a push.'

'Tomorrow is the funeral thing, so I get to see his body and then they'll bury him in the grave. And I know it's fucked up, but I'm looking forward to it. Looking forward to seeing him finally and all the love and goodness he has around here. I really hope Allah forgives him and sends him to heaven though.' Jalaal exhales.

'*Inshallah*, he will,' I say.

'*Inshallah*,' he repeats and smiles. 'I have to go now, Sabs. I just wanted to speak to you, so badly.' He pauses. 'I love you.'

It feels right. 'I love you, too . . .'

He waves goodbye before hanging up the phone.

There's something different about him. He's shifted in a good way. I'm glad he's in Somaliland and that he's finding his own version of peace. It's like he's embraced his pain and is taking everything in. It's time for me to do the same.

CHAPTER 33

JALAAL

Inna lillahi wa inna ilayhi raji'un. Verily we belong to Allah, and truly to Him shall we return.

Seeing Abo for the last time before he was buried was a mad experience.

I'm glad I was left alone to say goodbye. His body was still. Frozen. The hair on his head was completely gone and his beard was a greyish colour. He looked the same as I remembered him, he'd just aged. His eyes were shut. *Subhanallah.* He will never open them again.

I stood hovering over his body for ages. I wanted to be angry at him but all I felt was sadness and love.

The good memories were flooding in. I was remembering when Hooyo and Abo would pick me up from school together. The times that Abo would play football with me in the park. When Abo and I would rub Hooyo's pregnant belly together.

Abo made me deep how precious this life is. There's no point holding this grudge against him. What's done is done. I know Abo lived a better life in Hargeisa. And in a fucked-up way, I'm glad he did.

*

It's been two days, and I can feel something changing within me.

The sound of the *adhan* wakes me up and I find myself praying *fajr*. This is the first time I've woken up early to pray in a very long time. It feels good. It's also my last day in Hargeisa, and I'm glad that I decided to stay with Habo Salma and Shukri instead of my tapped uncle. He kept pestering me bare about the house and money. I don't know how to tell him that he's bad vibes. I deeped that all he cares about is money. It's mad to think that that is my dad's brother. I pray to Allah that me and Ibby never turn out to be brothers like that. His vibe is stinky, I'm happy to be keeping my distance from him.

The house is dark, but you can hear the quiet footsteps of everyone walking around for prayer. It's comforting.

When I go to the bathroom to make *wudhu*, the washing ritual before prayer, I feel clean.

After my prayer, I stay in *sujud*, my forehead planted on the mat, and make *dua* to Allah. I pray that Abo goes to *Jannah*. I wish for the forgiveness of my father's sins. Tears escape my eyes and I let them fall, tasting the saltiness in the crevices of my lips. I have never felt this close to Allah.

Back in my bed, I shut the mosquito net and rest my head on the pillow. I close my eyes and let sleep take me away for the next few hours.

The sun is beaming through my window, and I can feel the warmth in the room. Not suffocating like in the ends. I feel fresh. My mind is clear. It's bare weird but everything is starting to make sense.

After brushing my teeth and washing my face, I find Habo Salma and Shukri sat at the dining table, waiting for me.

'Hey Habo Salma.' I smile. 'Hi Shukri.'

'*Subax wanaagsan.*' She wishes me good morning.

Habo Salma puts a piece of bread and camel meat on my plate. She reaches to the flask to pour tea in my cup, and I tell her that I can do it myself. I don't know why they treat me like I'm some prince here. I know for a fact that if Hals was here, she'd be saying it's because they live in a patriarchal society and have a backwards way of thinking.

I haven't gone in Abo's room yet to sort out his possessions. Habo Salma wanted me to go through it yesterday but *wallahi*, it was too much for me. Today is my final day in the motherland. I have no choice.

'I was wondering where Abo's belongings are, as I wanna take some stuff back with me. Is that OK?' I flick my fingernails, avoiding eye contact.

'Come over,' Habo Salma chuckles knowingly.

I follow her like a sheep. She creaks open a door at the end of the corridor but doesn't step inside. Instead, she switches on the light and ushers me to go in.

I cross over and she disappears behind me.

Abo's room is not how I expected it to be. There is a huge double bed in the middle, a three-door wardrobe and a chest of drawers. For some dumb reason, I thought that Habo Salma would have packed all his belongings into cardboard boxes. But his room is tidy. As if someone is still living here.

There's bare random shit. Loads of cigarettes and lighters. Lots of *macawis* and white T-shirts. Some old cameras that I've never seen in my life. There are even my certificates from primary school. Abo never forgot about me.

*

I take the photo albums of us from when I was younger: me, Hooyo and Abo. I'm happy that I now have proper photos of Hooyo to show Ibrahim. I take a framed photograph of my parents on their wedding day. This one was hidden at the bottom of his chest of drawers, inside folded clothes.

The only thing that rattles me is a woman's perfume bottle. I take a sniff and my mind jolts. It was Hooyo's. I take it, too.

I turn the lights off in the room and leave.

Habo Salma lets me know that my adeero is on his way to pick me up.

'Will you guys come visit me in London?' I ask.

Shukri smiles and turns to her mum. 'Hooyo, please can we go see Jalaal in England. And I can meet my brother Ibrahim too, please Hooyo.'

'*Inshallah*, Jalaal we will come to see you soon,' she promises.

'I'm so happy that I came here, and I met the both of you. Shukri, you're the best thing that has happened to me.'

'Your Somali has improved Jalaal, you should've stayed here longer,' Habo Salma laughs.

'I'll come back whenever I can.' I smile.

I never thought I would come here and connect with my dad's other family. It's so fucking weird, but I guess it's what Allah wanted.

'Anyways, I have your WhatsApp, so we are going to keep in contact,' I say.

'I have packed some stuff for your Habo Hani, as she has been taking care of you all these years – make sure you put it in your suitcase OK?' She hands over a heavy blue plastic bag.

'Of course, Habo.'

We are disturbed by the loud honking of a car as my wasteman of an adeero arrives.

'That's your uncle then.' She gestures outside.

I sigh.

'Right come give me a hug, handsome Jalaal,' she stretches out her arms.

I walk into her embrace. She gives the best hugs.

'Your dad would be so proud of you,' she whispers into my ear as she begins to cry.

'Don't cry Habo. You're going to make me cry.'

I release myself from her grip and bend over to give Shukri a hug. Her skinny arms widen before she wraps them firmly around me, giving me the tightest hug I've ever had.

'You're the best big brother!' She jumps up and down.

'Shukri, you are the best sister I could have ever asked for.'

HONK HONK. This wasteman has no fucking patience.

'All right, I have to go now before he kills me.'

They follow me out and watch me as I jump into my uncle's 4x4, both waving me off. He doesn't even acknowledge them.

I put my seatbelt on as soon as I get in, and Adeero zooms out of Habo Hani's gated home.

'How did she take it?' he asks.

'Take what?' I act dumb.

'You know, what's happening with your dad's stuff,' he chuckles.

'Oh. Better than I expected,' I lie to him.

He grins to himself. 'Good boy.'

*

When we arrive at the airport and I grab my things out of his car, I look my adeero straight in the eye. 'Abo left the house to Habo Salma a long time ago, as he should have.'

His face drops.

I put in my AirPods and turn away, wishing my city goodbye.

The journey back to ends was long but necessary for me to deep the whole situation. There's a new sadness in the pit of my stomach, it's kind of big, and it's placed right next to a similar sadness from Hooyo's death eight years ago. This new sadness feels like a black hole right now, but it's going to subside over time, until it reaches the same size as the one next to it. And this sadness will stay with me forever. I'll get used to it and I'll be able to live a good life, because Allah only gives you the trials and tribulations that your soul can handle. I can do it. I've done it before. There's no point thinking 'why me?' – it's now 'why not me?'.

This whole shotting weed thing has to go. For good. There's no way it's going to run if I want to continue things with Sabrina, and I do, so badly. She is everything. More importantly, it's not what I want to do, and I don't know why it's taken me so fucking long to do something about it. And now that I've actually got some money, I can invest in myself.

I don't know how Shaah is going to take the news. I told him that my dad passed away while I was abroad, and he said we would link up once I got back to ends. Shaah is my boy, and he's been my boy since day one. I hope he's gonna understand once I tell him that I'm done with this life. He has to understand.

Habo Hani and Hals were shook when they found out we have a

sister. A whole sister.

I decided not to tell them until I got back cos I wasn't tryna deal with their stress. I still haven't seen Ibrahim. This whole trip made me realize how deep the love I have for my little brother runs. And he's gonna be so gassed when he finds out that he's got a sister.

Habo Hani asked straight away how much money Abo left me. It sounds mad, but I know it's not coming from a place of greed; she's just making sure that I wasn't mugged off. I told her that Abo left me forty thousand pounds and I explained the situation. And she cried. And Hals cried a bit, too. I thought about sharing the letter with them, especially Hals, but I didn't in the end. I want to keep this letter to myself.

I slowly open Ibrahim's door and peek inside. He's on his bed reading *A Series of Unfortunate Events*.

'Ibrahim,' I whisper.

He prods his head up and smiles widely as he runs up to me. He squeezes me hard and I hold him close, rubbing my hands on his little head.

'When did you come back?'

'Last night when you were sleeping.'

'Jalaal.' His face goes solemn. 'Is Abo going to hell?'

'Don't worry about Abo, this was his time to go and now he's in a better place.' I rub his shoulders.

'So will I ever see him again?'

'Yes. When everybody dies, they meet in heaven. So, when you're really, really old, and that's a long time away, and you die – you will meet Abo again. And you can finally meet Hooyo too,' I say with conviction.

'Really?' His eyes glimmer with hope.

'Yeah, obviously!'

'OK, Jalaal. Why does my heart feel sad?' he points to the middle of his chest.

'It's normal, it's gonna be like this for a little bit. But I promise you Bro, it's going to get better,' I convince myself too.

'O-K,' he mumbles before wrapping his arms around my chest again.

If Abo's death taught me one thing, it's that my family are everything to me. I need to be here for Ibrahim. And Shukri.

CHAPTER 34

SABRINA

I'm waiting by the Pizza Express at Paddington Basin for Jalaal. *Our place.*

I clock him and can't help but smile and run towards him. He opens his arms and I jump into his embrace, wrapping my legs around him. He holds on to my waist, carrying my weight. I plop kiss after kiss all over his cheeks. If this is what it feels like to be loved by someone, I wanna be loved all the time.

When I finally unwrap myself from him, he gets straight into it. 'I'm so sorry Sabrina. I'm so sorry that I fucked up. I'm sorry for what I did. I hope you know that I will never ever put you in a position where you'll doubt me ever again. *Wallahi*, I made a mistake. The biggest mistake of my life.'

I stop him mid-rant. 'Jalaal, you know I've forgiven you . . . we don't need to go through this again.'

He squeezes on to me tightly. I never realized how much he needed to hear and feel this forgiveness.

Everything seems to be falling into place. *Finally Sabs, finally.*

Jalaal takes my hands and intertwines his fingers with mine. The butterflies are fluttering around my stomach.

'Look Sabs.' He bites his lip. 'I don't think that I am the best at communicating how I feel, but everything that's happened recently has made me clock that I want you in my life no matter what. I know I ain't the best version of myself right now but I'm tryna pattern up.'

My heart soars. I've been needing to hear this from Jalaal. My insides are swelling with hope.

'Like actually do something with my life. My dad . . . passing away . . .' He looks up to the sky for a moment and I notice tears in his eyes. He squeezes them tight, and two tears roll down. 'It made me realize that this life is short. And I love you Sabs, like bare, I never saw this coming but *wallahi* I got mad love for you. And yeah . . . you wanna be my girlfriend?' He smiles nervously.

Relief seeps through my body. I was honestly starting to question whether this day would come. *Sabs, I told you that this guy is all for you.*

'Yes, I will be your girlfriend, Jalaal.' I peck him on the lips.

Once the words leave my lips, my heart warms. There's no unease, no questions, no doubt. I can't believe that the Jalaal I met at Shanice's house party, all those months ago, is now my boyfriend. No way did I think I would be sat here kissing him. *Ever.*

He holds on to me, and as our lips move in sync, my mind wanders. I start fantasizing about meeting each other's families, getting married, having children. *Sabs, you're getting carried away, you don't even know if that can happen.*

He backs away from my lips and places his forehead on to mine.

'I love you.'

'I love you, too.'

I inhale deeply from the mint-and-apple-flavoured shisha pipe before breaking down into a very short and swift coughing fit.

Amelia and Liyah both burst into a fit of giggles before taking the pipe off me, changing the mouth cap, taking their turns to inhale smoothly and exhale out cloudy air.

'Maybe shisha just isn't for me.' I sink into the velvet chair, taking a nibble of the triple-cooked chips on my plate.

'Nah Sabs, you just gotta practise. We were all coughing our first few times.' Amelia hands the pipe back to me.

'No, I think I'm done with the embarrassment.'

'So are we,' Liyah jokes.

I try my best to give a sour smile, but that was quite funny from her.

'I'm so glad we finally got to link up and do this together. It's been a long time coming.'

'Facts!'

I take in my surroundings – we've finally made it to Liyah's cousin's shisha spot. It's not quite what I expected: tacky fake plant wall installation with a cringey neon tagline, *Friday Night Vibes*. The loud volume of afrobeats that doesn't smoothly transition into R&B. The smoke clouds and phone flashes of people recording each other smoking and the aesthetics of the food.

My thoughts drift to Jalaal. I'm so glad that he's back. I can feel it in my bones that things are now starting to take shape in a positive way. *Sabs, you love this guy.* Yes, I do truly love Jalaal and I can't not see him in my future. My heart yearns for Jalaal. I choose him.

And I want everything that comes with him. I think I'm ready to go to the next level with him and explore my sexuality. If this summer holiday has taught me anything, it's that I need to stop being afraid of letting go. I can be so strict and uptight sometimes. I love Jalaal. I want to have this experience with him. And I love it because

I've come to this conclusion by myself. I have my insecurities, but I think I can get over it.

'What you daydreaming about, Sabs?' Liyah puffs out.

'Yeah girl, you're in another world,' Amelia playfully giggles.

'Well.' I scoot closer to them; the blaring of Burna Boy is burning my ears. 'Do you think it's too early to have . . . uhhum . . . sex?' I immediately quieten, my face warming.

Amelia giggles. Liyah's eyes widen.

'Don't judge me!' I fake surrender my hands.

'Nobody is judging you.' Liyah's words soothe me.

'I've been having sex for a while now,' Amelia confesses. 'At the beginning it wasn't that enjoyable but now that I've learnt what I like, it's amazing.'

'What you like?' I ask confusedly.

'Yeah, at the beginning I was just giving blowjobs thinking that's all there is.' She shrugs her shoulders. 'But now, it's all about me. And my man, he knows how to make me feel good.' Her cheeks redden at the intimate memories she recalls.

'Sabs,' Liyah interjects. 'There's no pressure, you go at your own pace and do whatever feels right. It's worked for you so far. And Jalaal, the way that boy loves on you. You got this.'

I smile. I needed this.

Later on, when I go to the toilet with Liyah, and Amelia isn't around, she gives me an extra boost of confidence. She suggests that we go to the sexual health clinic so I can be fully prepared. I don't know what I'd do without my best friend.

CHAPTER 35

JALAAL

Sohaib always brings me back to earth. Reminds me that I can make it. We've talked about the incident with his sister. He eventually admitted he was in the wrong. About fucking time. If he didn't switch up his attitude, that would've been some tapped behaviour – which I can't accept. During the time I've been chilling with him at Sainsbury's, he has been someone good to talk to about Abo's death. Just helping me to come to terms with it and he's always checking in on me. He always offers a good religious perspective too, ya know?

The store is calm today, probably cos Steve isn't on shift. 'Do you think it's too late for me to go back to education?'

Sohaib's head swings towards me as he abandons stacking the shelf. 'It's never too late. Whatever you wanna do – it's only gonna benefit you.'

'Hmm, I'm tryna figure out what to do next.'

'You thinking about doing that design thing?'

'Yeah, I did but that's a hobby innit. I think I need qualifications or something. I got some P's from my dad and I wanted to start a clothing business, but I really don't know how to do it.'

'Bro, that's calm. I would say holla at your college and try finish that course you were doing. You can start the clothing line for sure, let me chat my cousin though. He got his own business, and I can ask him how to start it up and stuff. Trust me, it'll be light work.' His excitement is gassing me.

'Really? You would do that?'

'Of course, I gotchu.'

Sohaib wanted to get munch after work, but Shaah already belled me asking to link up. And not gonna lie, I used to feel like a bum when comparing myself to Sohaib, and always used to feel better comparing to Shaah. But now, I feel like I could be as good as Sohaib.

Shaah rings the doorbell.

'Who is that?' Ibrahim shouts from upstairs.

'It's Shaah,' I yell back.

He dashes downstairs, but I manage to open the door first. I'm greeted by my best friend dressed head to toe in Trapstar with blue Air Jordan 1's.

'What you sayin' bro?' We give each other a brotherly hug.

'Nothing G, come inside.'

'Is your aunt home?' he asks.

I never actually deeped it until now, but Habo Hani and Shaah don't like each other. He's never said he don't like her but if she was here right now, he would be pressed. She knows he's low-key bad company. I wonder why I never clocked on to this.

'Nah, she's got a doctor's appointment with Hals,' I say. 'I'm looking after Ibrahim.'

He sighs relief. Ibby walks towards Shaah and gives him a spud. This little kid thinks he's gangsta.

'Ibrahim, go upstairs for a bit. I need to talk to Uncle Shaah about some grown-up stuff.'

Ibrahim frowns at us, but he knows what's up. He leaves us and we go into the kitchen, closing the door behind us.

'What you saying bro, how you doing?' I ask, leaning against the counter.

'I'm all right, fam.' He forces a smile. 'What *you* saying though, how was Somaliland?'

'It was good, *alhamdulillah*. Not gonna lie, didn't think I was gonna like it that much.' I find myself spilling into normal chatter even though I need to get something off my chest.

'Swear down? You seem a bit different.'

'Different?'

'Yeah, like you're more calm. Usually you got that serious face.'

My mind flickers to Habo Salma and Shukri, and warmth fills me. I need to do the right thing. Shaah isn't gonna like this. 'You know how I've been saying like I'm ready to go legit. And how I'm done with the road?' I change the subject.

He chuckles. 'Don't tell me you were being serious, bro.'

I don't laugh with him. 'I *was* being serious, fam. I'm stopping everything. I'm done. Like no more. I lost my mum and my dad now. Ibrahim needs me. He doesn't need me to be in prison or dead. You feel me?'

'I don't understand. What 'bout me? What 'bout us, fam? Nah, you're moving weird,' he says, his voice aggressive.

'How? I'm not *on this* any more. I'm gonna stop with all that fuckery.'

'It's not fuckery. It's how we live. It's how we make bread.' His words come out fast.

'Not any more,' I sigh. 'And not gonna lie, man's stopped with all the drinking and smoking too, gonna be on my *deen* and all of that. I'm tryna be a better person.'

'Jalaal.' He pauses and sighs. 'You know what, it ain't even that deep. If you wanna dip, then dip.' He shrugs his shoulders.

'Why you switching up?'

'You said you're on your *deen* and all that, so I ain't tryna tell you nothin'. Can't fight religion.'

'So that's where you draw the line. If it wasn't for Islam then you'd try persuade me?' Irritation pulsates through me.

'Allow it, Jalaal. It's calm. You're still my boy.' He nods reassuringly.

'Are you sure?' I remain composed.

'Nah fam, *wallahi*, I'm good, I'm your brother fam. It's all good.'

'All right, say no more.' I take it with a pinch of salt.

'So, what you gonna do instead?' His face is baffled.

'I don't know, I'm thinking 'bout going back to college to finish that design course and see where to go from there. Try start my own clothing business.' I hesitate in telling him my plans.

His face cringes before he masks it. 'Is that you yeah? Entrepreneur. Say less fam. Remember me when you leave the hood,' he jokes.

'Fam, you're leaving the hood with me!'

'I'm only leaving if it's better P's on the other side, which it ain't!' he laughs to himself.

'Shaah, I ain't gon' lie. Your parents are together, your older sisters are doing bits. One at uni and the other has a good job. Why you even on this road life?' I'm done with holding back.

'My family ain't all that you know. The road has always had my back. This is my real family. Not the one at home. You're my family.'

I don't understand why Shaah never opens up. I see no reason why he's on road. It's not even like he needs the P's. His family could buss him anytime.

But I don't bother fighting back. 'Anyways fam. Whatever you do. You know I got your back.' But I'm not sure that I do.

Shaah leaves before Hals and Habo Hani get back home.

'Ibrahim, Jalaal, come help with the shopping,' Hals shouts from downstairs.

We go downstairs to find bare Lidl shopping bags.

'Habo, I tell you all the time if you go Sainsbury's, you can get my discount!'

'*Iska aamus*, and just put everything away,' she snaps.

She isn't in a good mood. I start unpacking the shopping. I take the bag with the vegetables and fruits and start placing them in the fridge. Hals slides besides me, hands placed firmly on her hips.

'So . . .' I continue unpacking.

'So, what?' Hals is agitated.

'I have an idea about doing something special for Sabs's results day and I need your help.'

She swings her head to me, a grin emerging. 'Another surprise? Tell . . . me . . . more.'

This time, I want to rent an apartment so we can have some quality time. It's not like I can call her here or go to hers. I wanna order Sabs's favourite food, watch Netflix and chill, make sure we get a good view of the city. I know Sabs, she's the homebody type, she won't want a shisha date. She likes to be comfortable.

'Surprisingly, that isn't a bad idea.' She nods along. 'But, one thing, are you gonna decorate the apartment?'

'That's where I need your help.'

'I can do that. Easy. And I know how to make it extra special. Gotta buy the right things.' Still grinning with her full set of teeth.

'How?'

'Can you drive?' she asks. 'You got your licence yeah?'

'Yeah, I do but I haven't driven in a hot second. What the hell am I gonna do with a car?'

'Jalaal, you live in one of the most beautiful cities in the world and you spend all your time in ends. Drive around central, play music and embrace your youthfulness. When I got my Corsa at seventeen, best believe I was picking up all the girlies and doing loops around Piccadilly Circus and Tower Bridge. No motive, just vibes. Then take her to the apartment.'

I scoff. 'That sounds so moist. But I'm on it. That sounds like some romantic shit right there.'

'Right, I'm getting you a car to drive around.' She glances at me. 'I'll get you insured on my Audi A1.'

'Really? That's lit. I'm down.' I try to contain my excitement.

'Looks like we have a plan. Send that money over now,' she smiles.

This girl is forever rinsing my money.

CHAPTER 36

SABRINA

4*.32 a.m.*
Today is the day and I'm starting to freak out. Am I actually making it out of the ends? Soon it'll be 8 a.m. and UCAS will publish the results of my life online. I can't believe it.

I message Liyah.

> Are you awake????

Liyah
Yes lmfao, I can't fall asleep. Wallahi what is this?

> Nerves sis, nerves.

Liyah
We gonna do this, I believe in us.

> 100%.

I click the sleep button of my iPhone and place it on my side desk. I can't risk the radiation under my pillow. I close my eyes and try to concentrate on sleeping. I envision how everyone would react if I got into Warwick. Dad would be over the moon. Tasha would be overly gassed (mainly because she will finally get her own room). Izzy would be distraught at the fact that I'm leaving. Liyah and I would be doing bits. Jalaal would shower me with love and visit me every other weekend as he promised.

He is literally the rock that I need in my life.

I force my mind back to sleep.

5.37 a.m.

Is that really the time? Never in my life have I wanted to dash this iPhone across my room and hope it smashes against the wall. God, please help me sleep and naturally wake up.

Buzz.

Not long to go, I know you're gonna smash it. Love you long time, J xx

I genuinely have the best boyfriend in the entire world. I'll reply to him in a few hours with either tears of joy or tears of sadness.

6.03 a.m.

My eyes have barely been closed for twenty minutes. I'm tempted to open my blinds and allow the sunlight to forcefully wake me up. Until the moment of truth.

I can't be refreshing UCAS on my phone till 8 a.m. though, my eyes will fall out of my sockets. *Give it one more try, Sabs.* I promise myself that if I wake up, I won't look at my phone. I'll force myself to look at the ceiling.

7.28 a.m.

So, I haven't stuck to my promise as I'm currently glaring at my phone screen. Only thirty minutes left. I quickly check UCAS, praying they'll miraculously want to publish results earlier.

No update.

I twist open the blinds and allow the sunlight to seep through.

I can't stomach any food, nor do I want any. I don't want to be on my phone because I know that the minutes will drag like hours. Even scrolling through Instagram will make me anxious.

I place my Aztec embroidered cushions under my pillow and prop myself upwards. I close my eyes and allow myself to be consumed by my consciousness.

7.59 a.m.

It's time.

I turn my phone on 'Do Not Disturb'. I don't want Insta notifications distracting me. Shit. My fingers are shaking, and I can feel my heart in my mouth. This is too much.

I open up Safari. The UCAS page is still open from before. All I need to do is press the refresh button and I'll know. My thumb hovers over the circular arrow on the top right-hand corner of my phone. I take in a deep breath.

Welcome back Sabrina
Your status
Congratulations! Your place at University of Warwick to study Philosophy, Politics and Economics (PPE) has been confirmed.

I let out one ugly sob that is promptly followed by snot and tears. My blood pulses through my veins. Everything in my head goes quiet. I fucking did it. I actually did it. All those years of hard work. Endless revision notes. Anxiety-filled nights. The doubt. The hope. The struggle. The possibility. Everything amalgamated to this very moment. And I've done it. I've finally done it. And I deserve this. *You fucking deserve this, Sabs.*

Dad, Izzy and Tasha slowly creep into my room, confused expressions on their faces.

'So?' Dad tilts his head to the side curiously.

'Did you get in?' Izzy asks.

I sob.

'Oh sis, don't worry about it.' Tasha hurries to me, arms reached out.

'I got in,' I mumble before she reaches me.

She stops. 'What?'

'I got into Warwick.' I manage my first smile.

'Waaaaaaaahy, that's my gyal,' my dad's deep voice softly booms.

I get off my bed and Tasha embraces me in her skinny arms. Izzy squishes her arms around my stomach and Dad engulfs us all in a cuddle.

'My beautiful girls. I am so proud of you all.'

I can taste the salty tears in my mouth. At this point, I honestly don't know who they belong to.

'I love yuh all,' I cry.

'Me too,' Tasha chimes.

'I love you, Daddy,' Izzy echoes.

We all remain embraced together for what I wish could be forever.

As I get ready to go to school to collect my results, I open up Jalaal's chat.

I got in

He replies immediately.

Jalaal

I'm so fucking proud of you Sabs. You did it!

I love youuuuuuu, you're the best.

Jalaal

I love you too. Ima catch you later this afternoon after you done celebrating with your fam.

See you later

For what may be the last time, I meet Liyah at Paddington Station. Even though both Liyah and I received our acceptances into Warwick and UCL, I still want to know my grades. For this special occasion, I have the pleasure of Tasha and Izzy strolling behind me like fangirls. After our long family cuddle earlier this morning, Liyah FaceTimed me to let me know she got into UCL, and it was such a fucking emotional experience to feel that. We both did it!

I notice her lingering by the station turnstiles. She has her natural curls in a high pony with two long strands down either side of her face. She's dressed in a white T-shirt and a navy pinafore dress that's complemented with white Vans. I glance over myself and am overwhelmed by how underdressed I am. Puma cycle shorts, my notorious white Air Forces and an oversized graphic tee.

'LIYAHHHHH!' I shout at her as she runs into my arms.

She notices Tasha and Izzy, giving them huge hugs too. She's a proper hugger.

'What? I'm actually special enough to have the Campbell family in my presence.'

'Don't gas us,' I laugh.

'We aren't that special,' Tasha adds.

I wonder where she gets her sass from. I hold Izzy's hand and tell the squad we need to head off because the anxiety festering inside me is becoming unbearable.

'Promise me you won't open the results without me?' Izzy pleads.

'I promise I won't.'

Liyah and I collect our A4 vomit-scented brown envelopes and practically run back outside to where Izzy and Tasha wait in the courtyard. On the way, we bump into Ms Ross who congratulates us both and squeezes us with hugs. I'm surprised at Liyah's patience. I thought she would've opened them in the classroom.

She gives me a quick, reassuring smile.

'Sabs.' Izzy runs over to me while Tasha follows behind her, arms crossed.

I cautiously hand over my envelope to Izzy and she clutches it excitedly.

'Don't get too gassed Izzy, we have to open them together on the count of three,' Liyah tells her.

'OK, OK!'

'So, I'm going to count down from three and when I say "open", then we will open it together. Does that make sense?'

Izzy nods her head.

'Three, two, one, OPEN!'

Simultaneously, Liyah and Izzy pull out the white sheets from the envelope. Liyah's eyes whizz around the paper and when they focus, her pupils dilate.

'OH MY GOD!' she yells and jumps in excitement. 'I got three A's, I did it!'

She smashed it! I'm so happy for her.

Izzy's eyebrows are furrowed in confusion.

'I don't understand it,' she exclaims. 'There's so many numbers and letters.'

Tasha peers over Izzy's shoulders. Her face relaxes and she smiles warmly. She places her finger on the sheet to help Izzy. I'm beyond anxious now.

'English is . . . "A"!'

A slight tension eases off my shoulders and Tasha moves her finger again.

'Politics is "A" with a small star.' Tasha and I softly chuckle.

The chatter of students in the courtyard blur and all I can focus on is Izzy. 'And . . . Sociology . . . you got another "A" with a star!'

Tears fall down my face. Tasha wraps me in a big hug and Izzy jumps up and down yelling, 'YAY YAY YAY!'

'I'm so proud of you sis, you're actually doing bits,' Tasha whispers in my ear and I feel the wetness from her tears slide over my cheeks. My heart is both lifted and hurt at the same time. This year has been a fucking whirlwind and I'm just so happy that I can finally get some kind of peace.

I unwrap myself from Tasha and place my hands on her shoulders – looking into her teary eyes. 'That means the world to me. You're gonna do better than me, so I'll be waiting to celebrate you.'

She sobs harder and rests her head on to my chest. It's only at this point that I realize Izzy and Liyah are stood there watching us.

'We did it,' Liyah mouths to me.

'I know,' I mouth back.

*

McDonald's breakfast always hits the spot. Liyah devours her Egg McMuffin meal while the rest of us munch on our pancakes. I need to drench mine in syrup to get the right texture. *Sabs, you're too picky sometimes.*

'So, have you told . . .' Liyah quietens her voice and mouths 'Jalaal'.

'Yes, I have, we will be celebrating later,' I grin.

'Celebrating, yeah?' She wriggles her eyebrows.

'Don't get excited,' I snort. 'But don't forget I'm telling Dad that I'm staying with you.'

Jalaal had asked for my curfew and I told him that I don't have one, which is a semi-lie. I technically don't have a curfew, but I think Dad will be OK with me 'staying over at Liyah's'.

'I got you, sis. Anyways, I can't wait for you to spill the tea tomorrow morning.' She takes a bite into her hash brown.

'There will be no tea.' I roll my eyes.

'Don't worry Liyah, I'll find out for you.' Tasha adds her two cents.

I didn't even realize she was eavesdropping on our conversation. Izzy is busy, consumed with her McDonald's toy. Thank God.

'Natasha!' I widen my eyes at her.

'You're not that discreet, sis.'

I'm not sure about this dress. Jalaal hasn't told me where we are going or what I should wear. He just mentioned that I need to be ready for 7 p.m. What is up with boys and not letting girls know about dress codes? It's so jarring. I think it's always better to be overdressed than underdressed so I've settled for a LBD, you can never go wrong with a little black dress. I know Jalaal will never take me somewhere where I need to wear heels, especially after the PTSD from the party we met at. I pair my outfit with all-white New Balances. He always appreciates my crep game. Or lack of.

Make-up? I settle with a beat face, dark eyeshadow and even some false lashes. It is *my* day after all. The thought of having my hair tied up is stress-inducing so I've decided to wear my hair natural. The 3C curls are here to stay. *You're finally feeling like yourself.*

My phone pings.

Jalaal
I'm around the corner. Black Audi A1.

Coming now xx I reply.

I slip on a cropped leather jacket, grab my Calvin Klein side bag that has all my essentials, and walk out the house.

I turn the corner from our flats and am surprised to see Jalaal's head propped comfortably against the headrest of the driver's seat. Am I seeing things?

I pace towards him, and he shoots me a cheeky smile while revving the engine. I fling open the passenger door and plump myself next to him excitedly. He looks me up and down in awe.

'Beautiful,' he breathes.

'So, you're whipping now?'

'Just for today, Hal's treat.' His brown eyes stay still.

'Aww, you're adorable. Tell her thanks, as well!'

'Buckle up, B,' He releases the hand brake and presses on the acceleration.

We've driven for what feels like forever to the other side of London. We pull up to a part of Canary Wharf that consists of high-rise apartments and lavish city hotels. Jalaal stops the car by the security box of one of the towers and keys in a code on the touch screen. The diamond-patterned shutters begin to rise open. It leads to an underground car park that Jalaal drives us into. As we slowly drive through, I'm amazed by the expensive cars that I'm surrounded by: Mercedes-Benz GLAs, Lamborghinis, Rolls-Royces and loads of other luxurious cars. This is gonna sound so weird, but this is the kinda life I envision for myself. I can imagine myself having my own apartment in this area and having my sisters over for sleepovers and brunches. It warms me.

'I love you Jalaal, so fucking much.'

He abruptly stops the car and turns his head to me. 'Sabrina, I love you.'

By now our eyes are welling up. We are both actually wet wipes.

'Fuck.' I laugh. 'Just go park the car, I can't wait in suspense any more.'

He laughs too. 'You're bare high maintenance, you know.'

'Shut up, you don't even know what that means,' I joke.

He rolls his eyes.

I get out of the car and pull down my black dress, which has somehow managed to ride up my thighs during the long car journey here.

'You're gonna hate me but,' Jalaal starts.

'But what?' I tilt my neck.

He's dangling a blindfold while he looks at me with a face of fake innocence.

'Really?' I raise my eyebrows.

'Sorry,' he mouths.

'You do realize that my eyes have been open this whole car

journey, like I know we are in some boujee area.'

'That ain't the point.'

It's like dating your match in stubbornness. I surrender and walk over to him, sighing extra loud.

'High maintenance,' he mutters.

He delicately places the blindfold over my eyes, making sure that every inch is completely covered. I know he's gassed from the way his fingers are trembling.

'All right then, lead the way!'

It takes us fifteen minutes to get through a few doors (including a very awkward revolving door) and up a lift to the eighteenth floor. And I know it's the eighteenth floor because the automated lady's voice on the lift announced it. Not so smart Jalaal, eh?

'OK, you're gonna be able to take it off in a moment,' he whispers in my ear. 'Give me a sec.'

I hear a beep and a front-door handle turn.

'Sabs, I'm gonna take your blindfold off.'

'Too late, I can do it myself.' I rip the blindfold off my eyes.

In front of me is a candle-lit corridor with a trail of lilac-coloured rose petals. I recognize the scent of the candles – fresh linen, my favourite. Decorated along the high ceilings are confetti-filled rose-gold balloons that have 'congratulations' written cursively on them.

The tears begin to roll. Jalaal wraps his arms around my waist from behind, smothering his cheek on to mine and smearing my tears on his face.

'Walk in, babes.'

I enter the apartment cautiously, walking towards the door at the end of the corridor that has an 'open me' sign hanging off the handle.

I carefully tread around the candles with Jalaal's guidance.

I wrap my fingers around the door handle. 'Am I gonna cry more?' I half laugh.

'Course you are,' Jalaal smiles.

I turn and push open the door.

I'm met by a window wall with a scenic view of East London. It's speckled with glitzy beaming lights from the towers of the HSBC and Citi buildings. The smell is divine. The open-plan living room is dimly lit with candles and spotlights in the kitchen area. Scattered along the window wall are lilac-coloured rose petals and more balloons on either side. There is a huge flat-screen TV in the living space that is set on the Netflix home page with a coffee table in front of it, decorated by my favourite snacks. Sweet and salted popcorn, Galaxy Salted Caramel and McCoy's Thai Sweet Chilli crisps. And there are even Volvic bottles of water. My heart leaps.

'How did you do all this?'

'Hals helped me decorate.' His dimple deepens.

My eyes focus on the dark-grey marble island in the kitchen. There are Vapiano containers on the table and a gift bag.

Jalaal clocks me eyeing up the gift bag. 'Open it,' he says.

With a sense of urgency, I dive into the bag and find the new-season Chelsea shirt in there.

'No way!' My jaw drops.

'Yeah way,' he mocks.

I embrace him. 'What haven't you done?'

'I was gonna do a heart shape of petals on the floor, but I knew you would cringe out.' Jalaal brings me out of my trance.

'It's the best decision you've made.' My voice is hoarse, and my face is slobbered in snot and tears. 'Ugh, you've ruined my make-up.'

'You always look better without it.' He twirls me around and kisses me on the lips, his mouth intertwining with the saltiness of my tears.

'Bare salty,' he comments.

'Kiss me more.'

He presses his face against mine and we continue kissing till my tears are no more.

'This Vapiano is so fucking good.' I scuffle down my arrabbiata (with tagliatelle of course). 'I can't believe it tastes this good when it's not fresh. How did you do it?'

'Habo always told me the best way to reheat pasta is in the microwave. And that's what you watched me do. Put it in the microwave.'

'Haha, very funny, we get it, you understand sarcasm now.' I mimic his tone and lightly slap his chest.

He grabs hold of my hand and doesn't let go. My left hand is still holding the fork in my mouth. I slowly use my teeth to scrape the pasta off and remove the fork. He looks at me intently as I slowly chew my food. Still staring back at him, I place my fork in the Vapiano container and set it on the coffee table and turn my body to him. He takes hold of my other hand and breathes in a deep sigh.

Suddenly, the room goes silent. The TV in the background becomes mute and I'm no longer attuned to my surroundings. The lights are off, with only the candles burning and radiating warmth. I focus on Jalaal, and I feel his whole presence. His chest rising and falling as he breathes. His Adam's apple bobbing as he swallows. He's rubbing his thumbs against both my palms and looking at me closely. *I wonder if there's any pasta sauce on my face.*

Jalaal takes a gulp of air. 'Look Sabs, I know we are in an

apartment, and we have time together, finally. But . . .' He pauses. 'There's something that you need to know.'

Shit, I'm scared. Is he back on road? I nod along, pretending my heart isn't racing.

'There isn't any pressure or expectation for anything to happen.'

Sabs, what is your man talking about?

He notices my confused expression.

'I mean like sexually and stuff. We are here for you and for you only. I know you said you haven't got a curfew so we can go home whenever you want, but if you wanna stay over, I'll sleep on the sofa here if that's what you want. Or if you wanna cuddle in the bed. We can do that too. Just know that yeah basically, I want you to be bare comfortable and know I'm not thinking sideways. *Wallahi*, I just wanna make today special for you. And every day after.'

I'm happy that he's done this. I'm always wishing that we could have our own space, even if it's just for a couple hours, and he's done that. I was initially a little bit apprehensive about what Jalaal was expecting from me in an apartment, but that was just my insecurities coming through. I trust him. And I trust that he cares for me and would never rush anything. He's put me at ease. It's like the weight of something I was carrying has been lifted off my shoulders. I smile at him.

'Jalaal,' I sigh in relief. 'Thank you for making me feel comfortable. Firstly, I need to take advantage of this freedom. And I would never let you sleep on this sofa. I know I'm high maintenance OK, but I'm not a bloody dictator lol.'

'Why you always gotta say lol. It's bare cringe.'

'Oh, my days, let me finish my speech!'

'OK, OK, go on.'

'I really appreciate it and all of this, you make me feel so special. I know you don't have any expectations and I don't feel any pressure. And um yeah . . . I love you.' I raise my head to look at him.

'Ily2,' he jokes.

'Say it properly,' I sigh. He knows this agitates me.

'All right, all right, I love you too.' He leans over me, kisses my lips, and gently presses me down against the sofa.

'I wanna go to the bedroom,' I slip out.

'We don't have to if you don't want to,' he reassures me.

'But I want to. This sofa is also very uncomfortable for my back.'

'If we are goin' then you gotta cover your eyes, cos there's another surprise.' He smiles modestly.

'Jalaaaaaaaal! You didn't have to.' *You are being spoilt and it feels so good.*

'Of course I did, you're my girl.'

I raise my eyebrows at him; he knows I find that patronizing.

'We are each other's.' He corrects himself.

'OK fine, no blindfold though. I'm going to cover my own eyes.' My stubbornness prevails in all situations.

'I'm good with that.' He leaps up and holds his hand out for me.

I lace my fingers in between his and he pulls me up. He snakes his arms around my waist, nuzzling himself close to me.

'Cover your eyes then,' he instructs me.

I let out another exhausted sigh and press my fingers against my closed eyelids. I let him direct me to the room. I take a step in, and my feet sink into the soft carpet. I allow my toes to wriggle in its cushiness. My nostrils are met with a delicate lavender incense and a weird feeling of warmth emanates from the room.

'OK, you can open your eyes now.'

I blink my eyes open and see the bed yet again covered in lilac-coloured petals and a Selfridges bag placed on it.

'This whole surprise! And now Selfridges? Is a ring coming next?'

'You got jokes init. Go open it please.'

Unable to control myself, I unwrap the box, carefully unwinding the beautifully gifted bag and removing layers of gift wrapping. Inside are SKIMS pyjamas and slippers.

'I didn't think you would want to sleep over but just in case, I wanted to make sure you sleep like a princess. I know we're both not designer fiends, but SKIMS silk pyjamas are too comfy to pass up on. Anyways, I got a good discount on them,' Jalaal says.

'Jalaal, I can't accept this! It's beautiful. Way more than I deserve.'

'Listen, I want you to have this, you have to accept it. I want you to have the best, now and when you're going to uni,' he says so genuinely.

I can't believe this. *Well, it's best to start believing.* 'OK. I appreciate it so much, ohmagawd, I don't know how I feel about this,' I chuckle.

'Like a princess, I hope.'

'Of course.'

I carefully place the gift box on the bedside table and push myself back on to the bed, resting my head on the elevated pillow. I watch Jalaal. *My man, my man, my man.* His eyes widen at my motion and he wastes no time in climbing the bed to reach me.

He comes back on top of me and my body softens against his touch. We're still fully clothed, but I feel naked. His hands cup my face, and he gazes deeply into my eyes.

'I'm so fucking proud of you. Do you know how gassed I am to call you my girlfriend?'

My heart is whole. Jalaal makes me feel whole. He softly kisses my neck, his lips trailing up to my face. He pauses at the corner of my lips. Then our mouths collide. Warm and wet. I let him take charge as his lips move in rhythm. This feels just as magical as our first kiss. He nibbles my top lip and I quietly moan in response. I part open my mouth and allow his tongue to come in. He tastes good. His right thumb caresses my ear, sending sensations downwards.

I notice Jalaal pull his shirt off and his broad shoulders emerge, propping him up on top of me. The cute hairs on his chest remind me of the man he promises that he's going to be. I pull off my top and bra, our bare skin finally mixing.

We remove all our clothing until Jalaal is completely naked and I'm in my panties. The panties that I bought from Victoria's Secret just in case this day would ever come.

His hot breath hovers over my panties and I can feel its warmth touch my lips.

'Sabs baby, can I make you feel good?'

'Yes.' I press him against me.

He uses his teeth to pull off my underwear and I get goose bumps as I feel his plump lips trace from my hips down to my feet. Jalaal licks his tongue against my right leg, moving upwards towards my inner thigh, and then presses his lips against my lower lips. My neck crooks back as I suck in a breath and let out a soft moan. He opens up my lips and trickles the tip of his tongue in an up-and-down motion. Blood rushes there and it begins to pulsate. It feels so good, and I don't want it to stop. I want him to stay down there forever. He firmly holds on to my legs and pleasures me for what feels like eternity.

*

We both lie facing each other, one of Jalaal's hands stroking my face and the other one intertwined with my hand. I want to go all the way.

'Jalaal?'

'Yes?'

'I think . . . I think I want . . .'

'We don't have to do anything.'

'No, no, no, I want to.' I'm being honest. 'I'm ready.'

'Wait . . .' He half leaps up. 'I need to go get a condom. Can you wait like ten mins while I go to the shop? Sorry to kill the mood, but I didn't bring any, I didn't think we . . .'

'Stop,' I halt him.

He gives me a confused look.

I reach over to my CK bag on the floor and fumble through to find the array of condoms I picked up from the sexual health clinic when I went to get tested.

He shyly chuckles when I hand him a random-flavour condom.

'Have you been tested?' I hold his gaze.

'Yes, at the start of the year,' he says with a straight face, opening it. 'I haven't been with anyone since.'

My muscles relax.

'Just let me know if you're in any pain, OK?' I nod and we both take a deep breath.

'Always.' I lie back, close my eyes and wait.

'Um Sabs, could you open your legs a bit?'

'Oh, sorry.' I'm embarrassed. I part my legs, and I don't feel anything but an empty breeze. *Is this meant to happen?*

Silence.

'Is something wrong, Jalaal?' I ask him worriedly.

'Nothing at all.' He holds my hands. I can feel him trembling. He's as nervous as I am. 'I . . . I love you. And I just want you to know that I love you and we are only doing this if you want to.'

My heart warms.

'I want to.' I press myself against him again, letting him know that I'm ready.

He sucks his breath in, and I sense the mixture of pain and pleasure he's feeling.

Afterwards, Jalaal and I crave dessert, so we drive to the nearest Creams Cafe. We cruise through Canary Wharf, London Bridge and Waterloo. The streets are empty, and I'm in my new SKIMS PJs, my head out the window, letting the warm night air brush my face while Roddy Ricch's 'Late at Night' blasts through the speaker.

CHAPTER 37

JALAAL

It's mad that I feel like Sabs is my everything and ever since she came into my life, she's given me purpose. It's 5 a.m. The sun is rising, a line of light on her body. She's lying bare in front of me and it's the most beautiful thing ever. Not gonna lie, I'm bare gassed about this moment right now.

I wrap myself around Sabrina in a spooning position and hold her tightly into my chest. Her body temperature is warm, and I can hear her heart rate starting to slow down. It's a mad experience to have her lying in my arms. All I want to do is take care of her forever.

She turns around to face me. I look at her. Like properly. Her face is beautiful, speckled with cute freckles, her hair messy, and her collarbones are bare. My babes is so fucking peng.

'What is it?' She's going all shy on me.

'I love you.'

'I love you too, Jalaal.' She traces her fingertips against my lips.

She gives me a peck and my heart legit feels like it's going to jump out of my chest.

'I wanted to tell you something,' I say.

Her body immediately stiffens up.

'Trust me, it's nothing bad.'

She relaxes.

'I'm going to go back to college and finish my A Levels. I spoke to Ms Ross, and she said I could come back on a probation ting as an exception.'

'Really?' she grins.

'Yeah, really. It's about time I do something with my life, and not gonna lie, you did inspire me a bit.'

'I'm so happy for you.' She cups my face. 'I will support you either way.'

I wake Sabs up at 10.30 a.m. to eat breakfast together. Hals messaged me last night to let me know she was going to pick up the car at 10 a.m. She also said that I need to leave the apartment by 11 a.m. and drop the keys back in the letterbox once I leave. The way this girl tells me what to do is actually mad.

'We need to leave in like thirty minutes, do you think you can get ready and pack up?' I ask Sabs as we scoff our croissants.

'You underestimate my efficiency.'

'I dunno. You could be one of those girls with two-hour skincare routines.' I shrug my shoulders.

'You wish.' She shakes her head.

'Also,' I hesitate. 'We gonna catch a cab back to ends. Is that OK?'

'Yeah, that's fine but what happened to the car?'

'Hals collected it this morning while you were knocked out, she's always got somewhere to be.'

'I was that tired? Usually I'm a light sleeper.'

'Who lied to you?' I laugh at my joke.

Sabrina spends twenty minutes getting ready and we use the final ten minutes clearing up the mess of balloons, candles and petals. I purposely wash the dishes to impress Sabrina, which is successful. I tease her that she needs to 'unlearn her gender stereotypes'. She laughs and jokes that Hals has trained me well.

We're good to go at 11 a.m. and the cab aims to drop Sabs off first.

'Hey.' Sabs holds on to my hand. 'Thank you so much for everything, I really appreciate it. I appreciate you. Best boyfriend, yeah.'

'You deserve it.' I don't want the cab driver to hear us. 'I would do it over and over again. My girl is doing up A* and going to a top university, of course we need to celebrate.'

'You're too cute!'

I'm not that moist. 'Cute? You mean I'm a G.'

She rolls her eyes and squeezes my hand tight. 'Anyways, we are going Carnival in a few days. It's your first time, right?'

'Yeah, kinda looking forward to it,' I half lie. I'm not looking forward to the madness of Carnival, but I'm gassed to be spending time with my girl.

'It's gonna be so fun! Ima have to give you wines.'

I can't help but smile. I have the love of my life in front of me. I've got new family who love me. I'm off road. I'm going to college. I've got a future to look forward too. 'I'm not complaining.'

CHAPTER 38

SABRINA

I lost my virginity. Well, virginity is a social construct so let me rephrase that. I've had sex for the first time, with a boy that I really love. It was weird and wonderful. *That's one way to put it.*

I thought I'd be in excruciating pain and that my womanhood would be taken away from me. The truth is . . . it kinda naturally happened. And I didn't feel this big innate change afterwards. I was liberated, in an unusual way. *In the right way, though.*

Jalaal was patient and careful with me. And when it got uncomfortable, he stopped and reassured me. The love I felt in those moments is something I didn't believe I was capable of receiving from a guy. Especially Jalaal. *You were wrong Sabs.* And now, I can't wait to do it again. And I can't wait to tell Liyah.

I feel so silly for putting so much pressure on myself in having to *perform*, I definitely was giving into the male gaze. Reminds me of *The Great Gatsby*. I was worried about nothing because I can't wait to explore this side of my relationship with Jalaal more.

I was sore this morning, but I didn't want to tell him as I know he'd probably overreact and make a big deal out of it. Running around Canary Wharf looking for painkillers. It's OK though, the soreness has subsided.

It's not that I was actively practising celibacy, but I never had the desire to go out and seek sex. I wonder if God will see me less in his favour now that I have committed a sin. *Almost everyone you know has sex before marriage, Sabs, are they all going to hell?* That's true. God is all-forgiving, and to be honest, I don't even feel guilt. Am I meant to feel guilty because this feels like a natural thing that happened between two people who are deeply in love? I'm probably gonna marry him anyway, so what's the matter. *Sabs!* As long as I don't have a teen pregnancy, I don't think Dad will mind. *Slow down.*

I've been thinking about the first time I met Jalaal at Shanice's party; I never thought he would be this caring and attentive. *You were too judgy.* It's going to sound wild, but I genuinely love this guy so much and want to spend the rest of my life with him. I don't know if we have a soul tie, but I can't help feeling that this has cemented everything for me.

I told Dad that I would be celebrating yesterday, but let's be real, showing up at 2 p.m. the next day is a bit mad. I don't know if I can even justify that. He's due home from work any minute now and I'm legit shook of his reaction. Especially because he didn't call or text me to check up on me like he usually does.

I pull out my phone to text Liyah and spill the tea. Just as I'm about to unlock my phone, the front door opens. He's here.

I peep from the top of the staircase and see my dad waiting at the bottom in his work uniform. He's done an early shift today.

'Hey Dad.' I sweeten my voice.

'My golden child. When did you get home?'

Tasha is out with friends, so she can't chat shit on my behalf.

'Oh, a few hours ago. I slept at Liyah's house,' I lie. 'I know I'm not allowed to sleep over, but I was super tired after celebrating.

Sorry!' I rush downstairs to face him.

I pray the fact I bussed my exams and got into a Russell Group university has buttered him up.

'You know you're not allowed to.' He looks at me sternly. 'But I forgive you because I know that you needed to celebrate all your hard work. Never again though, you hear me?'

'Yes Dad.' I can't believe he's actually being calm about this. 'How was work?'

'It was all right. Let me get out my work clothes and shower, then we can talk over dinner.'

'All right,' I say too eagerly and rush upstairs into my room, closing the door.

I attempt to call Liyah but she doesn't answer. My phone pings and she texts that she can't answer because she's at a family function.

> Gurlllllllll. Let me fill you in about last night.

Liyah
Go on. I'm here sis.

I type out the first half of the night. I know that my fucking fingers are going to ache by the end of this.

Liyah
So, what happened after?

My best friend knows when there is more to a story.

> I did it! Finally a woman now. Jk Jk! It was nothing like I expected it to be. I thought I'd be crying the whole time in pain. But I kinda enjoyed it. Anyways, this is NOT a convo for texting.

Liyah

Yes Sabs!!! So happy for you.
You made it to womanhood. Let's FT later,
like you said, not for txting. Btw, what
you wearing for NHC?

Idk sis, wbu?

She sends me a picture of a red lace crop top and black denim shorts.

Liyah

Kl, ima bell you l8r.

I do something that I haven't done in ages. I snuggle in bed and read a book that isn't for an exam. *The Hate U Give*, my favourite book. I re-read it for what feels like the hundredth time. I know this sounds crazy because the book is somewhat tragic, but I love the political message, and I die for an interracial love story. I don't know if that is a by-product of being mixed-race, but I love it. Liyah would say that I'm obsessed with *struggle love* and maybe I am, I'm not ashamed. *You're living it*. There's something so powerful in beating the odds for love to prevail. That's why I hope that Mum will return one day. I have a feeling that she will.

CHAPTER 39

JALAAL

Spending Carnival with Sabs is a good change. I haven't actually done Carnival properly before. I've only ever been to after-party motives with the mandem.

Sabs looks banging. My little yardie babes. No make-up and her hair in two big braids. She's wearing black cycle shorts and a cropped yellow top, and is parading the Jamaican flag on her back. She's got some mash-up shoes on her feet though, but we ain't going to talk about that. I'm gonna have to let that slide, she can wear dead creps today.

The most adorable thing is that she's got a Somaliland bracelet on her wrist. I'm wearing both a Jamaican and a Somaliland bracelet on my wrist. If any Somalis caught me slipping, they'd look at me sideways for wearing the Jamaican one. But she's mine and I'm hers so I don't give a fuck.

We get off the train at Notting Hill Station and wait at Paul's bakery. I'm doing boyfriend duties today. There are so many fucking people on the streets, but I'm happy with Sabs stood in front of me, waiting together for her friends. She turns around and lifts a Volvic bottle of water to my lips.

'Babes, what is it?' I ask.

'It's water, you nitty. You're looking kinda parched, drink some.' She taps it on my lips.

'You look kinda parched,' I mock her voice.

I take a few gulps and feel the coolness travel down to my stomach. Shit, I *am* thirsty.

'I told you.' She twirls one of her braids in between her fingers.

I pull her into my chest, squeeze her in my arms and I kiss her hard against her forehead.

'Jalaal,' she groans into my chest.

I loosen my grip on her so she's able to arch her head backwards. I press my forehead against hers.

'Who told you to take care of me, huh?' The husk in my voice comes out.

'Don't get used to it.'

She's too sassy for her own good sometimes.

'I love you, you know that.'

'I love you too.' She rests on me.

I hold her protectively in my arms and turn to face the crowd in front of us. There are so many fucking people. So many fucking shades. And so many bottles, cans, glasses all over the place.

The feds are everywhere. At first, it makes me tense, but then I remember I have nothing to hide. I'm free of that. Not gonna lie though, having so many of them at this celebration is wrong. People are here for good vibes. It's a fucking cultural celebration. It's bare intimidating the way they are stood in every corner, screw-facing.

'Saaaaaaaabz.'

Sabrina slowly unwinds herself from me and our eyes search for the source of the voice.

Liyah emerges from the crowd, her long thick curls winding

down to her waist. I thought Liyah was coming with others. Sabs walks right into her arms, and they immerse in chatter. They are talking so fast that I have no idea what they're saying. There's just a lot of 'oh my god' and 'seriously'.

'Yo Jalaal,' Liyah says to me.

'You good, Liyah?'

We give each other a quick side hug. Them awkward ones.

'Yeah, never thought I'd see you like this . . . at Carnival,' she jokes.

'Neither did I,' I smile. 'Anyways, thought you were coming with more people?'

'Yeah, a few of my cousins are coming through.'

I'm going to be chilling with Moroccans today. That's new. Shaah said he's coming thru later with Nico. I don't think it'll be a problem.

'SABRINA! JALAAL! Is that you two, yeah.'

Our heads snap in the direction of the voice, trying to make sense of the countless faces in the crowd. Soon enough, Shanice emerges dripped in red costume; she must be part of Mas band. I try not to look at her as she half hugs me and pounces on Sabrina, completely ignoring Liyah.

'Oh my god, you two are too cute. And you lots met at my party, innit? That's craze-e!' she squeals.

'You look good Shanice, body is bodying,' Sabs gushes.

'Mi haffi look good yuh know, a Carnival Time!' she twirls and shimmies.

I glance the other way.

'This is my friend, Liyah,' Sabs introduces her.

'Hey girl.' Shanice eyes her before smiling.

'You all right,' Liyah replies.

Sensing the slight awkwardness, I randomly add my two cents. 'What you saying Shanice though, Carnival lit?'

'Yes, you better hold Sabs's wines you know, her waist don't play. I hope you can handle it, rudeboy,' she jokes.

'You're too funny!'

'Trust me. Got to go but love seeing you all. Stay blessed.' She waves, before running back into the crowd.

'Anyways, shall we go?' Liyah breaks the awkward silence, and we all move on.

CHAPTER 40

SABRINA

I have loved Carnival ever since my parents started taking me as a five-year-old. Obviously, only on Family Day. I have fond memories of the sun glazing, steel drums banging, clothes smothered in powdered colour and us freely dancing. As I've grown older, I've figured out which floats are my fave, which houses have the cleanest and cheapest toilets, and where to get the best jerk chicken.

'Guys, we have to go to Rampage,' I shout to the others as we squirm through the crowd. I'm no different to a sardine.

'You love Rampage Sound System, we go every time!' Liyah moans. Rampage is pure vibes; they play everything from reggae to dancehall to hip-hop. It's not all the time soca and calypso.

'Yeah, and Jalaal hasn't been, so we are going.' I grin at them as we all interlock hands and manoeuvre through the people.

There is no surprise that when we get there, it's decorated with the colours of the Jamaican flag and filled with people our age. The bass of the sound system vibrates through my body, my heartbeat in sync with the music. The waft of weed lingers in the thick air. Bodies are moving and so are we. *This is the summer of your dreams, Sabs.*

It's getting to around 7 p.m. and this part of Carnival feels proper scatty. OK, visually it's not that scatty because we are in one of the richest parts of London; but it's more about the people. Along the pavements, outside flats and houses, there are loads of mandem stood around watching everyone intently. I can't lie, it is kind of intimidating, especially for me as a girl. It's a different vibe from earlier with the lively floats and colourful costumes.

I wonder how Jalaal is feeling though, he's doing Carnival sober. I'm proud that he's turned a new leaf and has stopped with the drugs and drinking. He's tryna focus on his future and be more religious and I respect that so much. Shaah and Nico joined us earlier and are walking ahead of us. It must be hard for Jalaal, navigating that friendship with Shaah. It's not that I hate Shaah, but there's something off about him. *Are you sure, Sabs?* He doesn't have Jalaal's back. I wonder if he ever has. I don't want to ruin the vibe so I don't say anything to Jalaal.

We are both following the crowd down the Carnival route. Jalaal is walking behind me, hands firmly gripped on my waist and his upper body looming over me. I feel safe. There's no chance of a random guy bending me over.

The crowd are dispersing, and I finally see the road in front of me. It's not like earlier when we were all mushed against each other.

'Babes, are you hungry?' Jalaal whispers into my ear. *Music to the ears – he's a finding a new way to your heart, through your stomach.*

'Ummm.' I try to decipher whether I'm hungry. I know I'm defo tipsy from the drinks I've had.

'I haven't seen you eat since we got jerk chicken from that stall like three hours ago. Let's get you some food to eat.'

'Cool, let's go get food. I kinda want to leave anyways.' I squeeze his hand.

'Say no more, let's get out of here. Shall we ask Shaah, Liyah and them lots if they wanna come?'

'Yeah, sure.' I hesitate, but convince myself this is a good idea for all of us to mesh. It's safer to stick together.

Jalaal calls out to Shaah and his friend Nico from the distance, and I call over Liyah and her cousins from behind us.

It's well past Carnival curfew and the streets are empty, except for us, really. The sun has set, and the streets of West London are scattered with empty cans, questionable liquids and discarded flags. It's kinda eerie seeing London in this state. To think that one million people were squirming through these streets today is crazy.

Everyone getting food turned into being banterful and boisterous as we make our way down the streets. Most of the stations are locked off and now we're getting deep into the depths of NW. No one's complaining. It's fun just being out late. Jalaal, Shaah and Nico are reminiscing on old school times. Liyah and I have our arms interlinked, chatting shit. Her cousins are goofing about and imitating the wines they were taking earlier. The streets are quiet apart from a few other people tryna find their bearings, just like us.

'Yo, mandem, I really need to piss,' Shaah shouts at us.

'We don't need to know that, go piss somewhere!' Liyah shouts back at him before cackling at me.

Shaah laughs, throws up his middle fingers, before running down a small residential side street. We all slow our pace and continue chatting.

After a few short minutes, I hear muffled shouting.

For a second, I think Jalaal went with him to tease. But I see him standing behind me. He looks confused.

'Babe, what's happening?' I nod towards the side street Shaah just went down.

I can now hear faint voices.

'Hold on.' Jalaal steps back to look down the street.

'Fuck, it's Shaah.' He stares at me. 'Don't move!'

My heart drops.

'What happened?' I ask, but he's already gone.

He's not leaving me here by myself.

'Sabs, what are you doing?' I hear Liyah call as I run after him. Nico clocks on and runs ahead of me.

I come to a halt when I see there are two boys with huge zombie knives cornering Shaah. They're wearing balaclavas and gloves. Shaah, who has blood dripping down his forehead, has his arm lifted, trying to defend himself.

'STOP!' I shout instinctively and then start crying.

Before I know it, my body is turned to face the other direction, and Jalaal is in front of me.

'What the fuck are you doing here? I told you NOT to come,' he yells at me.

Before I can respond, there's a deafening screech. Our necks snap in Shaah's direction.

I see the two boys with balaclavas run down the street in the opposite direction.

'Oi, hurry up fam!' one shouts at the other who just dropped his zombie knife.

My focus immediately shifts, and I see Shaah lying on the floor, a pool of blood around his head and chest.

I freeze. My whole body turns numb, and I can't move. I crook my neck slowly towards Jalaal. The fury in his eyes is scary. His fingers are trembling, and his knees weaken as I see him lose his balance.

'JALAAL!'

Without warning, he dashes towards Shaah. He pauses ever so slightly when passing the knife on the floor, before kicking it away. He runs towards Shaah, Nico not far behind him, and drops to his side. Jalaal's lips are moving, but I have no idea what he's saying. He places his ear against Shaah's chest for a few seconds. He then lifts himself upwards and shouts something incomprehensible. He begins to cry and starts shouting as if he's possessed.

'OI, YOU FUCKING PUSSYHOLES, COME BACK HERE.' Nico sprints in the direction in which the guys ran.

'Call a fucking ambulance, Sabs!' Jalaal screams at me. I'm twenty metres away from him and Shaah, and my fingers tremble to get my mobile out. Fuck. There's no service. The tears fall harder, and my heart is thumping in my ears.

Before I can even speak up to Jalaal, five figures swoosh in from all directions and floor him. They're pushing and grappling with Jalaal on the floor. Once I start blinking, and my vision clears, I see the police have Jalaal against the ground.

'LEAVE HIM ALONE!' I force my feet forward.

With every step, I feel the force of the world against me. *It's happening all over again.*

'STAY BACK YOUNG LADY!' one of the police officers shouts at me.

I can see Jalaal clearly on the floor now. His forehead is grazed and there's a cut with a bit of blood coming out.

'STOP HURTING HIM. YOU'RE HURTING HIM.' I start crying and push my back foot off the ground to get to him.

But this time, arms and hands hold me back. I cry louder and push harder.

'Sabs, leave it,' I hear a familiar voice tremble in my ear.

The background noise blurs into one.

'Sabs, it's me, it's Liyah. Stop sis, it's too late now. You can't get involved. Just hold back.'

The arms around my body. They're more than just Liyah's, it's her cousins too. There is no way that I'm getting out of this. I won't be able to save Jalaal. *You can't let him go, Sabs.*

I stay frozen in this locked embrace and look onwards. The rest of the police officers are bombarding Shaah, ripping his clothes off. I can't see too much because there are so many arms flinging about. The paramedics arrive and put Shaah on a portable stretcher. Oxygen masks and tanks. My heart plummets. The police have Jalaal in handcuffs and have thrust his body upwards. He keeps shouting at them.

'Is he OK? Is he alive? Please tell me he's going to live. Stop being a wasteman and tell me he's OK.' He's bawling his eyes out as the police push him in the opposite direction to Shaah. *He doesn't deserve this, not after everything.*

'GET BACK.' The police officers usher us away. They place a tape around us.

Everything is a blur. Flashing lights. People talking to me. The tears have strained my eyes. Liyah's hand grips mine. Hard. She's not letting me go. *What the fuck just happened, Sabs?*

'Excuse me. I'm going to need your statement,' a policewoman says.

She's hovering over me but I'm looking beyond her. *Jalaal.*

'Hello . . .' She waves her hand in my face.

'Sabs.' Liyah squeezes my hand.

I blink multiple times to force the salty tears out. She looks at me, worried. Her eyes are sympathetic.

'Did you see what happened?' she asks again.

'Ummm . . .' I struggle to find my voice. 'Yeah, I did.'

'Do you think you could provide a witness statement?'

All I can think about is if this will get Jalaal into trouble. *He's innocent. He was trying to protect his friend.*

I look at Liyah and she gives me a nod of reassurance.

I nod in agreement. She walks ahead of me, and I follow behind.

I wonder if people think I'm some kind of snitch. This is the only way to help Jalaal. I don't even know what he's been arrested for. I thought he stopped all that drug shit. *He did, Sabs.* I have no fucking idea what's going on and how to help Jalaal. This is too much for me. *You didn't sign up for this, Sabs.*

I sit next to the officer as she pulls out a red notebook.

She looks kindly at me and says, 'So, tell me what happened.'

CHAPTER 41

JALAAL

The police station is cold. The cell is disgusting. This meeting room is dark.

Arrested for attempted murder and affray. Apparently, I'm lucky because I'm seventeen and considered a child. I'm in a room with the duty solicitor and Hals, my appropriate adult. Habo Hani is too heartbroken to be here.

'How the fuck did this happen?' Hals clenches her fists.

I explain to my solicitor and Hals what *actually* happened. No details are missed out.

'We can get the attempted murder easily discontinued, there's eyewitnesses and luckily the victim is alive. The prosecution doesn't have a leg to stand on. The affray may be an issue because you have had a drugs possession offence where you got a Youth Caution. Might be tricky because the victim, Shaah Navid, was adjacently involved in that case. It could be complicated. I wouldn't be so worried though, we should be able to squash the affray charges as you were simply helping your friend. Seems like your other associate, Nico, was more motivated for revenge.'

'Will Jalaal get bail?' Hals asks.

His fingers tap against his laptop keys. I'm gonna be sick.

'If we can get the attempted murder charge dropped immediately, then he should be home.'

Hals starts crying.

'It's a lot. Just stick to the facts that we've gone through during the police interview. I need you to keep it together, Jalaal,' the duty solicitor instructs me.

I'm fucked.

There's a knock at the door.

'Are you guys ready?' a police officer asks.

'Yes.' My solicitor stands up.

'OK, come through.' The police officer ushers us out of the meeting room and into the interview room.

Why did you try to kill him? Are you part of a gang? Do you owe someone money? Did someone force you to do this? Why did you lead this disorder?

The interview room is dark blue, no windows. My solicitor, Hals and I are sat opposite the two police officers. They speak their formalities.

'You understand that we have reviewed the witness statements and CCTV. We will no longer be proceeding with the charges of attempted murder,' the wrinkly one says.

I exhale. Thanks Allah.

'However, we are still investigating the charge of affray.'

I look to my solicitor for reassurance. He nods at me repeatedly. I don't even know what that's supposed to mean. But I'm going to stick with what we have rehearsed. It's not a rehearsal for some show though, is it? It's my fucking life.

After a long-ass interrogation and Hals being threatened to be removed from the interview because she was interrupting too much, we finally make it out. The police officer tells me that I'm going back to my cell while he discusses my release with his boss.

'How long will it take?' I ask.

He looks at me with bare pity. 'Not too long.'

I'm fucking pissed that I got myself into this fucking situation. This was not in the fucking plan. I lost my whole fucking dad, and I promised him that I would pattern up. How the fuck am I supposed to fix up when these lot are on my case for no reason?

'JALAAL,' Hals snaps.

It's only then that I notice we are still in the interview room; my jaw is clenched hard, my fists are tight.

'We have to leave you, but I will wait for you outside the police station,' she says.

I check my solicitor for support but this brudda just looks at me blankly, continuing to nod half-heartedly.

I give Hals a goodbye hug and she starts bawling her eyes out again. I try hard to keep my tears in, because I know it's not good to show her that I'm suffering. I lift my shoulders up high and allow the police officer to escort me out of the interview room, back into my cell.

Just as the officer is unlocking the door, I find the courage to ask him.

'Is . . . my friend . . . OK?'

He looks at me confusedly.

'My best friend, Shaah, who got stabbed, is he alive?' I ask him desperately. 'I just need to know that I'm gonna see my brother again.'

One small tear escapes.

The officer sighs to himself – he knows he could get into trouble for telling me this. I couldn't give a fuck; I need to know if my best friend is alive. I can't lose another person in my life.

'He's alive but in a coma right now.' He forces a smile at me.

Fuck. A coma. He hasn't left me yet.

'All right, get in mate.' He ushers me into the cell.

The officer locks the door with a hard thud and the silence hits me quick. I make my way over to the bed and sit down. It's not a bed though. It's a slab of stone with a blue, flimsy plastic mattress on top. In front of me is a silver toilet bowl – no toilet paper. It fucking stinks too.

I deep my surroundings, it's fucking ugly. Four walls closing in on me. A window with barely any sunlight coming in. My parents didn't die for me to end up stuck in a prison cell.

Even when things are going well, something must come along and fuck things up. Ever since I came back from Hargeisa, all I've done is try my hardest to do things right. Stopped selling weed. Stopped drinking. Stopped smoking. Treating Sabrina like the queen she is. Spending more time with my family. Being on my *deen*. Back in education and doing somethin' with my life.

The only thing that I haven't done is let go of Shaah. He's been my best friend since I was single digits. The truth is that if he wasn't with us at Carnival, none of this would have happened to me. That's facts. For so long, I wasn't ready for that truth, but now, it's in front of me. Imagine if I was the one who got stabbed up today? Because that could've been an easy possibility. I love Shaah to the death of me. He is my boy. But this right now, it has to be a sign from God. It must be a sign from God.

CHAPTER 42

SABRINA

I've locked myself in my room. The hours have been excruciating. Everything is a blur. *How the hell did this happen, Sabs?*

Dad thinks that Shaah was a friend from school and I'm going through this 'state' because I witnessed a friend get stabbed. He has no idea I watched my boyfriend get beat by police and dragged away from me in handcuffs. And there ain't no way I can tell him. He'll believe Jalaal is a roadman and is getting exactly what he deserves. But Jalaal is not a roadman, he left that life. I can't face Dad right now. I don't have the capability to lie about something like this to him. And I can't have my dad disappointed and angry at me while I'm already going through all this shit.

Hals called to explain everything late last night. The police accused Jalaal of attempting to murder Shaah. *This is why our justice system is failing us.* That makes no sense at all. But they reviewed the evidence and realized that he's *obviously* innocent. They've released him under investigation for the charges of affray. I have to google what it is, and I'm shocked they think that Jalaal was involved in some kind of public disorder. I was literally with him the whole time, he did absolutely nothing wrong. *Am I also involved for being there, too?*

There's no word on how long it will take for Shaah to make a full recovery. But he will. I'm just glad that he's alive. I don't think Jalaal could survive losing another person in his life. My boyfriend has gone through too much grief. *God, why are you doing this?* My heart breaks for him. He doesn't deserve any of this. And neither do I. It's my whole boyfriend that's going through all of this. He's going to college, and he's patterned his job at Sainsbury's. He wants to start his clothing business. This is just how fucked up the police and court system are – it doesn't even make sense. *None of this makes sense, Sabs.*

I blame Shaah. And I don't feel bad saying that. Shaah is the reason that Jalaal is in this situation. The truth is, if Shaah wasn't hanging around us, this would never have happened. Shaah is also Jalaal's best friend and I'm not in the position to tell him who he can and can't hang around with. It's too late now. *Sabs, you're his girl-friend, you have a right to set boundaries.*

There's no reason in hypothesizing, I need to speak to Jalaal. He should be getting released any minute now this morning, I'm just waiting on his phone call.

Ring.

'Finally!' I exhale.

'You don't wanna know the madness I been through. It's OK now, *alhamdulillah*. I'm home now!' He sounds almost normal.

'What happened? I was so worried; those police officers are so fucked up!'

'Trust me! They will call me when they have decided the outcome, but it'll be light work, I'm not tryna let it affect me, I'm innocent.' He sounds brave; his voice doesn't falter. There's no despair, not like when he lost his dad. *Well, duh, it's a different situation, Sabs.* I hope it's not an act. It doesn't seem like it. 'Just going to carry on patterning my life. I'm more worried 'bout you. Are you OK? Those were some fucked-up scenes. I never want you to see shit like that again.'

'I'm OK Jalaal, it's OK. I haven't really slept since last night but I'm just happy to hear you're safe.'

'Sabs, not gonna lie, I thought that you might wanna break up with me. I'm not meant to get tangled up in this mess. I left this life. I'm doing good . . .' His voice falters.

'Yeah, you're doing good, you don't have to worry about me. I saw everything with my own two eyes.'

'And also . . . I feel low-key bad for saying this, but I don't think Shaah can be my boy like that any more if he's so fixed on road. It's not gonna run. But . . . I'm gonna see him in hospital later, prolly chat to his family. It's the right thing to do. Right?'

'Course it is, you don't want to leave things on bad terms.' I think of how things ended with his dad.

'I don't know Sabs, it's peak. I'm just tryna focus on me. How did this happen?'

'I'm not sure, but whatever you do, I'll support you. But if something like this happens—'

He cuts me off. 'It'll never fucking happen again.'

CHAPTER 43

JALAAL

Alhamdulillah. Praise to Allah for allowing me to come home. The way that I prayed in that cell, I've never prayed like that in my life. If anyone tries telling me that God isn't real, they haven't been in a situation like that.

I deeped it ya know, while I was at my most vulnerable and fucked up, no one could help me. My solicitor is not a fucking magician. He can't control what happens to me. Neither can Hals, Habo Hani or even Sabs. In that moment, I knew that only God could save me. And since I've been home, I haven't missed one prayer.

I called Habo Salma and Shukri on WhatsApp video yesterday. I'm not gonna cap, I was a mess. Habo Hani advised me strongly against speaking to Habo Salma, but this was my decision. I feel like me and Habo Salma have an understanding. More of an understanding than Habo Hani and me. I spoke with Shukri for a while, pretending everything was all OK and showing her what London looks like. Basically, our shitty house and the estate from the window. Ibrahim took the phone from me and started talking to Shukri. Her English is very basic, and his Somali is very basic. Almost non-existent. Somehow, they managed to have a full-blown conversation, and I had to take the phone back after thirty minutes.

Shukri gave the phone back to Habo Salma and I enclosed

myself in my room. I asked Habo if she was alone, and she went outside to the conservatory area. It reminded me of when I was there not too long ago. She sat on the outdoor chair and asked me what's wrong. I told her almost everything that happened. I missed out the part about Sabrina, because she wouldn't understand. Telling her that I've got a friend who got stabbed is bad enough; telling her I'm in a *haram* relationship with someone who is not even Somali, let alone Muslim, is worse. I'll figure that out later.

Her response was everything I needed. She told me that sometimes God puts challenges in our way to allow us to make the right decision. What's happened has happened and I must move forward. She said she is going to make *dua* that everything goes well, and the police conclude their investigation, but I should use this experience to find ways to better my life and strengthen my faith. She kept it short and sweet. And kept it moving. There was no sympathy or pity. Just an understanding and a practical way to look forward. And that's all I wanted.

St Mary's Hospital. It's crazy to think that this is where I was born. The same place as Ibrahim. And where Hooyo died. And now my best friend lies in a hospital bed, somewhere, unalive and undead. He is in an induced coma, and they believe he will come out unscathed or with very minimal changes.

When I enter the room, Shaah's family kindly greet me, his mother weeping gently into my shoulder, reciting prayers in a tongue I don't understand. I engage with his family, showing empathy and patience. I ask them to have a couple moments with Shaah. They give me the time alone. It's a long time coming and I'm relieved to be speaking freely, with no resistance from him.

Shaah lies in bed, the sheets pulled up to his chest. His arms rest outside the covers, connected to a drip and other tubes. His face is kind of swollen and he's got small plasters across his eyebrows. His lips are fat and blueish purple.

I sit beside him.

'Shaah. Where do I start? From the beginning. Fam, can you even hear me? I don't know. I don't wanna stress you out cos I know you can't reply or anything. But what I'm tryna say bro is that I got mad love for you, and I'm so happy you're alive and that you're gonna make it out of this alive. *Alhamdulillah*. Ever since we were young yutes, you have been there for me, and I love you for that. Been there for me since day one. The thing is that I'm done with this life, bro, deep it, you could've lost your life. I just can't be around that any more. I've already lost my mum and dad; I can't lose any more people in my life. I won't make it out.

'Anyways, the point I'm tryna make still is that we can't be bros the way that we are now, if you're still on that lifestyle. I'll get dragged in or put at risk somehow, and it ain't worth it. I got mad love for you and I'm always gonna be your boy. I hope that when you make it out of this, you choose to leave this madness and then we can be bros like old times. I hope you understand *wallahi*. I'm praying every day and making *dua* for your recovery *inshallah*.

'I'm not the best at this talking thing so I'm gonna stop now, Shaah. Love you bro.'

He's unresponsive. Makes sense.

I watch my best friend one more time before exiting the sterile hospital room.

CHAPTER 44

SABRINA

'Dad, I need to tell you something.' I cannot contain this any more. I move into the living room where my dad is sat on the sofa. Tasha and Izzy are upstairs. Alone time is difficult to achieve in this house.

He pauses his TV show.

'What is it?' he asks softly.

'Ummm, promise you won't get mad.' I briefly look at his eyes before focusing back on my fidgeting fingers.

'I promise to listen.'

That's good enough. I inhale deeply. 'Well, uhm mm, you see, uhm mm . . . I have a boyfriend.'

'OK . . .' He narrows his eyes.

'He's not the guy who got stabbed, don't worry. But we have been together for a couple of months. And there's a lot going on with me moving to Warwick and I don't know Dad, I feel like a mess. I miss Mum. I wish she was here.' I start blubbering into tears.

I wish Mum was here to talk about boys. I feel like Dad doesn't understand. I just want Mum. She would know exactly what to say and how to make me feel better.

To my surprise, Dad reaches over to me and pulls me into a hug. He whispers in my ear, 'I miss her too sweetheart, and don't worry, I knew you had a boyfriend.'

I immediately jump back, putting my tears on hold. 'You knew and didn't say anything. How did you know?'

I swear to God if my sisters said anything, that's going to piss me off.

'Sabrina, I'm not stupid. It was obvious – especially when you went to Warwick – I knew it was a boy.' He smiles knowingly. 'Does he treat you well? Is he respectful? Does he respect his parents?'

'Dad.' I stop him in his tracks. I don't know if I should mention this, but I feel like it's going to come out of my mouth anyway. *Be brave, Sabs.*

'He got arrested.'

The look on my dad's face says it all. He clenches his jaw and the vein across his forehead begins to bulge.

'He's innocent, though.'

My dad rolls his eyes.

'I was there.'

Now, he's infuriated. 'What?'

'Just let me explain, please!'

I tell my dad everything. Well, almost everything. I miss out the part that Jalaal used to sell weed and has been in trouble with the law before. And the fact he kinda got kicked out of college. I basically tell him all the good parts about Jalaal and the fact that he got arrested was just a wrong place/wrong time kind of thing.

My dad pauses.

I hope he hasn't realized that I missed out half the story. He's not an easy man to fool.

'And I know you got some weird thing against Somalis, but Jalaal is an amazing person. He accepts me and I accept him. And yeah, I know Muslims are different too, but God is God at the end of the day, so what does it really matter? Although we are different, we are on the same page about so many things. Especially family.' I allow myself to take a breath.

He sighs. 'Sabrina Campbell. I do not have anything against Somalis. If I recall clearly, you asked me about Somali people in general, and I gave you my thoughts based on my experience and understanding, which may be limited. But that is, or was, my truth.'

'OK . . . so you're not *that* bothered about culture?' My heart is in my mouth. 'What do you think about the situation then?'

'Times like this I do wish your mother was here. She would've known the right thing to say. But Sabrina, your boyfriend, he's a young black boy, that inherently brings him problems and challenges just because of the colour of his skin. You and your sisters haven't really experienced that sense of racism because, well . . . you're girls and you're mixed.'

I bite my tongue. This isn't the right time for me to go on a rampage about the discrimination mixed-race people face. I know what's best for me.

'Whether he is innocent or guilty, there is one thing for certain, he does not keep good company. And the company that a man keeps can tell you a lot about his character.'

I open my mouth to defend him. He halts me with his fingers.

'Let me finish,' he says sternly. 'I can see you're already upset and torn up about what happened a few days ago. Is that how you want the rest of your life to be?'

'No.'

'Did you have any of this emotional turmoil before this boy came into your life?'

'No.' *Well yes, Sabs.* I have emotional turmoil, because of Mum. I've accepted she isn't here to support my future. *But you have Jalaal.* He supports me, and that's what counts.

'Do you see where I am going with this?' He raises his eyebrows.

'Yes . . .' I reluctantly admit.

'You don't have that long till you leave to go Warwick, you decide how you want to spend that time.'

I get up from the sofa and walk upstairs to my room. I close the door gently and crawl under my duvet. The tears just keep coming out. I muffle any sounds by pressing the duvet to my lips. It smells. It smells of sweat and sadness.

I'm not going to let Jalaal go. Dad didn't even give me time to explain that Jalaal is on the straight and narrow, as he would put it, and he's not chilling with Shaah any more. *Even if you told him that, would he really be persuaded?* Probably not. Dad is a man of action. If only he could meet Jalaal, then he would see how amazing he is.

Knock knock.

I rush downstairs to get the door.

'Sabrina Campbell?' A Royal Mail postman asks.

'Yeah . . .' I hesitate in accepting the package.

He rushes off as quickly as he knocked on the door.

I've been ordering bits for uni, but I'm not expecting anything right now.

The package is in a rectangular box. Shoes? Who the hell sent me a pair of shoes? I'm still stood in the corridor with a confused face. Tasha and Izzy come down the stairs.

'What's that?' Izzy asks.

'Yeah, what's that?' Tasha chimes in.

'No idea, we are about to find out.'

We all huddle as I delicately open the package to reveal an orange Nike box. There's a note attached in a familiar cursive writing. Just one letter in bold. *B.*

Jalaal. He's so annoying!

'Is that from your boyfriend then?' Tasha comments.

'Oh, her boyfriend, I've met him,' Izzy grins.

'What, when?' Tasha is suddenly alert.

'Guys! Shut up!' I indicate towards Dad in the living room. *Not sure why you're hiding, Sabs, cat is already out of the bag.*

The anticipation kills me, and I fling open the box. Inside lies a pair of white Air Force 1's, the Nike tick filled with the green, yellow and black of the Jamaican flag. The detailing is sharp and subtle. I can't believe he made me custom shoes.

'Ayy, those are cool. You better let me wear them.' Tasha tries to grab a shoe, but I pat her hand away.

'Absolutely not! They're mine.' I close the box and take them upstairs to my room. 'Don't follow me,' I shout down.

'You're whipped, sis, absolutely whipped,' Tasha calls back.

> Thank you for the custom shoes, I am so very thankful and gassed! You're legit the best. ILYSM <3

Jalaal
No worries B, ily2

CHAPTER 45

JALAAL

Sohaib and I are decked out in our *thobe*. The sun is beating down on us as we swim through the crowds leaving *Jummah* prayer at Regent's Park Mosque. This is the first time I've been here since a couple of Eids ago. I was apprehensive about wearing my custom shoes, so under the advice of Sohaib, I put on my distinguishable Crocs. Now, none of the hundred brothers will 'accidentally' take my shoes.

Kneeling in *sujud* with all these brothers did something to my soul. The few faces I noticed during the *khutbah* sermon greeted me warmly with *salam*, and for the first time in a while, I felt a sense of warmth and wholesomeness.

I prayed and made *dua* for a lot of things. Firstly, that I buss this affray case; even though I know I haven't done anything wrong, there's still that feeling that the system is against me. I prayed for all the people I love. Prosperity, good health and happiness. Habo Hani, Hals, Sabs, Ibby, Habo Salma, Shukri, Sohaib and of course, Shaah. For his recovery, and for Allah to guide him on the right path.

I finally feel my life is coming together. Only one more obstacle to overcome.

*

We find ourselves in Cafe Helen on Edgware Road. Best shawarma in these ends but the price is steep, not gonna lie. I tell Sohaib this is my treat for him as he's been so helpful and instrumental to me these past couple days and weeks.

We scoff down our juicy, zesty shawarmas, dabbing our napkins on the sauce leaking down our faces.

'Is this how calm my life can be?' I take another big bite.

He chuckles, swallowing his food. 'Jalaal, life can be whatever you want it to be. This is like any other Friday for me.'

'I didn't realize I was missing out on this. I only have one thing to sort out and then I'll finally be free.'

'The police investigation,' he says, his voice solemn.

'Yeah, bro.'

'How are you feeling about it, still?' He clears his throat.

I sip on the water given to me at the *masjid*. 'Well, I know I'm innocent, but you know how the feds work. I'm just leaving it in God's hands. There's nothing else I can do. And with Shaah . . .' I take a deep breath. 'I had to let that one rest. I can't be rolling with him and not find myself in trouble. This is how things have to go.'

'That's brazy. I hear it though. And I'm glad you came to this conclusion by yourself. So, you said you're going back to college? How did that all go? You going to be doing that and working at Sainsbury's still?'

'Yeah, they're letting me finish my course, I'm going back on Monday *inshallah*.'

'And the clothing brand thing?'

'Yeah, that's calm. I've patterned a supplier, thanks to your cousin, so just kinda figuring that shit out now.'

'Wow. I'm proud of you.' He squeezes my shoulder.

'Thanks, bro.'

'Do you wanna grab some *kanafeh* or something after we finish?'

'Nah, I can't still, I told Sabs I'm gonna take her uni shopping in a bit. Next Friday *Jummah*, let's do it though, *inshallah*.'

'Say no more, bro.'

CHAPTER 46

SABRINA

'You look handsome in that,' I tell Jalaal as we walk hand-in-hand down Oxford Street.

'It's called a *thobe*, and I was low-key nervous about wearing it in front of you.'

'What? Why? You look fine,' I overcompensate. 'Plus, it makes sense, you just came back from the mosque.'

'Fairs. Anyways, let's swap places.' He shifts my Nike, Zara and JD bags to his other hand, then moves to my other side, creating a barrier between me and the road. His fingers intertwine with mine again. *You could get used to this princess treatment, Sabs.*

'You know I'm a grown adult, I won't walk into the road,' I laugh.

'Probably, but I won't take that risk.' He squeezes my hands. It's so weird that he's doing the small acts that I usually do for Tash and Izzy.

'Anyways, where are we going? I think I'm done with shopping now. Should probably get home to Dad, actually.'

I've got it in my head that Jalaal needs to meet Dad. I just think if Dad actually met him and spoke to him properly, he would understand.

Like today: Jalaal has taken me to nearly every shop along the main street, urging me to pick out anything I might like – not just what I need, but anything that would be nice to have for university. He is adamant and has paid for everything, despite my vocal protests. Dad has to see how good that is.

Bite the bullet, Sabs. 'Jalaal, quick question – do you think you could meet my dad? Random, I know. But I think it would help me. Us.' Now that he's all lovey-dovey, he might be inclined to say yes.

He scratches his head. 'Are you sure that's a good idea? Especially after the whole Shaah situation.'

'It will help him understand that we are serious and for real, I do want his blessing. I need it.'

'Let me think about it.' He scratches his head.

'Thank you.' I squeeze his hand.

Jalaal made it clear he doesn't want me to *lift a finger.* The feminist in me is gagging to overcomplicate this by stating this is his way of exerting patriarchy, but I know the truth. *Jalaal sees how hard I work to keep everything together and just wants to make me feel loved and cared for.* Something I have been craving since forever.

In the end, I only purchased relevant bits and bobs, but Jalaal had this weird thing of making sure I buy two pairs of shoes in case something happens to the first pair. I told him he's paranoid, and luckily for me, they only had one pair of shoes in stock.

'I have one final surprise for you.' We rush down Carnaby Street.

'Please Jalaal, don't you think you've done more than enough?'

'No, not for you.' He stops. 'Anyways, this is for *us*, and we are here.'

I turn to my right and the pastel pink of *Astrid & Miyu* is facing me. Jewellery. If he's planning to do some sort of engraved J + S thing, I'll be so embarrassed.

'Don't worry, nothing to do with initials.' He must've clocked my reaction.

'Come.' He gently pulls me into the store.

He takes the lead and approaches the store staff. 'Hey, we have a welding appointment for 5 p.m.'

Welding?

'Yes, yes, come through.' A lady with blonde, pixie-cut hair leads us downstairs.

'What is going on?' I whisper to him.

'We are getting matching gold-plated bracelets,' he says like it's normal.

My heart melts at this thoughtfulness.

'You know, they weld so its stays on forever,' he adds.

'Really?'

'Thought this could be a goodbye present for you.'

'For us,' I correct him. 'You're acting like you're gonna get locked up or something. The police are still investigating and you're innocent so . . .'

'Sabs, relax, you're right. Legally, morally, it shouldn't be an issue. It should be calm, but you never know. I'm not that bothered though. It's in God's hands.' He squeezes my hand.

'Yeah, and God has your back. I'm not worried. Thanks for the present.'

'Anything for you.'

CHAPTER 47

JALAAL

*R*ing. *Ring.* No caller ID. Ever since I got rid of my trap phone, I've become bare wary of who calls me on my main line.

I pause *Power* on the TV to answer the call, waiting for someone to speak.

'Hello,' says a cockney accent.

'Yo.' I deepen my voice.

'Is this Jalaal Abdi?'

'Yeah, who's this?'

'This is PC Palmer from Paddington Police Station. I just wanted to inform you about the outcome of your case.' He pauses.

My heart sinks to my stomach. Fuck.

'Yeah . . .'

'We will not be continuing with the case, and it has been NFA'd. No further action.'

'Really?' My heart leaps into my mouth. 'That's sick. I told you man I was innocent; I was just helping my friend who got stabbed.' I jump and punch the air.

'We will send you a letter in the post to confirm this, also,' he adds.

'Say no more. See ya later officer.' I hang up the phone and immediately shout the good news to Hals and Habo before belling Sabs's line.

'Sabs, guess who is a free man?' I sing through the phone.

'Hey, what the hell are you talking about? I can't really talk, I'm out for coffee with my Auntie Maureen, she finds it rude when I'm on the phone to people.' Her tone is hushed.

'The police closed the case! Nothing holding me back any more. I'm so fucking happy, Sabs.'

'Oh my god! That's amazing news. You must be so relieved. I am so relieved for you. Let's talk about it later!' Her voice is quick and quiet.

'Say no more! I love you,' I tease her, knowing she won't respond in front of Auntie Maureen.

'Me too!'

I recline back on the sofa and deep it. Everything is falling into place. There's only one thing left that I need to pattern. Sab's dad.

I adjust my posture, taking a deep breath as I stand outside her door and make a quick *dua* to Allah. I don't know how I'm going to impress this man.

I knock on the door and wait.

I didn't tell Sabrina that I would do this. No warning. Her dad might not even be home.

The door swings open, and it's none other than the main man himself. Tall and hench, with waves in his hair and a face that means business.

'May I help you?' He hovers over me.

I clear my throat. 'Yes. Are you Mr Campbell? I'm Jalaal. Sabrina's . . . boyfriend.'

'Uh huh. And what are you doing here? She's not home.'

'Well, I was hoping,' I force confidence, 'to meet you and explain to you why I deserve Sabrina. I understand that you think I'm not the best person for her . . . and I'm here to prove you wrong.'

He raises his eyebrow. 'Is that all?'

'Uh, no. I have more to say.'

He turns around. I brace myself for him to slam the door in my face, but instead, he opens it wider and says, 'Close the door behind you and take your shoes off.'

'Yes sir.'

It feels bare weird to be sat in Sabs's living room, especially when she's not here. Her dad is sat on an armchair and I'm sat on the other leather sofa, directly opposite an ancient china cabinet filled with dishes and framed pictures. I'm dying to get up and have a look at them, but I know not to overstep my place.

'So, Jalaal.' He pronounces my name perfectly as he clasps his hands.

He waits.

'Yes, well . . .' How the fuck am I more nervous now than I was when I was with the police? 'I need you to know that I really love and care about Sabrina. She is the most amazing girl I've ever met in my life. She's clever and . . .'

He raises his hand to interject. 'So, here is the thing. You are telling me things that I already know about my daughter. At this moment, all I know of you is that you're someone who keeps bad company and has been arrested.'

I gulp in my fears. She told him about that.

'Well, I was accidentally arrested and that's all sorted right now. The point is, yes, I did *have* bad company. But I realized that I can't have bad company and also be with Sabrina. And I'll pick her every time. I'm done with all that crap. I'm in education, I've started my own clothing brand. I look after my family and I'm gonna be a successful man that's going to provide for your daughter.' My shirt is saturated with sweat at this point.

I pause for a breath, waiting to see if he wants to validate me.

Just as I'm about to further fight my cause, the front door opens and I hear her comforting voice. 'Family, I'm home.'

'Sabrina, come into the living room.' Her dad is suddenly soft-spoken.

I take in a deep breath.

She freezes at the door when she clocks me sat on the sofa. Her cheeks grow red, and she switches glances between us both.

'What is going on?' Her eyes widen.

'Well . . .' Her dad stands up, and I follow suit. 'Jalaal was coming over to get my blessing and I have given it to him.'

'Really?' Sabs gushes.

'Oh, yes, thank you, sir.' I bow my head at him.

Sabs looks at me sideways.

'Thank you for coming over, son.' He presses my shoulders and ushers me towards my shoes, which I quickly squeeze into, not bothered to do my laces.

'It was great to see you both,' I manage to get out my mouth before leaving the house, Sabs signalling that she will call me later with a big fat grin on her face.

CHAPTER 48

SABRINA

It is amazing to have my closest friends and family here to wish me goodbye before I'm off to Warwick for this new chapter of my life. I've had to accept that it's without Mum. But not gonna lie, I don't feel any more resentment for her absence; she has her own demons to face. *And she will face them in God's timing.* If this summer has taught me anything, it's that life is too short, and we need to forgive. Forgiveness is a big healer, and my heart feels so much lighter. I'm lucky to have a great support system and people who I can rely on. And I deserve to have this. I just couldn't see it before. I'm trying to love who I am today. *I am loving who I am today.* I accept I have different responsibilities to my friends, and I have to remember that there are other people out there who have it worse than me.

I had planned to have my goodbye dinner at a gastropub, but Jalaal was adamant we hire a private room somewhere nice and intimate. So here we are, in a private room at our local Hilton Paddington. Due to the boujee location, I had to impose a dress code of course, and everyone is looking gorgeous. Liyah. Tasha and Izzy. Amelia. Shanice. The twins from college, Fatima and Ayan. Jalaal and Ibby of course, and even Hals is here.

We have provided catered Italian food; I mean you can't go wrong with pizza and pasta. Plus, Jalaal said it's my day, so it must be my favourite food. I love that he pushes me to put myself first. I was so used to always placing others above me, but now, I feel more confident in asserting my needs.

'OK, hey . . .' I stumble on my words. 'Is it OK to get everyone's attention?'

The chatter doesn't die down.

'Yo!' Shanice shouts. 'Everyone shut up, Sabs is tryna speak.'

Everyone quietens down and Shanice chuckles.

I smile at her warmly, before commencing my monologue.

'So, I just wanted to thank everyone for coming today and I'm ready to give my speeeech.'

The small crowd cheer. *You got this, Sabs.*

Jalaal squeezes my hand before I stand up and unfold my paper.

'Thank you everyone for showing up and sharing this special day with me today, you honestly don't realize how much it means to me. These past few years have been a rollercoaster and I'm so grateful to have made it to the finish line. Warwick has always been my dream, even though I had never been there until Jalaal took me.

'I am low-key kinda shook about starting this new chapter, but it is great to know that I have this support system here. I love all of you guys so much and I'm gonna miss you loads. I will obvs be visiting during holidays, and I can't wait to catch up with everyone, but you're all welcome to visit me. In fact, you have to visit me because that's what friends and family are for.

'Anyways, enough of me rambling and being emotional. Yeah . . . thank you for being here today and in this moment, I love you all endlessly.'

*

Everyone is dancing, but Jalaal and I stay seated in a corner, just enjoying the vibe. His FaceTime rings.

'It's Shaah,' he tells me.

'Answer it,' I smile. 'Do you want me to go?'

'No, stay, it's cool.' He answers the phone.

'What you saying, bro,' Shaah's voice echoes before his face appears on the screen.

He's still at the hospital. He's wearing a hospital gown, a white one with the green polka dots. His face is unkempt, he looks rough.

'Man like Shaah,' Jalaal says.

He smiles through his battered face. 'Thank God I'm alive still. Man could've been in the grave right now.'

'*Alhamdulillah.*' Jalaal pauses.

Shaah shakes his head. 'On a real one Jalaal, I've got my mum bawlin' her eyes out in the hospital room. My dad is bare angry and disappointed. My sisters are in shock and bare emotional. All cos of me. You know how mad it is to watch them cry? You know how mad it is to feel like I'm the reason . . . *wallahi* . . . I don't know, bruv.'

'It's a lot fam, but it's good to know you're out of the coma. What's the recovery time saying?' Jalaal asks.

'The knife just missed a major artery, otherwise I would've been dead. They said I can leave in a week but it will take time for things to go back to normal. Listen though.' He hushes his voice. 'The feds are talking about moving me and the fam out of London. Said it's too risky for me to live here in case these man try finish the job.' His eyes widen.

'And . . .' Jalaal raises his eyebrows.

'I don't know what to do. I told them no at the beginning because this is man's home, I ain't tryna leave my ends. But now that I'm thinking about it, it might be a good move. They said if I change my mind, I should let my social worker know. Yeah fam, I got a social worker now.' He rolls his eyes.

'That's mad,' Jalaal manages to say.

'Yeah, for real . . .'

The silence is loud.

Jalaal's voice shakes the slightest. 'Did you hear what I said you while you were unconscious?'

Shaah's face dims. 'I did.'

Oh shit, that's so awkward. Jalaal told me about his confession.

'And I hear you, bro.' Shaah's eyes well up. 'I don't think I am where you are yet. I'm not ready to leave. I don't have any dreams or nuttin'.'

Shaah is choking on his words; I sense Jalaal is trying his hardest to hold his emotions in by the way he's biting his bottom lip.

'It's hard, fam,' he finally says. 'But when you decide you're done for good, *inshallah*, I'll be here.'

'*Inshallah*. Anyways, I got to go now.' Shaah's voice trembles.

'Stay safe.'

'You, too.'

The line goes dead.

I wrap my arms around Jalaal and hold on to him.

After a minute of silent embrace, Jalaal holds my hand. 'Let's go back to the party.'

Catching up with everyone and opening my gifts, I'm buzzing. Shanice got me a rice cooker and cookbook; Ayan and Fatima, a journal and books; Amelia, an electric blanket. Hals and Ibby give me a Polaroid camera, Tasha and Izzy (which is basically all Dad) a brand-new MacBook Air. Jalaal's sorted this whole evening, paying for everything. *Sabs, he is the gift that keeps on giving.*

'Before everyone leaves,' Liyah announces, 'there is one final present from Jalaal.'

Everyone says *ooooo* simultaneously.

'What?' I blurt out. 'What did you get me? You shouldn't have.' I give Jalaal the death stare.

He smirks at me before handing over a gift bag.

'Sabs, this is the first sample piece from my clothing line *LDN Nomad*, and it is inspired by you.'

I'm already crying before I've seen what it is. This is honestly the most generous, loving thing anybody has ever done for me. I feel the pressure of everyone's eyes watching me as my fingers tremble. I pull out a small, black hoody from the gift bag, slowly unfolding it to see the design that is artfully printed on to the soft fabric. The logo *LDN Nomad* is sketched on the right crest of the hoody and in the middle, it's me. An illustration of me from Shanice's party in my black dress and red heels. My hair in a bun with my fresh edges and a plastic plate of Caribbean food.

The day we first met.

Sabs, you know it was love on sight.

EPILOGUE – TWO MONTHS LATER

JALAAL

'Sabs, do you have to watch every Chelsea game? This is a Carabao Cup game so it's not even a big thing.' I snuggle closer to her in the bed. 'Please, I'm so bored of all of this.'

She smirks.

I won't tell her that I'm low-key getting into it. Her passion for Chelsea is rubbing off on me. I've watched more Chelsea games in the last three months than in my whole life. I find myself often checking the Premier League table to see when Chelsea is playing, but I'm not watching. I can't give her that satisfaction.

'But Jalaal, the last time you came, you made us watch *Ozark* and I didn't even want to watch that. I had to miss Chelsea playing Tottenham. It's my turn now.'

Not gonna lie, she does have a point.

'Maybe you should stop inviting me over then,' I joke.

'Maybe you should stop being a dickhead,' she mimics my tone.

'Maybe you should give me a kiss.'

'Maybe you should relax,' she fires back and sticks her tongue out at me.

'Whatever.' I roll my eyes and glue them back on her laptop screen.

*

It's mad to think that this is my fourth time visiting Sabs in Warwick now. She's settled in bare easily and not gonna lie, my girl is thriving out here. Her flatmates in her accommodation are calm – one of them even bought a hoody from my sample sale, which was sick.

Sabs is into all these societies and clubs; I don't really understand myself, but she told me she's on the committee for the Afro-Caribbean Society. I'm not surprised.

I'm so proud of her and how she's settled in. Sometimes I'm high-key shook at how she's able to manage all this stuff while getting a first in her essays. It makes me want to do better, and I am doing better. And whenever I come over to these ends, she has time for me. No distraction.

Sabs is such an amazing person. I know that I'm one lucky guy to have her in my life, let alone have her as my girlfriend.

Not tryna sound moist or anything, but I do enjoy coming up to these ends and visiting her. And it feels much better knowing that Habo Hani knows as well. I had to come clean and tell her truth – there was nothing to lie about. Hals backed me up though, so Habo Hani wasn't as pressed about it. I think she might even be open to meeting Sabs at some point. Small steps though.

Shaah has moved out to Kent somewhere, I have no idea what he's on. I haven't heard from him yet so it's probably not that good. I meant what I said, I'll be there for him so long as he's on the right path.

College is wavy, I'm on track to achieving distinction for my course. I sold out the first drop from my clothing line. *Alhamdulillah, everything is going well.*

Hals has gone back to Bristol for uni, but we still FaceTime every other day. I don't actually know what I would've done without her.

This whole summer that passed has been such a fucking shitshow, but she has had my back. She helped me with everything. I love her bare. And I can't wait for Habo Salma and Shukri to visit us during the holidays.

'What you thinking about?' Sabs disrupts me from my thoughts.

I clock that the game is on mute.

'What do you mean?'

'You literally zoned out, babes.'

I still love it when she calls me babes.

'I was thinking about how mad this summer was,' I say quietly.

I know Sabs doesn't really like thinking about the past. Especially after everything that I put her through.

'It was mad, wasn't it? But we are here now, and we got through it.'

'Only upwards from here.'

ACKNOWLEDGEMENTS

ٱلْحَمْدُ لِلَّهِ

To my parents. I HAVE SO MUCH LOVE FOR YOU! For believing in me, for guiding me and for understanding me. My endless gratitude to *Hooyo,* who instilled in me a love for reading, and to *Far,* who cultivated the space to be creative. The countless books, pens and notebooks over the past twenty-nine years have set the foundation for the writer I am today.

To my family, who have supported me throughout this whole journey, even when I was in the trenches. You always showed up for me and never doubted my dreams of becoming a published author. Thanks to Abbie, Asli Issa, Adam B and Hamdi. A special shout-out to my cuzzy Saiad, the first person to have read the book in its entirety and the one who gave *Love on Sight* its name.

To my friends, who showed up in ways that you may not have realized. Roop, my soul sister, championing me in this journey of life. Mahek, for the countless book events and networking. Lena, for the thoughtful gifts that motivate me to write. Zahra, for your endless support since those Jonas Brothers fanfic days lol. Rahma, for always gassin' me up and making me feel like *that* girl. And to Taylor and Amreen, my international babes, for allowing me to dream big, and celebrating my every milestone along the way.

To DWHS and GLE, for raising me. Through hardship comes reward.

To the women who believed in me and my vision when navigating the complexities of the Youth Justice System. You taught me perseverance, self-belief and power.

To everyone at Chicken House; Barry, Laura, Ruth, Emily, Jazz, Rachel H, Rachel L, Esther and Elinor, who helped bring this book to life, but especially to Shalu Vallepur, who has been there from the very beginning and believed in *Love on Sight*. I will never forget that first email telling me that I'd been longlisted for the competition. I'm so happy to have had an editor that I vibe so well with 😊 And to Emma Draude from EDPR and to Dark Matter, for paving the way so *Love on Sight* can meet the world.

To my wonderful agent, Saff Dodd, for making this overwhelming new world feel seamless. Thank you for having my back, always <3

Big shout out to Ali Al Amine for this beautiful beautiful beautiful book cover!!!

The Curtis Brown Creative, and Yvvette Edwards, my first mentor who helped get *Love on Sight* into shape.

To my MA crew, the group of students who edited the very first pieces of *Love on Sight*, helping to manifest a few chapters into an entire book. A special mention to my tutor and lecturer, Jodie Kim, for being the calm during a storm and a trusted soundboard when the heart was heavy.

And to everyone that turned me down, thank you! I'm being dead serious. Every 'no' brought me closer to this 'yes'.